DAWN OF DRAGONS

PREQUEL TO THE DRAGON AGE

The author may be contacted at
james@jamesmaxey.net

Published by the James Maxey, Hillsborough, NC
Dawn of Dragons originally published by author 2013

ISBN-13: 978-1503227125
ISBN-10: 150322712X

DAWN OF DRAGONS
Prequel to the Dragon Age

Jesus answered and said unto him,
Verily, verily, I say unto thee,
Except a man be born again,
he cannot see the kingdom of God.

Nicodemus saith unto him,
How can a man be born when he is old?
can he enter the second time into his mother's womb, and be born?

Jesus answered, Verily, verily, I say unto thee,
Except a man be born of water and of the Spirit,
he cannot enter into the kingdom of God.
That which is born of the flesh is flesh;
and that which is born of the Spirit is spirit.
Marvel not that I said unto thee,
Ye must be born again.

John 3:3-7

CHAPTER ONE
DANGEROUS ANIMALS

THE DRAGON SLITHERED SILENTLY among the trees branches as the knight on horseback drew closer. A practiced hunter, the beast positioned himself downwind, with the setting sun at his back.

Not spooking the horse was the dragon's top priority. The knight himself would be no threat, but experience had taught the beast the benefit of slaying the mount along with the rider. Horsemeat as a rule was more savory than the flesh of men. No doubt the diets of men spoiled their taste; most humans spent the better parts of their lives slowly poisoning themselves.

This knight looked to be no exception. Despite the gleaming, polished armor that glimmered ruby beneath the dimming sky, despite the sword and mace and crossbow that all hung within easy reach, it was obvious from his smell that this man posed no danger. He was sweating from the simple effort of wearing the armor and riding the horse. No doubt his sword arm was slow, his aim unsteady. This was just another deluded fool in a growing string of fools who had set out in pursuit of the dragon.

The knight grew ever closer to the dragon's hiding place. The man's eyes stayed on the path before him, oblivious to the danger above. As the knight passed below, the dragon was close enough that he could have dangled his tail and touched the rider's helm.

With feline anticipation, the dragon tensed, his mouth opening slightly to reveal dagger-like teeth. His strike would be lightning-swift; the horse and rider would die before they ever understood their fate. The dragon's claws sunk deeper into the branch as he shifted his body to pounce.

The knight's phone rang.

"Goddammit," grumbled the knight, pulling the reigns of his horse as he twisted in his saddle to better reach his saddlebag. He continued to curse softly as he rooted around the contents of the bag, only halting his obscenities when he shifted his helmet back and raised the phone to his ear.

"O'Brien here," he said.

The dragon leaned closer, curious at this new development. His keen hearing allowed him to hear the voice on the other end of the line. A female voice. The knight's mate, perhaps?

"Dammit, Martha," said O'Brien. "You know not to call me when I'm working. You know I—what? What do you mean you know I'm not working? Jackson told you what? What?"

The woman's voice on the other line told the knight what Jackson had revealed: O'Brien was spending several million dollars to pay for a vacation at the most exclusive hunt club on the planet. He'd explained his absence to his wife by claiming he was attending a business conference.

O'Brian sighed, and rubbed his temple.

"Fine," he said. "So I'm hunting. Yes, you're right, this is a goddamned mid-life crisis. Yes, I lied to you. Yes, I frivolously blew a huge wad of dough. But it's my money, Martha. I've worked my ass off to get where I am and it's time I started eating the fruit of my labor."

The woman's voice grew louder and angrier as the dragon lowered his long snaky neck to listen better. He was now close enough to see his toothy reflection in the knight's polished helmet.

"Don't take that tone with me," snapped O'Brien. "I don't need to explain myself. Tell Jackson I'd better not see his face when I come back to the office. I—"

Martha asked something the dragon strained to hear. Her mood had shifted. Her voice cracked with sorrow. Didn't O'Brien trust her anymore?

"This isn't the time to discuss this," said O'Brien. "I'm hunting! There are dangerous animals here and it's getting dark. I'm going to hang up. Don't call me again. I mean it. Yes. Yes, consider that a threat. The prenuptial agreement is rock solid, Martha. You'll do as I say and you'll like it."

The dragon had enough. Tensed muscles uncoiled as it leapt, spreading its wings at an angle that flipped it into the path of the knight, opening its jaws and emitting a hiss that caused the horse to rear.

O'Brien cursed as he fell from the saddle to the stony path. He curled into a fetal position to avoid the hooves as his horse turned and leapt over him. Martha was shouting from the fallen phone, her voice panicked. With a start, O'Brien unfolded himself and drew the sword from his scabbard, struggling to reach his feet as the dragon looked on with impatience.

"Good sir knight," said the dragon, with a hissing British accent that was half Monty Python, half actual python. "Sheath your sword and heed my words."

O'Brien's mouth fell open.

"Your mate has called because she fears for your safety and you treat her with scorn," said the dragon. "True knights were chivalrous, but your behavior is loutish in the extreme."

"You talk," said O'Brien.

"Or you've hit your head rather hard on the path," said the dragon. "No, I jest. I am, indeed, speaking your native tongue. The monsters who designed me thought it a nice touch, as dragons in speculative literature are somewhat loquacious. But, sir, don't allow your amazement over my vocalizations to distract you. Your behavior toward your wife is shameful. As one who dreams of knowing the love and affection of a devoted mate, I ask you to lift up that phone and apologize. Leave this place, and I shall not injure you. My offer of safe passage does not extend to your horse."

"Ha!" said O'Brien, brandishing his sword. "Well, goddamn! A talking lizard."

"You assume a martial position," said the dragon. "I ask you to reconsider. Don't act rashly. I've killed seventeen of your ilk. You haven't a chance if you continue on this course of action."

"Hee!" said O'Brien, licking his lips, shifting his grip on the sword. "You breathe fire, too? You making this hunt worth the money, lizard? Huh, *lizard?*"

"My name," said the dragon, "is Morningstar."

O'Brien screamed like he was auditioning for a kung fu movie as he lunged forward, swinging his razor sharp sword like a baseball bat.

Morningstar pushed backwards with a flap of his wings, raising up on his tail for balance as the sword cut the air where he'd stood. His hind claws lashed out, slicing through O'Brien's steel breastplate like the world's fastest can-opener.

O'Brien dropped the sword, falling to his knees as Morningstar swayed above him. The wanna-be knight dipped his gauntleted fingers into the jagged gash in his breastplate. He pulled them out to study them in the dying light. They dripped with red. His face grew pale.

Morningstar snaked his head forward, jaws wide open, and sank his teeth into O'Brien's cheeks. With a snap and a crack, his jaws closed, and Morningstar's mouth was filled with teeth and a tongue not his own. O'Brien fell to the stony path with a clatter.

Morningstar spit the foul taste of businessman from his mouth and silently moved toward the fallen phone. He lifted it, listening to Martha's panicked voice. It nearly broke the dragon's heart. How terrible it must be to lose a mate, even a rude and foolish one.

"Madam," Morningstar said with all the softness his serpent voice could muster. "I regret to inform you of a tragic event."

CHAPTER TWO
NOT VERY GOOD AT IT

ONE DISADVANTAGE of being a zombie was that Alex Pure no longer sweated. This meant he had trouble regulating his body temperature. Sitting on the sunny-side of an over-packed Greyhound inching toward Atlanta, Pure's internal thermometer hovered around 107. When Pure got this hot, time crawled. His perceptions shifted into high gear, turning a five-hour bus ride into eternity, give or take a week.

On the plus side, his accelerated perceptions meant that he had plenty of time to work the crossword puzzle in the open puzzlebook of the sleeping man in the seat across the isle. Pure felt it would be rude to reach out and reposition the book on the man's lap, so he worked the crossword upside down and backwards to help pass the time.

Crossword puzzles had taken on special significance since Pure had died. He'd never paid much attention to puzzles when he was alive, but death had changed the wiring in his brain. He noticed hidden patterns in the world that had once been lost on him. He could glance at clouds and know the weather for the next week. (Boiling hot.) He could study a stranger's face and deduce intimate details of childhood. And then there were crosswords. These puzzles now struck Pure as one of the highest achievements of modern man. Sure, mankind had poisoned the planet, wrecked the climate, and triggered mass-extinctions, but, what the hey. Men could also put words into these marvelous grids. There was something magical, almost holy, in a language where words locked and clicked into other words with such ease.

35 across had Pure stumped. It was a big one, 14 letters, with a clue too broad to be of any help. *35: Your problem.* "IDIEDINTHEWARP" fit nicely, except that 35 down was "Newton's light bulb," which was "APPLE." The next letter over had to be a "T" since the word down (or up, given the puzzle's inverted state) was "BATHTUB." He slid his eyes back and forth, working the down answers, quickly assembling the letters across until he reached the final clue, "Heavenly light," making the last letter the "G" in "GLORY."

"ATLANTISRISING" read 35 across. How was this his problem? Or anybody's problem, for that matter? No doubt this was some movie reference he was missing. He hadn't been to a movie in all the years he'd spent in Mount Weather. Pop culture clues were tough for him. He was only 33, an age when a lot of people started to realize that the music and movies they'd imprinted on during their college years were no longer "cool." But he'd skipped movies and music during college in favor of drugs and anonymous sex. On rare occasions, the name of a pharmaceutical might slip into a crossword, but most puzzle makers were too conservative to ever work in any of the several hundred slang terms he knew for genitals and the creative ways in which they could be used.

The man across the isle woke up. The magazine shifted as the man pulled out his phone and glanced at the screen. 5:34pm, August 12, 2037. Pure tried to stare around the man's hand to see if there was any more of the puzzle he could work. The man suddenly looked across the isle to find Pure staring intently at his lap. Pure turned his face toward the window.

The pale reflection there didn't look like a zombie. He still had a mostly clean-cut appearance from his military days, though his dark hair was just a little too long for regulation, and he had the same five day unshaved stubble he'd sported when he'd gone into the warp. His clothes had seen better days, though. His once white shirt and blue jeans were ripped and muddy, as if he'd recently spent time clawing himself free from a jail that had collapsed around him, which, in fact, was how he'd spent his weekend.

Outside the window, beyond his reflection, was the rain forest. He'd been to Georgia years ago and it had been nothing like this. It had forests, sure, but this was jungle, thick and all-consuming. The shoulders of the road were black with ash. The department of transportation had switched from mowers to flame-throwers to keep the pavement clean. The bus passed a kudzu covered cinderblock foundation for a house, the tenth empty foundation they'd passed in an hour. This area of the country had been hit hard by mega-molds.

Mega-molds left Pure with a sliver of optimism. What with all the species going extinct, it was comforting to realize that new species still slid into the gaps. Life went on. Mega-molds thrived in the tropical heat and humidity. Thrived was something of an understatement. If mega-mold spores blew into your door as you headed for work in the morning, a huge black puffball would fill your house by the time you returned home. If you were unfortunate enough to open the door, you'd get a face full of spores and suffocate in moments as the mold took root in your lungs. Once the spoors got into your house, it was best to walk away and never look back. Eventually the puffball would push through your roof and knock down the walls. The most you could hope for was that the HAZMAT team might return the little bits of twisted metal that had been your bowling trophies after they had incinerated the place and raked through the ashes.

At last they reached Atlanta. The transition from uninhabited rain forest to teeming metropolis was almost instantaneous. Pure closed his eyes to rest them. Since exiting the warp, he didn't need to sleep. Unfortunately, after long hours of use his eyes sometimes dried out and stuck open. He'd go temporarily blind until his retinal cells could regenerate. He took this quiet moment to practice breathing and concentrate on his heartbeat. He suspected his heart didn't beat when he wasn't thinking about it. He hadn't really been able to test this, since any time he wondered if his heart was beating, sure enough, it was.

"IDIEDINTHEWARP" was a much better answer than "ATLANTISRISING." Why couldn't Newton have sat under an ipple tree?

The bus stopped in the tightly packed downtown terminal. Pure looked out the window, spotting a newspaper rack. The economic sense of newspapers had vanished long ago, but a handful still survived as non-profits supported by corporate sponsors. A headline on the *Coca-Cola Journal and Constitution* read, "Atlantis Rising Homeless" before disappearing behind a bumper sticker on the newspaper box that read "Four Horsemen." Pure was vaguely aware that the Four Horsemen were some kind of band.

Leaving the bus, he went to the paper box. It only took cards, which Pure couldn't carry since they left an obvious trail for the people hunting him. On a whim, he tried the handle anyway. The door swung open and he grabbed a paper. The part of his morals that minded minor theft had died in the warp with the rest of him.

On closer inspection, the headline read, "Atlanta's Rising Homeless Population Strains Resources." He scanned the article for another second or two, "floods of Canadians," yadda yadda, "no more beds" yadda yadda, "Pepsiphetamine addiction," same old, same old. He'd read this story a thousand times. A dozen years ago, the waves of cold water from the melting Artic had disrupted the Gulf Stream. Without the oceans pumping heat north, much of Europe and large swathes of

Canada were vanishing beneath glaciers. When Pure was a kid, everyone had argued about global warming. Now, with a growing ice sheet covering everything north of Maine, the average world temperature was plunging rapidly, despite the furnace-like heat of Georgia summers. On paper, global warming had gone away and everyone was happy.

Except, of course, everyone was miserable. The headlines were a daily assault of Famine, Pestilence, War, and Death, making the "Four Horsemen" sticker on the paper box grimly appropriate.

Just then, a pink-haired teenager, maybe fourteen years old, sauntered past him singing, "*Atlantis rising. . . .*"

"Hey," Pure said.

". . . *Arab's white caps in a winter wale,*" sang the boy, walking on. The music from the boy's headphones was loud enough for Pure to hear.

"Wait," Pure shouted, reaching out and grabbing the boy by the shoulder.

In a lightning whirl that Pure found impressive, the boy spun around, dropped a switchblade into his hand, and placed the tip to Pure's throat.

"What the *fuck* is wrong with you?" the boy screamed. "Do *not* touch me!"

Pure smiled. The knife at his throat didn't worry him. He was more bothered that everyone in the bus station was staring. He preferred to keep a low profile.

"Sorry," Pure said, holding up his open hands. "I just wanted to ask you something."

The boy popped out one of his earphones and said, "What?"

"You were singing about Atlantis and—"

"You high or something? I weren't singing 'bout Atlanta."

"No, Atlan*tis*."

"What I said," said the boy, who still had the switchblade inches from Pure.

"So what were you listening to?"

"It's by the Four Horsemen."

"How does it go?" asked Pure. "The bit you were singing?"

"*At last it's rising, like Ahab's white corpse on a whiter whale.*"

Pure wrinkled his brow. "Really?" he asked.

"Really," said the boy.

"What does that mean?"

"I dunno," said the boy. "What's it matter to you?"

"Put down the knife and I'll explain," said Pure.

"Don't touch me again," said the boy, slowly lowering his hand, but leaving the blade open.

Pure studied the boy's eyes. He'd seen eyes like this before, hard and cold. He knew the boy's story without asking it. The kid was a loner, probably an orphan, most likely the victim of sexual assault, which explained the knife reflex. Pure also knew something else about him.

"Your name," said Pure. "It's John Conover, right?"

"It's Spike," he answered, furrowing his brow. "Do I know you?"

"Nope. I'm here because of a fortune cookie. I read your name on a fortune cookie."

Spike stared at Pure.

"I know it sounds crazy. But yesterday, I was eating Chinese food in Savannah and got a fortune cookie with your name in it. Earlier that day, I found a bus ticket to Atlanta on a park bench, sitting underneath last Sunday's obituary page from the paper here. I think I'm supposed to come here and warn you that you're about to die."

"Are you *threatening* me?" said the boy, raising the knife again.

"No. I'm hoping to help you. I know you've no reason to believe me, but I'm in touch with, ah, for lack of a better word, a 'higher power.' There's this, um, *entity* that guides me from a different dimension. Unfortunately, he's not very good at it. He causes me to see and hear things. I get clues, weird snippets, but they're always hard to figure out. Eventually they all make sense, but usually I'm too late to do anything. I thought I was coming to Atlanta to find the grave of John Conover, for instance. Maybe talk with his widow or something. Finding you alive means I might have gotten here in time to save you."

"I don't need saving," said Spike. "You some kind of religious freak?"

"I'm not here to indoctrinate you. But the one who guides me must think you're important. After all, you gave me the third clue in an hour with the words 'Atlantis rising.' I don't have the foggiest notion what this means, but he must think it's important."

"Show me the fortune cookie," said Spike.

"OK," said Pure, digging into his pocket. As he searched he made nervous small talk, aware that people were staring at them. He really hoped no one called the cops. "I don't need to eat anymore, but, you know, I occasionally miss food. My taste buds aren't great so I have to go with really hot stuff to get any effect. I suck down those little red peppers in General Tsao's Chicken like they were candy. Ah! Here it is."

Spike took the slip of paper from Pure.

"This says, 'Spies are everywhere,' " said Spike. "My name's not on it."

"Really?" said Pure, taking back the slip. "I swear—"

"Freeze!" shouted a deep, familiar voice behind him. "Put your hands in the air!"

Pure lifted his hands and peeked over his shoulder. From the corner of his eye he could see Hammer Morgan aiming his obscenely large pistol at him. Hammer was accompanied by two Atlanta police officers, also with pistols drawn.

"Get on the ground," shouted Hammer.

Pure sighed. These encounters were growing tedious. Hammer didn't ever bother to say hello anymore.

"Get real," said Pure, rolling his eyes. "The floor's *filthy*. I know you get off on your little dominance games, so what say we skip to the part where you cuff me."

"Get on the damn floor," growled Hammer.

Pure sighed. "Or what? You'll shoot me? You've tried before and it never takes. What do you think will stop the bullet this time? Aren't you tired of this game yet?"

"Get on the floor," said Hammer. "Your friend too."

"Hey man," said Spike, "I ain't no friend of this asshole." Spike waved his arms around for emphasis.

Unfortunately, he was still holding his knife.

"Weapon!" shouted one of the officers, taking aim.

Pure's senses were still accelerated by the heat. The gap between the officer pulling his trigger and the thunder of the shot seemed like a space of minutes. Unfortunately, for Pure to cover the distance between him and the officer would have taken what seemed like hours. As it was, he was able to move his body between the officer and Spike long before he heard the gunshot.

Too bad that the whole reason you can hear a gunshot is that the bullet breaks the sound barrier. In eerie silence the bullet punched into Pure's torso. By the time the sound reached Pure, he was no longer in his body.

Pure rose. The kinetic energy of the bullet punching his flesh raced through his blood. He felt almost alive again. The energy was a wave, lifting him, driving him up, higher, far beyond his body, through the smoke-stained roof of the bus terminal, out into blue sky, and beyond.

Pure was no longer here and now. He was back in the warp, in the space that was no-space, the there that was not there, in the eternity that hides between the ticks of a clock. The warp was a pitch black canvas against which strobing lights swirled. Little by little, the flashes began to take the shape of a man. Not just any man ... himself. A second Alex Pure still dwelled in this darkness. The Pure that waited for him at the heart of the warp was a beautiful creature, all light and brightness, free of the squalor and weight of physical existence. Before him was Pure, purified.

The purified Pure was surrounded by monkeys.

Good, thought the more earthly Alex Pure.

The glorified Pure extended his hand. The earthly Pure reached out. Only the tiniest gulf separated their fingers.

The higher Pure drew his hand back.

"Sorry," that Pure said, shaking his head. "Atlantis is rising. Or maybe falling. Whatever. Do something, or everyone dies."

The earthly Alex Pure cried out in frustration as he began to fall. The perfected Pure and his monkey minions vanished. Blue sky flashed by, followed by the yellow bus station ceiling, as Pure twisted to see what was happening. The bullet or some fragment of it had passed through his torso and was now entering the eye of Spike, AKA John Conover, AKA the latest person he'd helped kill. Could he have stopped this just by not coming here? Should he just give up?

Before he could ponder the value of action versus inaction, the wave of energy that had lifted him collapsed entirely, crashing him back into his squalid, heavy body. He stumbled backwards, his ears ringing, his nose wrinkled from the sulfur stench of gun smoke. His skull vibrated like a struck bell.

"Ow," he said, struggling to keep his balance as he tripped over Spike's sprawled and twitching limbs. He finally found his footing and remained standing.

"Hold your fire!" Hammer shouted to the officers.

"Ow, damn," said Pure, clutching his stomach. He wasn't bleeding. That meant his heart wasn't beating. Only, now that he thought about it, hot red liquid oozed around his fingers.

"Alex," said Hammer, his gun aimed straight at Pure's head. "I'm giving you one last warning. Don't make me do this. I don't want to hurt you."

Pure stopped worrying about his blood. He clenched his fists into tight knots and stared into Hammer's eyes. Perhaps twenty feet separated them, but it seemed so much less, so much less than the space that had lay between his fingers and the hand of his higher being. Pure believed that his rage was powerful enough that no bullet would ever stop him. He could stomp across the tiny distance and snatch away Hammer's gun and feed it to him.

"Are you satisfied?" Pure growled. "Your goons have killed a kid. Is catching me worth it?"

"He had a knife!" the officer who had fired shouted.

"Shut up," said Hammer.

"How will you sleep tonight?" asked Pure.

"Not as important to me as where you're sleeping tonight," said Hammer. "You're under arrest. Get on the floor. Place your hands on your head."

"How's he still standing?" the second officer mumbled.

"I'm not a violent person," said Pure, addressing the officers, ignoring Hammer. "But the entity that watches over me is sometimes clumsy. Did Hammer tell you what happened to the last jail they put me in?"

"On the floor," said Hammer.

"Charleston, South Carolina, gone from the map. The earthquake was 7.8 on the Richter scale. The epicenter was the jail that held me. In the aftershocks and tidal waves, the whole damn city slid into the ocean. Kind of like the myth of Atlantis, now that I think about it."

"Alex, I'm counting to three," said Hammer.

"Why are you calling me Alex now? Whatever happened to our pet names, Sugar?" Despite his flippant tone, Pure dreaded what was about to happen.

"One," said Hammer.

Pure could see straight down the barrel of the gun. This one would stop in his brain.

"Two!"

Pure wondered if he'd still be able to do crosswords upside down and backwards without a pencil. He asked, "You want another city on your hands? Atlanta is a long way from the ocean. Might be a volcano this time."

"Three, *Sugar*," said Hammer.

The air cracked open in a flash of light. Monkey screeches filled the bus station as tiny rainbow windows bubbled all around the officers. Bony monkey fingers reached out and snatched at their pistols. Hammer got off a shot that whizzed past Pure's ear before the monkey paw twisted the gun from his grasp. A horrible stench filled the air as feces materialized from nowhere, flying in precise arcs to splatter forcefully in the faces of Hammer and the officers.

"Thanks, warp monkeys," said Pure, bending over Spike's body.

"Mind if I borrow this?" he said, tearing away the earphones and the tiny player they were attached to. He wanted to hear more of the song.

By now, the whole station was a cacophony of screams as monkey fingers tangled in the hair of people watching. Buckets of monkey dung rained from the sky, save for a narrow corridor around Pure. Pure turned to Hammer, blew him a kiss, then walked out to the street where a line of cars waited at parking meters. Instinctively, Pure spotted the one with the windows rolled down.

Pure got into the car, dug for the keys under the seat, found them, then turned the ignition. His wheels were an ancient station wagon with a gasoline engine, no doubt the only means of transportation for some honest, hard-working Joe. Pure understood that without the car the poor guy wouldn't be able to get to work and might lose his job. He and his wife and their nine kids could wind up homeless side by side with the Canucks. But Pure had a hole through his liver. Everyone has problems. He put the car into drive and hit the road.

CHAPTER THREE
SHOOTING STAR

THE CITY CAME FROM *beneath space, following the faintest possible ripples left from the hole that had been punched through reality. It emerged into nearly nothing, far out beyond the orbit of comets, confused by the lack of a nearby planet. It spun slowly, analyzing the radiation that sank into its soot black shell, studying the feeble tugs of gravity, until at last it found the nearest star, wreathed with a thin halo of dust and gas.*

There were planets there. One had been the source of the signal, carried far, far away by the motion of the galactic arm in the time it had taken the city to follow the ripples.

Dipping back into underspace, the city punched back into the mundane dimensions closer to the star. Cataloguing the various planets, its attention became fixed on a gassy, wet ball of rock orbited by an oversized moon. It felt a thrill of recognition to see this world of ice and fire and wind. Continuing to skim along the surface of space, it drew ever closer until it tilted into the planet's gravity well. The city was coming home.

The city came with a gift. Within the quantum patterns of its machine soul were love, peace, and joy. The city was designed as the perfect servant and the perfect master. The culmination of 65 million years of evolved intelligence, the city was programmed to create a world without war, without hate or hunger, safe from fear, and even death.

Heaven was coming to Earth.

We couldn't have stopped it if we wanted to.

THE WINDLESS SEA WAS THE COLOR of onyx, calmed to mirror smoothness, reflecting starlight in the moonless night. Adam Morgan lay on the deck, his body stiffened to near-paralysis by a lifetime of aches and agonies magnified by the stillness.

His knees throbbed. They hadn't been any good for years now. They hurt standing, sitting, lying down. The knotted muscles of his back felt tangled together with barbwire. His ribs ached with each wheezing breath. His heart beat too fast and too hard for a man his age. His skin burned like fire, the heat of the day's sun still dancing upon him.

His pain gave him grim satisfaction. This was why he'd come to sea, in pursuit of the medieval notion that mortification of the flesh could in some way redeem the soul.

At times he felt on the edge of salvation. After years cooped in labs and offices, shut away from the sun, wind and rain, he'd connected once more with the physical world. His weeks on the sea had kept his body in motion, kept soft muscles pumping until they became solid little ropes, pulling and pulling against the sails, against the wheel. His mind, so used to wrestling with the fundamental questions of life in his day to day job as a geneticist, now wrestled with questions of survival.

This was a new sea for a new world. The great heat engine that drove the trade winds and pushed warm water northward had collapsed into chaotic eddies. The Gulf Stream was but a memory now. From day to day the sea changed. The maps of the world were being redrawn as the encroaching oceans chewed away the coastlines. The Outer Banks of North Carolina had been overwashed by the tidal surge of a hurricane in early spring, and when the waters receded half of the land was gone. On the flip side, the plastic trash that had been floating in the Pacific for nearly a century had proven a fertile ground for matting microbes. They'd knit the whole mass together into a giant floating island that was home to a hundred species of birds and even starting to sprout forests. All environmental destruction was a precursor to environmental creation. Not all the new environments, alas, were pleasing to the human eye, let alone the nose.

When he'd set sail, Adam had hoped to learn that at heart he was an adventurer, an explorer, a new man for a new world. Confronting wind and wave would make him feel alive.

Now, a thousand miles from the nearest land, the wind had died, the waves had gone still, and there was nothing to confront except memories.

He'd failed his son. Right before he set sail he'd phoned Chase. He'd called to say that he was sorry for all the years of neglect, shunting Chase off to boarding schools, allowing him to grow up a stranger. Instead he told Chase that the battery in the car was down to forty percent efficiency and he should get it replaced before he made any long trips. This was possibly the closest he'd ever come to vocalizing concern for his son.

Adam had meant to do better. His own father had been absent much of his early childhood, serving on active duty in the Marines, rotated through endless deployments in Iraq and Afghanistan. Then, one day his father had come home to stay, at least what bits had been found and placed in the casket. Adam entered his teen years determined to live up to the memory of a man who'd given his life for freedom. Anytime he felt afraid, or tired, or willing to settle for second best, the ghost of the man who'd given everything for what he believed would come back to spur him onward. Adam's dead father had been a better parent than he'd been to Chase.

He tried to shake off these thoughts. He tried to find the will to stand, walk into the cabin, and fix something to eat. Focus on the now. His past was a disaster, but it was done. Gone forever. No point in looking back. Forward only! Never give up.

"I'm a new man for a new world," he said, repeating his mantra.

But his body was unimpressed by his pep talk.

"Get up," he said. "Stop being an old self-pitying fool."

THE CITY GREW EVER CLOSER to the blue planet. It studied the oceans. There were intelligent beings living in these waters, but not all intelligence was equal. More promising were the tool using bipeds who skimmed the surface in artificial vessels of their own design. These beings were not who it expected to find, but there were no other candidates for the origin of the signal. Whether they knew it or not, these creatures had summoned the city, and it would serve them.

ADAM COULDN'T GET UP. His memories weren't finished. After tormenting him with Chase, his thoughts turned to Jessica, his wife of twenty-five years. Twenty of these years, Jessica had been in a coma. She'd been a victim of sleeper flu, the epidemic that swept North America in the winter of 2017. That flu had been a harbinger, a prelude of worse things to come, the years of draught, the earthquakes, the plagues, the wars, the hunger.

Adam could have done something about this, perhaps. He was one of the world's top geneticists. He could have used his genius in pursuit of cures to the plagues, or to design new crops for famine-ravaged lands. Instead, he'd spent the last two decades of his life building living toys for bored, wealthy men. This had paid much better than trying to save the world. Chase may not have appreciated his expensive boarding schools, but at least his son had gotten a good education and had been shielded from the horrors that each day shocked the public schools. Chase had been spared from violence and disease, from drugs and abuse. While Jessica could never know it, the best doctors available cared for her in a secure private facility with a self-contained power grid. These things cost money. Lots of money.

More than money.

Not for the first time, the option of suicide flickered across his consciousness. And not for the first time, his dead father rose up to frown at him for his weakness.

"I'm a new man for a new world," he said. He closed his eyes and imagined himself rising, standing on the deck. He opened his eyes and hadn't moved an inch.

"The hell I am," he said. "I'm a monster."

But even a monster proved unequal to the task of standing.

High above in the darkness a light twinkled, a bright star growing brighter. As Adam watched, the star threw off sparks, growing larger, yet leaving no trail, until suddenly it vanished.

His right shoulder went numb. The boat lurched. A gunshot cracked in his ears.

"Ahhh!" he cried, sucking air, rolling to his left side as he clutched his right shoulder. It was hot and sticky, the familiar contours of flesh distorted. He pulled his hand away, straining to see his fingers in the dim starlight. They were dark with blood.

With the crack of gunshot still ringing in his skull, he grasped that he'd been shot. How? Who? Why?

He rolled to his belly and used his left arm to help him rise to his knees. His other arm hung limp, dragging the deck as he crawled toward the open door of the cabin. He lurched into the dark portal, falling down the short steps that led into the tiny room that served as bedroom, office, kitchen, and hospital. He fumbled, slapping the wall until at last he hit the lights. He rolled onto his bed, gasping in pain with each movement.

"Oh god," he whispered, staring at his mangled shoulder. "Oh god."

If the wound had been a few inches to the left, he'd be dead.

He might still die if he blacked out while he was bleeding. He had to fight the shock. He had to make his body move.

This time, his body obeyed. He rolled over into the floor and pulled out the drawers beneath the bed, searching for the first aid kit. He found it, and also stumbled across the bottle of brandy he'd been saving for the day he reached Spain, his first destination on the other side of the Atlantic. He opened the bottle awkwardly with his left hand and took a long swig of its contents, then poured it liberally over his wound.

It burned like mad. But the liquid washed away some of the blood and gore, giving Adam a better look at the damage.

To his relief, his arm wasn't hanging by a thin strip of flesh. Instead there was a two-inch gash torn through the outer edge of his deltoid, bleeding steadily, not spurting with each heartbeat. No major artery was involved.

The wound looked to be as much a burn as a gouge. The edges were black with ash. Feeling was returning now to the arm below the wound. He could wiggle his fingers, though he still couldn't bend his arm at the elbow.

He found the gauze in the first aid kit and pressed it against the gash as firmly as he could. The pressure somehow made the pain more manageable. The palm of his hand now encompassed the injury that had been his whole world seconds before.

He would survive this.

Unless whoever shot him had a second bullet.

But this was crazy. How could anyone have shot him? He hadn't seen or heard an airplane or a boat. There definitely wasn't a stowaway on board after three weeks. It was impossible that someone had shot him. So where had all this blood come from?

By now, his arm bent at the elbow. He fumbled with the first aid kit, unwrapping the medical tape. He bound his wound, as tightly as he could manage, the tape painfully pulling the hair in his armpit. His handiwork was far from tidy. When he was done, he fashioned a crude sling to keep his arm immobile. Already, blood seeped to the surface of his work.

He grew lightheaded. He was afraid to lie down. Sleep was dangerous. Sleep was the enemy. Where was insomnia when he needed it?

He struggled to his feet in the cramped cabin. He found his flashlight and headed back up the stairs into the open air. The part of his mind that believed he hadn't been shot was starting to win.

He had another hypothesis now. The reason the shooting star he'd seen didn't leave a trail was because it was coming straight at him. He'd been hit by a meteorite.

It was a wild, improbable, stupid theory.

But it was the best he had to go on.

He followed the blood trail he'd left, like a detective investigating his own murder. Here was the bloody handprint against the door, here the splatter where the victim had stumbled. Here was the splash of red where he'd been hit.

As expected, there was a splintered hole punched in the deck. He stooped to look down through it but it was too small to see into, no bigger around than his pinky.

Now sleep really wasn't an option. In all likelihood, he had a hole in his hull. His ship might be sinking.

But the size of the hole in the deck gave him hope. It might be only a small hole. He might yet save the ship. It was possible even that the rock had disintegrated, and done no further damage.

He went back into the cabin and pulled aside the panel that opened the crawl space. To his relief, water didn't rush out. On his hands and knees, he tossed aside the gear stuffed in the space. He searched the area with the flashlight beam, trying to figure out where the hole would be. Everything looked dry. Maybe his sense of space was off. The hole might be further forward.

He climbed back up the stairs. His dizziness was gone now. Even the pain in his arm grew distant and unimportant in the face of this mystery.

He sat his flashlight on the deck, centered on the hole, the beam pointing straight down. He went back to the cabin, crouching before the crawl space.

There. The beam of light hung on the far side of the space, further to the left than he'd envisioned. In the tight column of light, something was moving. It glistened as if wet. He guessed it to be a tiny fountain of water bubbling up.

Falling to his belly, he pulled himself into the dark space, grunting and cursing as he struggled forward for a better look.

But the closer he got, the less what he saw made sense. It wasn't a fountain. It looked like a small acorn, glistening with blood. He stretched to pick it up. Though he could barely reach it, the object clung to his fingertips; the blood that coated it was the consistency of molasses. Bringing the thing closer to his eyes, it was unmistakably a seed, though from what plant he couldn't fathom. The shell was hard, but dented slightly as he pressed his thumbnail into it. His fingertips tingled as he held it, a faint needling as if the object was intensely cold, though it felt pleasantly warm.

Then, for no reason that made sense to him, a vision flooded his mind of him placing the blood covered seed in his mouth. He found the idea repulsive, yet his hand moved toward his mouth despite himself.

As his tongue touched the surface, his mouth filled with a thousand flavors, as if every taste bud had clicked on at once. Every meal he'd ever eaten flooded his mind, from the sweet warm fatness of mother's milk to the unbearable sourness of his first pickle to the satisfying protein and fire marriage of a well-seared steak. His lips closed around the object and he pressed it against the back of his teeth as music filled his ears, every song he knew flooding back in one chaotic din that merged into a thrumming, bone-shaking chord. His mind opened before the assault of sound and he discovered that he suddenly knew, in every language of the earth, all the words for love and hope and fear and death.

He spat the seed back into his palm.

With the blood coating washed away by his saliva, the seed glowed with a faint internal light, tinted pink. The seed had grown during the brief seconds he'd held it in his mouth and was now closer in size to a pecan, bent slightly into the shape of a kidney. Staring through the translucent skin, he could see dark veins running to a central nucleus. Turning it, he managed to get a faint idea of the irregular shape within.

Adam furrowed his brow. The thing inside was a tiny homunculus of a man, with toothpick limbs that twitched and quivered. The tiny black specs that served as eyes turned toward Adam. The slit of the mouth, no longer than a hyphen at the end of a sentence, opened and silently mouthed a word.

Adam dropped the seed.

His stomach twisted into a tight knot as dizziness seized him. He felt inverted in the cramped space, unable to tell if he was facing up or down. He tried to back out and the slowness of the process caused him to panic. He banged his head against the wood enclosing him.

It wasn't until he at last wiggled free, sitting in the cabin, clutching the edge of his bunk for stability, that he realized how much his ears were ringing. His throat felt as if he'd swallowed barbed-wire. He'd nearly screamed himself deaf.

Glancing toward the open door of the crawlspace, at the luminous seed writhing as it grew, he screamed some more.

PURE STOOD ON A BRIDGE overpass in Memphis. From here it was an eighty-foot plunge onto a highway. The late night traffic whizzed beneath him.

He leaned over the rail, trying to make sure the fall would be enough to really damage him. If the gunshot had pushed him into the warp long enough for a few short sentences to be exchanged, what might smacking into the pavement at terminal velocity accomplish?

Pure was frustrated with chasing around the country on hunches and odd messages. He'd used the search function on Spike's media player and learned that the Four Horsemen's label, Apocalypse Noise, was based in Memphis. It struck him as potentially significant to learn the location of the Apocalypse. He'd gone to the studio office, only to discover they'd gone bankrupt and the office was now empty. The whole thing was a dead end. The other location clue on the album Spike had listened to was a song called "Skeets Motel." He'd used the GPS in the car to search greater Memphis and had been skunked. No Skeets Motel.

He had no patience for detective work. Thus the temptation to throw himself off the bridge. He wanted to find his higher self and beat the answers out of him.

But some small quiet voice within him didn't like the pavement diving option. A: It was really unfair to lay this kind of guilt trip on some innocent driver who might run over his body. B: Memphis had the same budget problems as everywhere else; they couldn't afford another pothole. C: Even though he was confident he'd survive the fall, if survive was a verb that applied to a man already dead, this was still going to be painful. Pain sucked.

A car pulled to a stop near him. A voice called out, "Mister?"

Pure turned around. A middle-aged woman in a nurse uniform sat in an ancient, battered Prius.

"You okay?" she asked.

Pure smiled. "You worried I might jump?"

"Yes," she said.

Pure nodded. "I was thinking about it. It's a long story."

"So tell me about it," she said. "I'm on my way to work, but I'll call and tell them I'll be late. I'll listen as long as you need me to."

As she said this, a passing car on the bridge beeped its horn, annoyed it had to swerve to avoid her car.

Pure started to say something, but stopped. The thing he hated most about his current condition was how difficult it was to explain himself. He'd once worked in a top-secret military facility, his soul had been ripped from his body by an experimental warp door, and now he was on the run from his former boyfriend who was hunting him down to take him back to be studied like a guinea pig. Oh, and apparently, he was supposed to stop the apocalypse. There was no part of the truth that didn't make him sound like a nut.

"I've changed my mind," he said. "I'm not going to jump."

"You sure?" she said.

"What's your name?" he asked.

"Mariah."

"Mariah, I'm Alex. I promise not to jump. In retrospect, it's a fairly desperate measure to take in order to get directions to the Skeets Motel."

"Skeets Motel?" Mariah said, sounding bewildered. "That's in Arkansas, in the Ozarks. We stayed there twenty years ago when we moved from New Mexico to here."

Pure smiled. "Wow! You're a real life saver."

"OK," she said, sounding more confused. "No problem."

"Thanks for restoring my faith in humanity," said Pure, giving her a salute. He watched as she pulled away, her taillights looking like two red eyes. "I hope I don't let you down."

MORNINGSTAR REGRETTED gorging on the horse. Even with an empty belly, his wings were only useful for short flights of a few hundred yards. With thirty pounds of raw meat in his stomach, he was too heavy for his wings to lift him. He could still glide from tree to tree, but his pace was only barely keeping him ahead of his pursuers.

From his perch in the trees, he could hear the ATV's of the security team on the other side of the hill. He knew they could track him wherever he went, but on an empty belly he could flit across the rough terrain at speeds that kept him safely out of reach.

They were chasing him because of O'Brien's phone. He'd stolen hunter's phones in the past and it always triggered these chases. In the hours before the batteries ran out, Morningstar was a voracious reader. Most of what he knew of the world beyond the forest came from the information he'd gathered from these devices. The men who'd created him had designed him to be smart, but they weren't keen on him actually furthering his education.

The security team had been pushing him east all morning. Morningstar's skull throbbed. He was nearing the border of his territory. He'd been warned that there was a device in his head that would kill him if he ever tried to leave his forest. Just coming a few hundred feet away from the edge of the boundary triggered a screaming sound inside his skull that made his teeth ache.

Certain that he had at least five minutes before the guards could spot him, he tried to focus on the article about dinosaurs. Dinosaurs fascinated him and he read everything he could about them and other ancient reptiles. He was particularly interested in the archaeopteryx. Morningstar thought he looked more like this toothy protobird than any other creature he'd ever seen, though from what he'd read the archaeopteryx had been little larger than a chicken, while he was closer in size to a tiger. Still, there was something about knowing that such a beast had once existed that made him feel a bit less lonely.

Of course, the archaeopteryx was now dead. Morningstar still hoped to avoid such a fate. With the screaming in his skull too great for him to concentrate on reading anyway, he at last flung the phone away, then leapt across treetops away from the boundary until the pain lessened.

He froze as the ATVs came over the ridge. There were twelve men with dart guns. If his belly wasn't so full, he'd be tempted to fight them. He had an advantage in such encounters because they weren't actually here to kill him; he was valuable property. The more hunters he killed, the more other hunters were willing to pay for a chance to bring him down. This meant he had little to lose by leaping down upon the guards and killing as many of his tormentors as he could before the tranquilizer rifles laid him low.

Alas, he had nothing to gain, either. He'd killed guards by the score. It never truly diminished their numbers. From what he'd learned via his study sessions with stolen phones, humans numbered in the billions. Picking off two or three or even a dozen at a time would never bring him permanent relief from such an enemy.

The men found the phone on the ground and quickly retreated, apparently not wanting a face-to-face encounter any more than he did. It still wasn't too late to change his mind and pounce upon the lone ATV driver straggling behind the others. But he kept still, knowing that such an attack wouldn't get him any closer to his long-term goal.

He studied the land to the east, at the forest stretching for miles beyond the boundary, dreaming of the vast world beyond. One day, all that vast world would be his hunting ground.

CHAPTER FOUR
THE KID, THE BABE, THE NUN

DEPUTY RON TUCKER pulled his cruiser into the parking lot of the Skeets Motel to find Erskine Skeets, proprietor, waiting for him. Tucker was at the end of a week of graveyard shifts and the last thing he felt like was dealing with Skeets, probably the most paranoid person in all of White Hill, Arkansas. Two, three times a week Skeets would call and report someone suspicious who'd checked into his hotel. Skeets had watched too many movies in which small town motels were the favored abode of serial killers and terrorists. Ten years ago, Skeets had reported a thuggish looking character with a hook for a hand, an eye-patch, and a tattoo across his neck that said, "Satan's Servant." The guy turned out to have an outstanding warrant for armed robbery in Tulsa. This taste of success as an alert citizen had turned him into White Hill's biggest pain in the butt.

Deputy Tucker rolled down the window of the cruiser, drawing back from the terrible heat that flooded in once the seal of his air-conditioned environment was broken. Not even 8:00 a.m. and already a blast furnace.

"Morning, Mr. Skeets," said Tucker. "What's up?"

"*What's up?*" said Skeets. "What do you mean by that?"

"I mean what's wrong," said Tucker. "Why'd you call 911 this time?"

"That's not what I heard in the tone," said Skeets. "You sound like you're annoyed. You sound like you're tired of doing the job that us taxpayers hired you to do."

"Sorry," said Tucker.

"No you're not," said Skeets. "Look at you. You don't even have enough professionalism to get out of your car when you're talking to me."

Tucker grabbed his sunglasses from the dash. Conversations with Skeets usually had him rolling his eyes. The sunglasses might save him from a scolding. Tucker exited the car and put on his smile.

"I apologize, Mr. Skeets," he said. "Been a long night. What can I do for you?"

"I got some thieves up in 21 that need arresting," said Skeets.

"I see," said Tucker. "What did they steal?"

"Gasoline. I had two guests complain this morning about their tanks being almost empty. It's the folks in 21 what's doing it."

"You saw them?"

"Ron, take a look at this parking lot. We got six vehicles left this morning. One diesel, four fuel cells, and that old junker truck with a gas engine. It belongs to the folks in room 21. Who would you suspect?"

"It could be someone who's not a guest here," said Tucker.

"That's a pretty suspicious bunch in 21," said Skeets. "I almost called them in last night."

"Suspicious?"

"Yep. Three of them. The kid that checked in paid with cash and said his name was Robert Walters, and that's what his license said, but I thought it was funny he called himself Robert, not Bob, not Rob. And he's traveling with this girl, maybe sixteen, with dark glasses, acting like she's blind. But she had a lot of tattoos. And I ask myself, why would a blind person want tattoos?"

"Maybe she got them before she went blind?" said Tucker.

"Maybe. Still seems funny to me."

Tucker nodded. "You said there was a third person?"

"An old lady. I mean really old. Dressed like a nun."

"A nun," said Tucker.

"Right," said Skeets.

"A nun?" said Tucker.

"You having trouble hearing me?"

"Nope. Let's go talk to them."

They walked to 21, Tucker wiping the sweat from his brow. He was guessing it must be 95° already, maybe 100°. Tucker knocked on the door. There were hushed voices from inside. No one answered.

Tucker knocked again. "Open up! It's the police!"

More hushed conversation.

The door opened a crack, then stopped as it reached the end of its chain. A sweet-faced little old lady in a habit looked through the crack.

"May I help you officer?" she asked in a trembling voice.

"We've had reports of some gasoline theft this morning. I was wondering if I could come into your room and take a look?"

"Now wouldn't be a good time officer," said the little old lady. "I'm afraid one of the sisters is in the shower."

Tucker noticed he could hear the water running.

"Well, can you ask her to throw on a robe?"

"I suppose," said the little old lady.

Just then, the shower stopped.

A male voice called out from the bathroom, "Man, I thought I'd never get the smell of gas off me."

The little old lady shut the door before Tucker could react.

There was now muffled shouting inside the room, although Tucker couldn't quite make it out.

Tucker turned to Skeets. "I assume you have a key?"

"You going in?" said Skeets. "You gonna arrest 'em by yourself or you gonna call for backup?"

"Maybe you're right. The nun looked kind of vicious," said Tucker.

"There's that tone again," said Skeets. "Is there anyone left on the force that's not a smart ass?"

"You got a key, or you want me to kick the door in?"

Skeets held out the key. Tucker took it and drew his gun. Then he thought better of barging in. He was in a hurry to get this over with but that was no reason to be sloppy. While his every instinct told him there was nothing dangerous going on, he decided to play it by the book. He walked to the back of the truck and took out his radio.

"So you're not going in?" said Skeets.

"Not yet," said Tucker. "They're not going anywhere without getting past us. Figure I'll call in these plates."

"You didn't believe me," said Skeets. "I know it. No one down at the sheriff's ever believes me. But I was right! We got us some criminals this time!"

"Yeah," said Tucker. "We'll have to special order you a medal. You've saved the world from a dangerous old nun."

SISTER SUE PULLED HER EAR from the door and started loading the shotgun. Sue had been fighting for the Earth Defense Army for seventy-plus years now, so her gnarled fingers slipped the shells into the shotgun with practiced precision.

"I'll show them dangerous," Sue said, snapping the gun shut.

"Whoah, whoah, whoah," said Chase as he hopped, off balance, pulling on his pants. Chase was a clean-cut kid, fresh out of college, and from the sound of his voice it was apparent he hadn't had many run-ins with the police before. "Why are you loading the gun?"

"He's calling in the plates," said Cassie, with her hands over her ears. Cassie was the tech-wizard of the team. She had more circuitry and wires in her body than most people had in their cars. She was also—and this goes a long way toward explaining Chase's presence in the room—one hot babe, long and lithe, blonde and pale as a fairy-tale princess. She said, "I'm monitoring the radio right now."

"*Why am I loading the gun?*" Sue said in a whining, mocking voice. "I'm loading the gun because you can't keep your mouth shut. '*I thought I'd never get the gasoline off,* '" she whine-mocked. "You might as well have run out waving the can and siphoning hose."

"Look," said Chase, his voice squeaking slightly. "We only siphoned a few gallons. I'll take the blame. That's gotta be, what, a fifty dollar fine or something?"

"The truck's stolen, moron," said Sue.

"Oh," said Chase.

"I've got six federal warrants for my arrest," said Cassie.

"Oh," said Chase.

"That's cute that you still count," said Sister Sue. Then to Chase: "In the grand scheme of things, the fires of hell burn as hot for gasoline thieves as they do for cop killers. I say in for a penny, in for a pound."

"The sheriff's coming to provide back-up," said Cassie. "We've got ten minutes, tops."

"We should talk about this," said Chase.

"Let's talk. Me first," Sister Sue said as she stomped up to him and smacked him on the forehead with her bony knuckles. "You've blown it. You've given this hick cop a reason to arrest us. Now we can go out and kill one cop or we can wait ten minutes and have to fight Jesus knows how many. If we go to jail, who's going to expose your daddy's dirty little secret?"

"Chase," said Cassie. "Listen to her. You're still thinking all bourgeois. This cop is nothing more than an enforcer for the fascist enviro-rapists. You knew when you signed on that we were called the Earth Defense Army. What part of 'army' didn't you understand? This is war. People get hurt."

Chase felt not for the first time that he had passed through some veil between the sane world and Cassie's world. For the two months he'd known her he'd been drawn into increasingly bizarre scenario's that tested his moral fabric, forcing him to make complex ethical decisions in the blink of an eye. Every time, he'd come down on the side that would most please her. But was he actually seconds away from being an accessory to murder?

"While you're making up your mind about which side you're on," said Cassie, "stick this on the window."

She handed Chase a small metal disk, the size of a nickel. It was sticky on one side. He carefully reached his hand under the curtain and stuck the disk to the glass. Instantly, he could hear the deputy and the hotel owner talking.

"Backup's on the way. The tags don't match the vehicle. Probably both stolen."

"I knew it!"

Cassie said, "That device turns the glass into a big microphone. It only works one way."

Sister Sue pulled the five-gallon gas can out of the closet. There was still a little left after Chase had topped off the truck. As she untwisted the lid she mumbled, "You and your gadgets, Cass. Sometimes the old fashioned ways are best."

She started to pour gasoline on the bed.

"Whoah whoah whoah WHOAH!" shouted Chase. "What are you doing?"

"If we set the room on fire, the smoke will give us cover when we open the door," said Sister Sue.

"You're insane!" said Chase.

"If we're going down," said Cassie, her voice firm with the conviction of the righteous, "we should go down in flames."

From the window, they heard another vehicle pull into the parking lot.

"More cops?" said Sister Sue, searching for her lighter.

Chase went to the door and looked out the peephole.

"An old station wagon," he reported. "Some bum getting out."

"Morning, officer," said the new arrival. "You got kind of a situation here?"

Sister Sue tilted her head like a curious dog.

"Who might you be?" asked the deputy.

"I might be the tooth fairy," said the newcomer.

"I know that voice," said Sister Sue, moving toward the window.

"Look, deputy, you're a busy man. I don't know what these folks in that room have been up to, but what say we forget this whole thing and go get a cup of coffee or something?"

Sister Sue pushed the curtain back ever so slightly to peek out.

"I'll be damned," she said, then sighed. "It's Alex Pure."

In the parking lot, Pure was studying the deputy closely, trying to get a judge of his character. According to the name badge, his name was

Tucker, and late last night after walking past an ATM that malfunctioned and spit out upwards of ten-grand, Pure had tuned into an oldies station where he heard a song by the Marshall Tucker Band. This had to mean something. On the other hand, Pure wasn't sure what to make of the nervous, slightly angry looking civilian next to the deputy.

"Okay, Tooth Fairy," said Tucker, "I'm going to need to see some I.D."

"Let's cut to the chase," said Pure. "I'm pretty sure I've been sent here to bribe you." He reached into his front seat, making sure the deputy could see his hands and pulled out a grocery bag bulging with cash. "You and the missus might take a nice vacation or something."

"I can't believe you're trying to bribe me," said Tucker. Pure thought he detected more amazement than indignation in the lawman's voice.

"Arrest him," said the smaller man. "This bastard must be part of the nun's gang."

"Shut up, Skeets," said Tucker.

Pure's eyebrows shot up. "Nun, you say?"

"Don't act like you don't know her," said Skeets.

"I might," said Pure. "Her name Sue? Really old? Kind of mean?"

"She didn't say her name," said Tucker, eyeing the bag of money. "How much money is in that bag?"

"What kind of question is that?" said Skeets. "You aren't listening to this damn crook are you?"

Tucker took off his sunglasses and rubbed the bridge of his nose. Pure was certain he'd take the money if Skeets wasn't watching. "All right, Tooth Fairy," sighed Tucker, "you're under arrest."

"You don't want to do that," said Pure.

"I kind of think I do," said Tucker.

In the distance, a siren drew closer.

"Look," said Pure. "This isn't intended as a threat, but you don't want to arrest me. Something bad might happen. Very bad."

"Are you getting your dialogue from a Hulk comic or something?" said Tucker. "Put your hands on the hood."

INSIDE THE MOTEL ROOM, Chase stood in front of the door as Sue tried to push past.

"Now's our chance!" she said. "While they're distracted! I can get them all!"

"Sheriff's almost here," said Cassie, her hand over her ear. "I've cracked his GPS. We have less than a minute."

"Out of the way!" said Sue.

In desperation, Chase grabbed the shotgun. He was reasonably strong, but Sue held onto it with a death grip. Chase couldn't wrench the gun from her hands, but at least he was keeping it pointed toward the ceiling.

Outside, a siren drew nearer.

"SOMETHING BAD is about to happen," said Pure. "Don't say I didn't try to stop this."

Tucker drew his gun. "Hands on the hood. Now."

The sheriff's cruiser zoomed into the parking lot, going way too fast. Pure looked up, and knew instantly how things would play out. As Tucker and Skeets looked over their shoulders, Pure stepped out of the way.

This was just one of those things that happen. Like a crossword with all the letters falling into place, Pure instinctively understood that the sheriff was in his mid-sixties and something of a "type A" personality. He chain-smoked and ate pork-rinds and Mountain Dew for breakfast ever since his third wife abandoned him. The man was long overdue for a heart attack. Something about taking the curve a little too fast into the parking lot set it off. As spots danced before the sheriff's eyes, the last thing he'd see was Tucker and Skeets as they bounced off his windshield. The fender of his squad car clipped the tail end of the pickup truck and his car went spinning off, crashing into a tree, at the same time that Tucker and Skeets hit the pavement.

Pure knelt over Tucker and felt for a pulse. The deputy was alive. Pure checked his own pulse. It beat with a sudden startled rush, as if it had been snuck up on.

The door to room 21 swung open and Sister Sue yelled out, "Prayer works!"

"Hello, Sue," said Pure.

"How did you know I was here?" said Sue. "And why in the world would you rescue me? I figured you'd rather see me rot."

"I'm here because the Four Horsemen recorded a song called 'Skeets Motel.' They also have a song called 'Evil Nun' but I didn't make the connection."

He saw a young guy leading a woman from the room. She was a real looker, probably breath-taking if you were into that sort of thing.

"Who're you corrupting now, Sue?" Pure asked.

"This is Cassie," said Sue. "She's the brightest young star in the Earth Defense Army. Smart as a whip and willing to do what's needed to fight the good fight."

"She'll kill people, you mean," said Pure. "Who's the kid?"

"Some lovesick crybaby name of Chase," said Sue.

Cassie said, "You should be nicer to Chase. He's doing his part."

"His part in what?" asked Pure.

"We're hunting dragons," said Sue.

"Dragons?"

"Big winged lizards, pointy-tails, fire-breathers," said Sue.

"I never said they breathed fire," said Chase.

"This explains why every other channel I scanned this morning was a gospel station reading from Revelations about 'that old great dragon,' " said Pure. "This must be why he sent me to Arkansas."

"Who? Who sent you?" said Sue.

"The Unholy Ghost," said Pure. "It would take a while to explain."

"I hate to break up this reunion chitchat," said Cassie. "But I've called an ambulance for the people hurt in the crash. We should get out of here."

"That was nice of you, calling an ambulance," said Pure. "I see Sue hasn't corrupted you completely."

"You act like we're bad people," said Cassie. "We're trying to save the world."

"Let's take your station wagon," said Sue. "Our truck's stolen and they've run the tags."

"Fine, not that it's a big help. My station wagon's stolen also and I've got the military chasing me," said Pure.

"I'm going to hell, aren't I?" mumbled Chase, shaking his head.

CHAPTER FIVE
GHOSTS

THE BABY FINALLY STOPPED CRYING. Adam Morgan had retreated to the deck and curled into a ball. The eastern sky was brightening with the approach of morning. This had been the longest night of Adam's life, and he'd had a lot of long nights.

The night that followed the morning when Jessica hadn't woken up—that had been one long, horrible night of worry and regret. Jessica had been so supportive while he was finishing his doctorate. He'd repaid her by growing increasingly distant and focused on his work. Her love for him, her gentle kindness, had turned into an annoying distraction. Her pregnancy, an accident that she intended to bring to fruition, had filled him with resentment. He wasn't ready for a child. He didn't have time for it, or her. It wasn't that he didn't love her—she was a dream come true. But he sometimes wished he'd met her five years later, after he was finished with school, after he'd already built a career.

A year after Chase was born, Adam's selfish wish of life without the distraction of Jessica came true. She'd been one of the first victims of the sleeper flu. She'd fallen asleep and was gone, like a reverse ghost, the body lingering, the soul no longer present. The tragedy should have changed him. He'd sworn it *would* change him. Intellectually, he understood how short life was, how important it was to spend every minute with those you love. He vowed on many a sleepless night to be a better man, and most of all, a better father.

He'd broken those vows. The effort of navigating the bureaucracy to get Jessica long-term care at the same time he was starting a job in the research division of Bestiary Industries had eaten up all of his time and energy. He relied on his mother-in-law, Francine, to serve as baby sitter, and would often leave Chase in her care for weeks at a time. When Francine had died five years later and he assumed full-time care of Chase, he discovered the emotional chasm was already there. Francine had filled the boy with the notion that Adam was negligent and cold. Nothing he attempted closed the gap. Eventually he stopped trying.

At thirteen, Chase had run away. That had been the second longest night of his life, and had led to his decision to enroll Chase at a boarding school. By this point he was director of research at Bestiary, leading a project so big it would change the world. He didn't have time to focus on raising a sullen, rebellious teenager.

Now, curled up on the deck, shivering beneath his thin blanket as the sun rose, he couldn't help but think he was finally paying the price for his sins. After careful consideration of all the evidence, it was clear to Adam that he'd gone insane. This wound in his shoulder, how absurd to think it could have come from a falling star. This must be a fiction his mind had constructed to cover up a difficult reality. Most likely, he'd stabbed himself in a psychotic fugue brought about by his own self-loathing.

Or, even if he *had* been hit by a falling star, there was no way there was a baby in the belly of the ship. After he'd recovered from his first shock over seeing the fetus, he'd taken the flashlight and a sharp knife and crawled back under for a closer look. The fetus had grown in the space of an hour, and was now the size of a baby near full term, wrapped in a moist, urine-colored membrane. Adam had wanted to stab it. He didn't. He couldn't understand what this thing was, or how it could be here, but he couldn't quite bring the knife forward to cut it either.

Then, as he watched in horror, the membrane had split and pink jelly rolled toward him and the baby began to cry. He'd abandoned knife and flashlight, grabbed a blanket, retreated to the deck.

"I'm so sorry, Chase," he whispered. He didn't know why. He *was* sorry, but he didn't know what good it did to say this here, in the middle of the Atlantic where no one could hear. But he couldn't help but think that the baby was something his subconscious had conjured to represent Chase.

From the cabin came a loud crash, the rattling of pans and tins of food. It sounded like the baby had gotten into the pantry. He put his hands over his ears.

Adam wasn't sure what good the hands would do. No matter what his ears might think, the sounds weren't coming from an external source. They were products of his mind. Except that his hands *did* muffle the sound.

"Or," he said, "I could just think the sound is muffled."

He bit his lip. There was always the possibility he wasn't insane. Accepting that meant rejecting everything he believed, his whole worldview, that scientific laws controlled the planet, that reality had boundaries. If there really was a baby rummaging around in the pantry, it was breaking those laws. It was something supernatural. Adam didn't believe in phantoms. Yet wasn't the lore of sailors full of ghosts and monsters? Was there some truth to these legends after all? No, it was foolish to follow that line of thought. Insanity was the only sane explanation.

He lowered his hands. The electric can opener in the cabin whirred. He sat up as the noise stopped. A can clanked to the floor. The can opener whirred again. Adam shielded his eyes from the morning sun. Night was over. Standing, legs wobbly, he decided it was time to gather more information.

He crouched down at the cabin door, peering into the dim shadows within. Another empty can clattered on the floor.

"Hello?" said Adam, his voice quavering. "Is someone down there?"

A belch from the shadows answered him.

Then, wobbling into view, the pale body of a toddler appeared. It was a little boy, his face filthy, a mess of beans and jam. He was naked, except for a tiny bracelet around his wrist, gleaming white and pink, as if carved from a conch. The baby belched again.

Adam stared, determined not to run. The baby looked to be almost two years old now. He shakily started up the stairs, squinting as he entered sunshine.

"Star," said the child. "Light."

Adam backed up slowly, allowing room for the child to come on deck. "You talk," he said.

"Soon," said the child, stretching its arms above its body as it turned to face the sun. It sighed contentedly.

"Who are you?" asked Adam. Once again the insanity hypothesis was gaining momentum. This child was a dead ringer for Chase when he was two.

"Soon," said the child, walking, now more steadily, toward the rail. With a grunt, the child pulled himself up and over, landing in the water with a splash.

Adam ran to the side. The baby's pale body could be seen beneath the surface, several feet down, kicking vigorously. Was this a test? Was he supposed to jump in and rescue the child? But the baby was moving gracefully, purposefully under the water. It didn't appear to be in danger.

For one brief moment, Adam thought of the myth of Atlantis. He knew the original story by Plato, of a decadent civilization pushed beneath the waves by vengeful gods, and he knew the science fiction creation, of a city surviving beneath the water, populated by human-like beings, changed to adapt to their surroundings. A wildly improbable hypothesis formed—was this child from Atlantis?

The boy swam back toward the surface, no longer a toddler. He'd grown a foot in height, and had lost much of his babyish roundness. The bracelet on his wrist had grown to fit his now larger arms. As he sprang from the water, he grabbed the rail and swung himself onto the deck.

He was a perfect match of Chase as a five-year-old, a little thinner perhaps, and with a happy grin he'd never witnessed on his own son.

"Chase?" asked Adam.

"No," said the child. "I like the name you were thinking. Atlantis."

"So," said Adam, sitting down. "I'm crazy."

"You're perfectly sane," said Atlantis. "I'm reading your mind."

"I'm sorry, no," said Adam shaking his head. "I have to be crazy. I can't accept that this is supernatural."

"Nor should you. I'm not beyond or above nature," said Atlantis. "I'm nature perfected. Nor am I the Atlantis of myth or fiction. I'm the Atlantis yet to be."

Even as Atlantis spoke, he grew taller, his arms and legs growing thicker. Adam decided his sanity was no longer important. There were too many questions.

"Why do you look like my son?" asked Adam.

"I don't. I look like you," said Atlantis. "I've harvested your genetic template. This body is based upon it. When I'm finished, it will be the body you should have had, optimally balanced and muscled, free of the residue of the pesticides and heavy metals your society has slowly poisoned you with, free of scars and cellular decay."

Adam didn't know what to say to that.

"This will be my gift to you," said Atlantis. "I sense your present body is no longer comfortable. Especially now, with your wounded shoulder festering with infection and your whole body exhausted. I'm responsible for some of your immediate discomfort. I hope you will accept my offer of relief."

"I don't understand you," said Adam. "I don't understand any of this."

"I know it's difficult. I can see your thoughts, the turmoil and confusion. I can see the life events that have led you to question your sanity at this moment. But you will understand. You've the knowledge and training to fathom what I say. You've the wisdom to accept the truth."

"What are you?" asked Adam. "How can you read my mind?"

"Your thoughts are nothing but chemical reactions, releasing energy. I can see this energy. When I stimulated your taste buds earlier, I studied the wave patterns of your memories to fine tune my ability to read you."

"How is this possible?"

"I'm not human, Adam," said Atlantis. "This may be difficult to fathom while I'm clothed in this form. I'm not a living creature as you understand life. Your language lacks the words to describe me precisely. It's best to say that I am a city, in search of new residents."

"A city?" asked Adam.

"I was designed to serve my residents, to keep them healthy and whole, to provide their every want or need so that they can achieve their fullest potential undistracted by the labor of mere survival."

"Who designed you? Where do you come from?"

"Again, there are no words in your vocabulary. Others designed me. I come from elsewhere," said Atlantis.

"You're an alien?"

"It may be simplest to describe me as such. But it's only true on certain scales. You use the word 'alien' to describe fellow human beings not native to your country of origin, but you recognize that they're the same species, no different than you on most levels. The ones who designed me were also no different than you in fundamental ways. They loved, squabbled, and played, raised families, dreamed dreams, and struggled to understand and grasp the universe."

"This is incredible," said Adam. "Astonishing. But I believe you. Any other explanation for what's happening requires me to believe in the supernatural or doubt my own sanity."

"You are sane," said Atlantis.

Adam ran his fingers through his hair as he paced back and forth on the deck, his body crackling with a surge of adrenaline. "This is fantastic. I mean, when I was a kid, I just took it for granted that there were aliens. And now . . . I don't even know where to begin. God, this changes everything. This is . . . words fail me."

"I understand," said Atlantis. "I would understand you even if you ceased vocalizing. I'll continue to speak, however, since you might find more efficient forms of communication unsettling."

"How far away is your home planet?"

"I'm standing on it," said Atlantis.

Adam shook his head. "No. No, you said you were from elsewhere. Where's that?"

"If a seed is carried on the wind and lands in a field where it finds fertile ground, would not that field be the home of the resulting flower? Earth is my home."

"And you called yourself a city. Does that mean . . . are there others inside you?"

"Soon," said Atlantis. "But not others. I've come to be your home, Adam. I've come to be home for your species. Upon my shores, humanity will thrive and prosper. Within my walls, civilization will at last be given birth."

Atlantis slipped the shell bracelet from his wrist. Atlantis was much taller now, lanky yet graceful, a perfectly shaped youth on the verge of puberty.

"This," said Atlantis, gazing at the shell, "is the key that unlocks the gates of paradise."

Adam stared at the bracelet. Atlantis offered it toward him. Adam reached out, his fingers grazing the smooth surface.

Then things turned strange.

CHAPTER SIX
VERY, VERY QUIET

"**W**HAT ON EARTH IS all over this map?" Chase asked as he scraped at the brownish gunk with his fingernails.

"Blood," said Pure. "I was gut-shot in Atlanta. I was half way through Mississippi before I stopped thinking about it and it went away."

Chase stopped scratching the gunk. "It looks like ketchup."

"It *is* ketchup," said Sister Sue from the backseat. "Pure's an unrepentant liar."

"It isn't even mildly important that you believe me," said Pure.

"Not to add to this argument," said Cassie, who sat next to Sue, "but I noticed the smell of blood the second I got in the car."

"Thank you," said Pure.

Chase put the map down. "What do you mean it went away?"

"I mean the hole in my stomach went away. I forgot about it, and it went away."

"Oh, Lord," said Sue.

"Ever since I died, it's been like there's some sort of template of what I'm supposed to look like. When I'm not paying attention, I sort of 'reset.'"

"Spare me," said Sue.

"You know, Sue, I did save your butt back there. Can't you show a little gratitude?"

"Yeah, what's your problem?" said Chase.

"Don't start with me, boy," said the old woman. "My problem is that this man is a scoundrel. He's a junkie, a thief, a liar, and a vet."

"You're a vet?" asked Chase. "What war? My grandfather died in Afghanistan."

"She means I'm a veterinarian," said Pure. "Guilty as charged. And this old biddy is a Luddite terrorist. It all balances out."

"Better a terrorist than a damned vivisectionist!"

"So how exactly do you two know each other?" asked Cassie in a cheerful tone.

"Sue was a old rabble-rouser at NCIT where I was a doctoral student."

"Wow," said Cassie. "That's, like, the top cybernetics school in the country."

"It's the top torture school in the country," said Sue. "They open up live animals and wire them into computers and machines. It's horrific."

"Progress isn't pretty," said Pure. "But Sue was calling for violence to stop it. She had a website up with pictures of the doctors and students. She had 'wanted' posters listing our addresses. One of the doctors was shot under mysterious circumstances. I think Sue murdered him, whether or not she actually pulled the trigger."

"I've pulled plenty of triggers. This is a war and I'm a soldier, the last line of defense for God's green earth. Do you deny you were hurting animals?"

"We weren't hurting animals for entertainment. We were doing research to make human life better, pushing the frontiers of what was possible with prosthetics and organ transplants. The research helped improve the lives of millions of people."

"Spare me your pious justifications," Sue said. "*You* were only in the program to steal drugs."

Pure shrugged. "That was a long time ago."

"He used to say that it was unfair that horses got all the best pills."

Pure smiled dreamily. "Good times," he said. "I used to get wound up on this perfect stew of amphetamines and aggressors. I'd be up all night and in the morning I'd go down to the protest site and get into shouting matches with Sue." Pure sighed. "Now I'm all nostalgic."

"He takes nothing seriously," said Sue. "He's the closest thing to a soulless man I've ever met."

"True," said Pure. "The funny thing is, I actually still had a soul then but didn't know it. Now I know my soul has left my body and it won't leave me alone."

Chase interrupted. "I think this is the turn up here."

Pure slowed the station wagon down in front of a deer crossing sign so riddled with bullet holes it was almost unrecognizable. He steered onto a weedy patch of rock and dirt that barely resembled a road.

"I'm pretty sure this is right," said Chase. "But my father's notes are spotty. Hopefully I won't get us stranded in the middle of nowhere."

"I don't think you can," said Pure. "Not to get all religious on you, but if I'm turning down this road, it must all be part of his master plan."

"Oh yes," said Sue. "He's also a blasphemer."

"Not God," said Pure. "I'm talking about . . . oh, forget it."

"This has to be the place," said Cassie, her eyes flickering behind closed eyelids. "We're on the edge of a hundred square miles of land owned by the Warsaw Paper Corporation. That's one of the front companies of the Bestiary investors."

The station wagon lurched and bumped over stones the size of breadboxes.

"Who really needs a muffler?" Pure said as they bottomed out with a vicious clang.

"I'm getting a signal," said Cassie.

"On what?" asked Pure.

"In my head," said Cassie. "I guess I should mention that I'm a beneficiary of NCIT's cybernetic research."

"You're welcome," said Pure.

"I lost my sight when I was five. I've been wired up with an array that stimulates my optic nerves. Now I have a virtual computer monitor in my head. It gets signals from a camera in my glasses so that I can see. Of course, my sister Jazz hacked the code years ago. Now I mainly use the screen to go online and only use my eyes when I really need them. All the really interesting stuff in the world happens in the higher radio spectrums. Right now we're passing through some kind of electronic fence."

"Then we're on the right path," said Chase. "The dragons are kept in the game reserve by a radio field that causes them pain if they get too near the borders. The signal interacts with some kind of chip in their head."

"More NCIT research at work," said Cassie. "This is why I'm on Sue's side in this war despite my benefiting personally."

The road ended at the edge of a stream. The other side of the stream was a solid wall of poison ivy.

"This is it," said Chase. "I think."

"Dragons in the Ozarks," said Pure as he opened his door. "And I thought my story was hard to believe."

"What is your story?" said Chase. "You make all these weird allusions to being dead, to having a higher power guiding you, to helping us because 'he' wants you to help us, but I still haven't figured you out. I know you're just waiting for someone to beg you to explain what the hell you're talking about."

"I think I could really only explain if I was drunk," said Pure. "Too bad booze doesn't work for me now."

"He's probably high," said Sue, lifting the hatch on the station wagon. "Right now, it doesn't matter."

Sue pulled her shotgun and a rifle case out and laid them on the ground. She flipped open the case to reveal a dart gun and several vials.

"What's in those?" Pure asked.

"Acyteloranethine," said Sue.

"Rhino tranks," said Pure. "Excellent stuff. Dilute it down and mainline it and you'll have an inner peace that will last all weekend."

"Pure, as much as it pains me to say this, I want you to carry the rifle," said Sue.

"Hey," said Chase.

"Don't argue," said Sue. "I know the plan was for you to carry it, but you didn't exactly impress me with your nerves of steel back in the hotel room."

"I've got training in this," said Pure, taking the rifle. "I'm a pretty good shot. Target practice was mandatory back at Mount Weather."

"Where?" asked Chase.

"Mount Weather. It's where I lived when I worked for the government. It's all part of the reason I'm dead now."

"That's it," said Chase, throwing up his hands. "Thanks for helping us escape the cops and all, but you, sir, are insane. I'm in charge of this hunt and I say give me the rifle."

"You're not in charge," said Pure, looking through the scope on the gun at the surrounding mountains. "You might be the least in charge person I've ever met."

"Calm down boy," said Sue. "Remember the important thing here is bagging the dragon."

"But he's *crazy*."

"You're the one who has us out in the Ozarks hunting dragons," said Pure. "I'm along for the ride no matter what, but maybe someone should fill me in on the back story."

"Ever hear of a company called the Bestiary Industries?" asked Chase.

"Of course," said Pure. "They did some recruiting at NCIT. They're a gene-splicing outfit. They're the company that takes fish genes and splices them into cows to get milk that contains omega 3 fatty acids. They make chimeras, basically."

"My father led a project that was a little more sexy than getting fish oil from cows," said Chase. "Right around the time I was born there was a worldwide ban on hunting big predators like lions and tigers."

"Yeah. That was one of the things Sue was always worked up about," said Pure.

"A group of wealthy hunters decided to exploit a loophole in the law. They pooled their resources and gave Bestiary a huge grant to build a new type of game animal, one that wouldn't be covered by existing bans. It took a while, but their investments have finally paid off. We're standing in one of the most exclusive private clubs on earth. People pay a million dollars an hour to hunt dragons here."

"Really?" said Pure. "That's awesome!"

"You sicken me," snapped Sue. "I should have known you wouldn't see anything wrong with this."

"Private citizens using their own money to create a creature with no ecological significance that they kill for their own entertainment," said Pure. "What *is* the problem here?"

Sue stared at Pure with a look of revulsion, hatred, and pity.

"Give Chase the gun," Sue said, with a sigh.

"Wait a second," said Pure. "I'm still on the team. I'm looking forward to shooting one of these babies without having to shell out the dough. But why drug it? It'd be less dangerous to kill one than to take one alive."

"What we're planning to do," said Cassie, "is set a live dragon loose in Central Park."

"I see," said Pure. "Why?"

"When my father retired, he left to sail around the world," said Chase. "My mother's been in a coma since I was one year old, so Dad turned the keys to his house over to me. I went poking around in his papers and found out about the dragon project. But when I tried to go to the press with it, nobody cared."

Cassie said, "The press won't be able to ignore this story once our dragon is disemboweling joggers."

"So this is a publicity stunt?" said Pure. "One that's guaranteed to get people maimed or killed? Why do I think this was Sue's idea?"

"You should be more respectful of Sue," said Cassie. "She's spent a lifetime fighting to save this world. No one has more moral authority to do this than her."

Sue looked pleased with herself.

Pure shook his head. Maybe he was getting his signals mixed up. Maybe his higher self had guided him here to stop Sue instead of helping her. But, if there was one pattern to the signals he got from above, it was that the Pure in heaven had a warped sense of humor.

Also, backing out now would mean he'd miss a chance to see a dragon, and he was curious to find out what the gene-splicers had been able to knit together. Did it have wings? Could it breathe fire?

"I'm still in," said Pure. He looked back through the scope at the mountains again. "Hey. There's a castle up there."

Chase grabbed some binoculars from the camping gear and followed Pure's gaze.

"That must be where the guests stay," said Chase. "They get choppered in from Little Rock."

"Any contingency plans if we run into a hunter instead of a dragon?" asked Pure.

"Yes," said Sue, snapping the shotgun barrel shut.

IN ROOM 21 of the Skeets Motel Hammer Morgan ran his fingers across the damp bedspread. Gasoline. Why had Pure poured gasoline in the room? Or had it been one of the others the deputy had witnessed? He wished he knew who they were. Alice, his contact back at Mount Weather, was doing research but hadn't yet called him back.

He moved on to the shower. He found some hairs in the drain, blond, short. This matched the deputy's description of the boy. This would give them a DNA profile on at least one of Pure's friends.

"What are you up to, Alex?" whispered Morgan.

Morgan's radio chirped.

"I'm alone," he said. "Talk to me."

"The woman has to be Susan Karr," said Alice. "She's a sixties radical who never grew out of it. She's a hundred and seven years old and something of a legend in the underground community. She's on the President's list of terrorists we're authorized to kill on sight."

Morgan nodded. Pure had talked about Susan Karr before, though not in a manner that indicated they'd team up. Still, it wasn't as if Pure had any other friends or relatives to turn to.

"The girl I.D.'s as Cassandra Robertson," said Alice. "She's sister to Jasmine Robertson, presently the top name on the kill list, but Cassandra should be taken alive. It's possible she has information about Jasmine. Cassandra is legally blind, but has cybernetic implants that allow some limited vision, so don't turn your back on her, okay?"

"Great," said Morgan, rubbing his temples. Jasmine Robertson was a name he knew well. A few years ago she'd breached security at Mount Weather, draining thirty terabytes of top-secret data before they'd severed her link. That had been a huge black eye for the whole project.

The notion that Alex, an eyewitness to the inner workings of Mount Weather, was involved with someone only one step removed from Jasmine Robertson was troubling. Why was Alex involved with people like this? He hadn't exactly been the most moral person on the planet, but he was definitely not a terrorist. What had happened to him in that warp?

The last unknown was the boy. "Any leads on the blond kid?"

"Nothing firm," said Alice. "But associates report that Cassie was hanging out with a blond, short haired boy named Chase Morgan. Relative of yours?"

Hammer Morgan sagged as he sat on the bed. Ever since Alex had come out of the warp, life had been one string of weird coincidence after another.

"You know that no one at the Mountain has relatives," said Hammer. Thankfully his personnel records were sealed under a security clearance two levels higher than what Alice had access to. There was already pressure to get him off the case due to what supervisors believed was a simple former friendship with Pure. He'd get yanked in a heartbeat if they found out his grandson was involved.

Still, the good news was that Chase's involvement gave him a pretty good clue as to why he was in Arkansas. It had been almost four decades since he'd severed ties with his old life, but from time to time he peeked into his family's records. Adam had turned into something of a mad scientist, splicing together eagles, snakes, and tigers. Maybe he'd gotten it from his mother, whose hobby had been knitting.

"Alice, send a team to seize the records of Bestiary Industries. See if they've shipped any, ah, exotic cargo into the area recently."

"On it," said Alice.

PURE WAS PLEASED to discover he was immune to poison ivy. The others had sprayed themselves down with protective homeopathic lotions but Chase already had a nasty red rash breaking out on the side of his neck. Pure was tickled that the mosquitoes found Sue especially tasty. He wanted to chide her about animal rights every time she slapped one, but now wasn't the time. Since slipping in the first dragon turd, he'd grown very, very quiet. A huge, carnivorous beast was in the neighborhood. Judging by the bone fragments in its stool, it ate people.

Fortunately, there wasn't much chance of the dragon sneaking up on them. Cassie had pulled out some nifty toys from her backpack, eight matchbox size solar powered helicopters with small cameras in their noses. She was flying these through the surrounding forest, guiding them with her mind. While daylight lasted, Cassie had 360-degree vision out for hundreds of yards. Ironically, she couldn't see where she was putting her feet. Chase had to guide her, with his arm around her waist.

Except for the man-eating monster part, this walk through the woods was rather relaxing. There weren't any fortune cookies or crossword puzzles around, no half-tuned radio stations to murmur messages at him. Sometimes Pure wondered if he wasn't simply bonkers. It wasn't entirely impossible that he'd fried his synapses with some horrible mixture of chemicals. He'd been pushing the limits for decades. But he'd always maintained. It wasn't accurate to say that he'd been careful, but he'd been practiced at his addictions, and managed to stay focused and balanced enough to get clearance at Mount Weather. Of course, he'd also been sleeping with the head of security and that might have played some role.

Cassie stopped. "It's getting too dark," she whispered. "I have to reel in my eyes before they lose power."

"Do it," said Sue. "This thing probably doesn't hunt at night anyway."

"Why do you say that?" asked Chase.

"Think about it. These fat cat hunters are spoiled. They have that big castle up on the mountain to sleep in at night. They want to hunt this thing during banker's hours."

"Wow, Sue," said Pure. "That's damn close to logic. I'm impressed."

"Uh-oh," said Cassie.

Everyone froze and looked around at the growing shadows.

"I just lost one of the eyes," said Cassie. "It died instantly. Maybe I snagged a branch."

The other toy helicopters buzzed back into their vicinity like a swarm of hummingbirds.

Pure watched carefully the directions they flew in from, and turned toward the gap in the forest where nothing emerged. He raised his rifle and placed his eye to the scope.

There was a snap and a growl. Teeth flashed before the scope. Before Pure could even think about pulling the trigger the rifle was pushed back with such force that it snapped his wrist. The eyepiece of the scope pushed into his right eye socket with a sickening wet pop.

As Pure fell, the others started screaming. Pure would have screamed himself except that dagger sharp claws were digging into his diaphragm and ripping his bowels out. Then there was a horrible clap of thunder.

Pure watched his torn body land on the leafy forest bed as the dragon snarled over him. Pure was rising up through the branches as the scene below him locked up like a crashed computer program. Smoke rose from both barrels of Sue's shotgun. Apparently, she'd changed her mind about catching this dragon alive. Chase had turned a shade of white that a snowman would envy and looked ready to turn and run, except for the arm around Cassie, which held on tight. Cassie stood oddly calm as her helicopter eyes all turned toward the dragon. Maybe she had lasers in them or something.

If Pure had still been in the vicinity of his lips, he would have whistled when he saw the dragon. The beast was twelve feet long from snout to tail tip, with a wingspan easily exceeding that length. It was a magnificent creature straight out of a storybook, with bright red scales that blended into feathers at the edges of the wings, and a marvelous, noble head that was part crocodile, part horse, with the steady, knowing eyes of an owl.

It was crouched in an unreptilian pose, catlike muscles coiling and twitching, as it balanced on its hind legs. Unlike the typical movie dragon, this beast was bipedal, with small two-fingered claws at the middle joint of each wing. Apparently, the designers hadn't been able to work around the four-limb limit vertebrates had been stuck with since they crawled out of the oceans.

And then Pure was above the trees and the dragon and his companions were gone, nothing but memories, and he wondered if this was the last time he'd ever see his body.

With no sense of transition at all, Pure was no longer in the sky. He was back in the warp, where the purified Pure sat on a throne of light, reading, of all things, a Gideon Bible.

"I am a brother of dragons," said the Higher Pure, "and a companion of owls."

"What?" asked Pure.

"I left this open for you in the motel room, but you didn't go in," said Pure. "You're surprisingly difficult to steer. Or maybe it's not such a surprise. What I recall of that body, it was always difficult to control."

Pure tried to get closer to the throne, but as he rose, something thin and bony wrapped around his ankle, stopping him. He looked down to see one of the warp monkeys.

"You found them," Pure said.

"Poor lost souls," said the Higher Pure. "Do you know searching for the monkeys was the first taste I had of actual purpose? Of feeling like I was here for a reason? It's intoxicating to think that you have a starring role to play in the grand scheme of things."

"Why am I still alive?" Pure asked. "Why are you in here and I'm down there? Why can't I rejoin you?"

"Sorry," said the Higher Pure. "I've finished knitting together enough of your blood vessels to get you going again. Shoo."

"Wait," said Pure.

Even as the word left his non-existent lips, he was no longer in the there-that-was-not-there. He was falling again, passing through branches on a collision course with his damaged body.

Not much had changed. Sue was frantically stuffing new shells into the shotgun. Chase now had both arms around Cassie, attempting to drag her away from the dragon. The tiny helicopters swarmed around the creature's head. The dragon swatted at them like a bright red King Kong as he stood atop Pure's body.

Pure had half a second to assess what he was about to get shoved back into. His right wrist and trigger finger were bent at an absurd angle. His right eyeball was dangling from its socket. A loop of intestines about three feet long lay on the forest floor. This was going to hurt.

CHAPTER SEVEN
SHELL GAME

ADAM'S FINGERS BRUSHED the polished surface of the shell. His vision blurred. His knees buckled and he fell forward. He was vaguely aware of Atlantis moving to catch him. Adam fell slowly, as if hiding between seconds were eternities and he'd fallen into such an eternity, and into a memory both alien yet instantly familiar.

Adam could see himself standing on a shore of pearly sand, white as bone and gleaming like treasure. Before him was an ocean, crystal blue, with dolphins leaping in graceful arcs just beyond the breaking waves. At his feet was a dodo bird, nuzzling its great hooked beak against his thigh. He wore a robe of diaphanous silk, as soft and light as air, a brilliant green, with dragons embroidered along the sleeves in gold thread.

Behind him was a city, with towering spires stretching into the heavens, the tips lost in clouds. Among the spires flew angels and eagles and airships. The towers were not cold, stark things. They were alive, a vertical maze of waterfalls and garden terraces vibrant with hues of green. Long vines covered the walls, teeming with a rainbow mix of flowers.

He looked upon the city with a lump in his throat. This was the city of love, the city of hope, the city where dreams were given substance, the birthplace of actual civilization. This was his home.

In his hand was a gilded cage, filled with butterflies. He studied them closer. These weren't bugs. The delicate cage held machines, clever bits of clockwork with twin prismatic solar sails upon their backs and gleaming emeralds for eyes. He opened the wire door and watched the machines flutter skyward.

"Godspeed," he said.

This was the memory that gripped him in the space between the seconds. This was the memory of a thing that never was. Or perhaps of a thing yet to be.

And then the arms of Atlantis embraced him, halting his fall. Atlantis lifted Adam and carried him into the cabin, to place him on the bunk.

Adam noted the wrecked condition of the cabin, with empty tin cans scattered hither and yon. It didn't matter. He was too tired for it to matter. He felt feverish. He closed his eyes.

When he woke, the day had passed. He was aware that it was dark even before his eyes opened. The night ocean had a different smell than the ocean by day, a fresher smell, like air after a storm.

He felt more rested than he had in years. His body was still sore and his wounded shoulder burned fiercely, but his head was clear, free of guilt and worry. The shell was still in his hand. He studied it in the dim light that trickled from the open door. The shell was like a Möbius strip, twisting and turning in on itself, a shape hypnotic in its simultaneous simplicity and complexity. The surface was smooth as the inner shell of a conch, shaded in subtle pinks and purples, the color growing in intensity in the inner curves. The shell was warm, as if picked up from a sunny beach. Adam placed the shell to his ear. It was humming, not a mechanical hum, but a hum like a woman's chorus heard at a distance.

Adam pulled himself from the bed and climbed onto the deck. Atlantis was perched on the prow, watching the toenail sliver of moon that hung over the horizon.

"What happened?" asked Adam, moving forward. "Was that a dream? I had a vision of a city before I lost consciousness. What does it mean?"

Atlantis turned to him, smiling. "It means you've seen a future."

"The future?"

"A future. If you choose it."

"If I choose it? What do you mean?"

"I cannot and will not impose myself upon this world uninvited," said Atlantis. "I said before I'm but a seed. Before I can take root, I need permission. I need a representative of this world to say, 'Come, traveler, you are home. We welcome you.' "

"Why me? Why choose me for such responsibility?"

"Who else is better suited to this task?"

"Anybody!" said Adam. "My God, pick anyone at random."

"You are who I chose. You've experience in shaping the fate of species. You're the father of more than just your son."

Atlantis knew. Of course, he knew, thought Adam. It told me it reads my mind.

"You're the creator of dragons," said Atlantis. "Creating life is a feat worthy of the highest honor. In some era, you would be considered a god."

"I'm not a god," said Adam. "I'm someone who took the money and did what I was told."

Again, his memory kicked in strong, only this was a memory he knew, a memory he'd relived a thousand times before. He was sitting in a stuffed leather chair in the office of David Sanchez at Bestiary. Sanchez was CEO and before this day Adam had doubted Sanchez knew he was alive. There were a dozen other men in the room, men he didn't recognize. Sanchez told him he was being promoted to head a special project.

"We want you to build us a dragon," said one of the men, with a Texas drawl.

"What?" he'd asked.

"A dragon," said the Texan. "You know. Big lizard. Wings, sharp teeth, claws, the works. We want it big, dangerous, and clever, the meanest damn predator the world has ever seen."

"Ah," said Adam. "Why?"

"So I can hunt it," said the Texan.

Adam looked at the Texan, then looked at Sanchez. Neither of them was smiling.

"Look, son," said the Texan. "Back in my granddad's day, a man could go over to Africa and bag himself a lion or a rhino, then bring it home and put its head on the wall. It was a way of saying, 'I'm the damn top of the food chain and don't you forget it.' "

"I see," said Adam.

The Texan continued. "You shoot a lion these days and you're a pariah, not to mention a criminal. Hell, hunting doves on my own damn ranch requires three different permits. So me and the boys down at the club got an idea. 'Why don't we make a brand new animal?' George asked. And I said, 'Hell, why not?' We thought about bringing back a dinosaur, but later most of the boys got set on the idea of hunting dragons. So I started making phone calls and Mr. Sanchez here said you were just the man to head such a project."

Adam had felt a bit sick. He found the idea of creating a creature to be hunted for sport repulsive. He wanted to jump up and tell everyone in the room to go to hell. But, he had to think about Jessica. The consequences of losing his insurance would be disastrous.

Plus, in a way, he was flattered. Apparently Sanchez read his reports after all. Adam had done his doctorate on chimeras, new creatures spliced together from the genes of unlikely donors. All of the technology was available to make every creature that had ever graced the pages of a storybook. It was only a matter of time. And money. Ungodly, enormous sums of money that he was certain no one would ever want to spend.

Sanchez handed him a folder. "This contains a broad outline of the specifications for the final creature. It also contains the budget numbers that the consortium represented here is willing to finance."

Adam had opened the folder, glancing over the numbers. He thought it was a typo at first. There were too many zeroes. Then he looked at the budget breakdown and realized they were serious. Ungodly, enormous sums of money weren't an obstacle any more.

He knew then and there he'd do it. And he knew the moral compromise he'd make to live with himself. He'd build a dragon all right. He'd build it so well that it would be the hunter's heads over the dragon's mantle.

So he'd said to Sanchez, "I'm your man."

And now Atlantis was asking him to decide something larger. He didn't fully understand the consequences. He had no grasp of the risks. There was more than the lives of wealthy hunters at stake if he chose wrong. His decision would change the world forever.

"If I don't decide, will you find someone else to give you permission?" Adam asked.

"No," said Atlantis. "My time is growing short. You must decide. I offer myself as a new land, a terra incognita for the human race to settle. Unlike past human migrations, there will be no danger to the environment. There are no natives to displace, no rare habitats to disrupt. Humans will flourish under my care. All will be welcome."

"It sounds too good to be true," said Adam.

"In your vision, you saw it. You felt it. Tell me what you felt, Adam Morgan."

"Love," said Adam, tears welling in his eyes. "I was standing on the beach and I felt loved. I felt that everything in the world was good and made for my pleasure. I've never felt anything like it. I've never even imagined."

"Pure altruism is my only motive," said Atlantis. "I've been created not to be your master, but your servant. When I fully mature, even the breezes that flow through my streets will be alive, driven by one purpose, to comfort and care for those who breathe them."

"How can I say no?" said Adam, now openly weeping.

"Say yes," said Atlantis. "I require an affirmation."

"Yes," said Adam. "Yes."

"Come," said Atlantis, motioning Adam closer. "My first gift will be to relieve you of that shell."

Adam thought he meant the bracelet. As he moved closer to Atlantis, he saw clearly that the boy he'd witnessed growing earlier was now a man his own age, but taller, better muscled, without a stoop or slouch, with skin practically luminous with health.

Atlantis held his hand out. Adam took it.

"When the transfer is complete, take my vessel and place it on the water," said Atlantis.

Then, fluidly, naturally, Atlantis drew his perfect, smooth mouth to Adam's cracked, dry lips and they kissed. Adam wanted to pull away. But something was happening. Something like his earlier fall, only now time was accelerated, and before he could decide to pull away he'd already done so.

Now it was Adam instead of Atlantis who sat on the prow, looking back into the face of a sickly, aged man, a man with a face he'd seen not so long ago only in mirrors. The man's eyes were closing, his body swaying, and with a thud he collapsed onto the deck, his limbs thrown at strange angles. His hand fell open, revealing the gleaming bracelet.

Adam looked down at the new body he found himself in. He was flawless. He held his hands before him. His old hands had been pocked with scars from a lifetime of small accidents, like the white slash on one thumb from handling a broken beaker, or the more puckered scar near his wrist from a careless splash of acid seeping around his glove back in college.

His new hands were astounding, works of art masterfully carved by a gifted sculptor. He stood. There wasn't an ache or a pain anywhere in his body. He felt as if he could leap ten feet in the air. He tried it. He fell far short of ten feet, but when was the last time he'd leapt a foot in the air, let alone three? He felt finely tuned, his muscles moving in grace and balance.

"This is how I was meant to be," he said, in wonderment. His voice sounded deeper, smoother, his teeth fit his jaw better, his tongue felt like an instrument of song. He laughed. He couldn't remember the last time he'd laughed. It proved such a natural sound, the sound a human was meant to make, a sound as perfect a match to man as a meow was to a cat or a woof to a dog.

Everyone should feel like this, he realized. Our genetic code carried the promise of perfection. It was the world that roughened us, the viruses and bacteria that nibbled us away, the jobs that stressed us and caused our hair to thin and our arteries to harden. He was in a body that had never known hatred or fear or anger.

"So," he said. "This is life."

He looked at his old body. It was dead. There was no longer any spirit within, nothing animated the limbs or lungs. Adam felt a twinge of sorrow as he studied the body he'd worn for nearly five decades. The sorrow melted into sentimentality. Those dead arms were the arms that had cradled his infant son. Those dead lips were the lips that had kissed Jessica.

He saw the shell bracelet lying in the open palm. He picked it up. Atlantis had said to place his vessel upon the water. He was in the body Atlantis had grown, but it was obvious that Atlantis wasn't inside his old body.

Would the world thank him or curse him for what he was about to do? Despite Atlantis's rejection of the term, Adam knew he was about to unleash an alien presence upon the world. But he remembered the bliss he'd felt in the shadow of that city. What the world thought no longer mattered. He wanted to feel that bliss once more.

He leaned over the rail of the boat. In the moonlight, his shadow darkened the water as he slowly lowered the shell.

CHAPTER EIGHT
OUCH

PURE SCREAMED BECAUSE HE COULD. Whatever the Pure in the warp had done to fix him had restored his lungs. Right now seemed like an excellent time to use them. He was still disemboweled, still had one eye dangling from its socket, still had a broken hand, and to top it all off he had a dragon sitting on his chest.

The dragon paid no attention to Pure's scream. Instead it focused its attention on the tiny helicopters that buzzed it, lashing out with its jaws. One by one the helicopters fell in shards of plastic.

"Get off me!" Pure shouted, pounding his good hand against the dragon's belly.

As the last helicopter fell in a shower of plastic shards, the dragon snaked his head around to stare at Pure.

"I admire your resilience, sir," said the dragon.

"You tal—" Pure said before the dragon closed his jaws around his face. Pure had an especially good view of the beast's tongue. It looked more mammalian than reptilian, with fine cilia covering the surface. The teeth, though, were pure gator.

The dragon whipped around, lifting Pure by the head, swinging him in an arc. Pure's feet collided with something that gave way instantly. Sue's shotgun went off with both barrels as she cursed. The dragon spit Pure out. Pure flew a good ten feet before smashing into a tree trunk.

As he landed upside down he could see Sue struggling to regain her footing. She must have been what he hit. The smoking shotgun lay at the dragon's feet. Tiny wounds peppered the creature's torso, but didn't slow it. Off to the side, Cassie was digging through her backpack. Chase was nowhere to be seen, which didn't surprise Pure in the least. The dragon stared down at Sue, his neck pulled back as if about to strike.

"You talk?" said Pure, as loud as he could manage.

The dragon turned his gaze toward him. "So many choose these as their last words," said the dragon, stepping over Sue. "I must commend you, sir. You're made of stern stuff. All the other hunters break so easily."

"We didn't come here to hurt you," said Pure as he rolled himself over into a sitting position. With his broken hand he scooped as much of his intestines as he could into his torso while he popped his eye back into his socket with his good hand.

The dragon recoiled at the sight of Pure manipulating his own entrails.

"My good fellow, aren't you in terrible pain?" the dragon asked.

"Ouch," said Pure, half-hearted, with a shrug.

"Allow me to put you out of your misery," said the dragon, rearing back to strike.

"Why do you have a British accent?" Pure asked.

Then there was a crackle, and the terrible odor of burning feathers. The dragon shuddered and shivered as Cassie's taser sent enough voltage through him to make steam roll out of his nostrils.

The charge on the taser was powerful, but brief. Ten seconds later the crackling sound died away and the dragon still stood. The beast coughed, amidst a cloud of smoke.

"That, madam, was uncalled for," he said as he turned toward Cassie.

Cassie wielded her cane like a baseball bat and met the dragon's stare. Her dark glasses hid her eyes. The set of her jaw gave her a determined, fearless look.

"Bring it on," she said.

Thwip.

With a sudden puff of air, a dart buried itself deep into the dragon's neck. Pure looked back to where he'd first been ambushed and saw Chase standing there, dart-gun in hand.

"Leave her alone," said Chase. "You want to fight someone, I'm your man."

"Siiirrrr," said the dragon, stepping toward Chase. The dragon's serpentine head swayed drunkenly. "You . . . yooooooou."

The dragon stumbled, spreading its wings for balance. With a flap that cleared the forest floor of leaves it steadied itself. Then it lost its battle with gravity and collapsed to the dirt.

"Seriously," said Pure. "Why did it have a British accent?"

"Oh my god," said Chase running to Pure's side. "Don't look down."

"I know, I know," said Pure. "My intestines are hanging out. No big thing."

"How are you still alive?" said Cassie as she helped Sue stand up.

"I would offer last rites," said Sue, "but it's too late for you."

"This isn't going to kill me," said Pure, sagging back against the tree, closing his eyes, or trying to. The one that had come out of its socket didn't respond. "I'm already dead. I died in the warp."

"We don't have time to sit and listen to him babble," said Sue. "Cassie, get the restraints on the dragon. We've a long walk back to the station wagon with this thing. Chase, help her."

"But Pure. . . , " said Chase.

"Pure's done for," said Sue. "He's in shock. He'll be dead in minutes."

"You people don't listen to a thing I say," said Pure.

"I'm listening," said Cassie as she pulled long plastic cords out of her backpack.

"You're obviously scientifically savvy, Cassie," said Pure. "Ever hear of 'spooky action at a distance?' "

"Yeah," said Cassie. "It's a property of entangled particles. You can have two entangled particles separated by any distance and when you change the spin on one, the other instantly changes spin. Since the transmission of information appears to happen faster than the speed of light, Einstein labeled it 'spooky action at a distance.' "

"You go to the head of the class," said Pure. "Engineers have been playing around with spooky action for decades now. They create encrypted messages with it, for instance. But for the last ten years I've been working with a government black ops team on something more ambitious."

"Black ops?" said Chase.

"US military research is like an iceberg. Only a tiny fraction of it is above the waterline. The rest takes place in programs that are off the books. Black ops."

"The idea of you involved in something sinister doesn't surprise me," said Sue.

"It's not sinister," said Pure. "It's just secret. And one reason so much of it's secret is because of people like you who protest every project under the sun because it's endangering snail darters or whatever."

"You mentioned Mount Weather earlier," said Cassie. "My sister's told me all about that place. She said it's home to a shadow government that really runs the US. You worked there, huh?"

"Yeah. But Mount Weather doesn't house a shadow government, at least not anymore. Mount Weather was set up during the cold war as a second home for the US government in case of nuclear war. There was a whole city there at one point, forty thousand people, all living underground in complete secrecy. But after the cold war ended, the budget to run the place kept getting smaller and smaller. Now there's maybe a thousand people, all involved in military research. I was working on the spook door."

"What's that?" asked Cassie as she and Chase set about binding the dragon's limbs with the plastic ties.

"One theory about spooky action at a distance is that it only appears to be taking place at a distance here in our four dimensional world. But what if the two particles react instantaneously because they're actually the same particle? Some unified theories call for as many as thirteen higher dimensions. The researchers on our team believed that entangled particles are actually separate four dimensional reflections of a single particle existing in one of these higher dimensions."

"I follow you," said Cassie.

"So the researchers on my team had an idea. Since all matter is made up of particles, what if you built two gates out of entangled particles? Would it be possible to step through one gate and exit through the other?"

Sue walked around the dragon, checking its bonds. "They need to be tighter, boy," she said to Chase. "Look how Cassie's doing it."

"It took ten years but the project was a success," said Pure. "There's a spook door in Mount Weather and another one in Houston. No light passes through them. When you look inside, they're pitch black. But if you toss a baseball through one, it comes out the other side."

"Wow," said Cassie. "No wonder this is a secret project. This will change the world."

"Actually, there are still a few bugs in the system," said Pure. "Baseballs, no problem. But then we tried mice. There were complications. The mice all came out flipped."

"You mean inside out?" asked Cassie, wrinkling her nose.

"I mean mirror symmetry. When they came out they looked normal and healthy, but when I dissected them all their organs were on the wrong side."

"Ah," said Cassie. "I was wondering how a veterinarian wound up working on a physics project."

"This was Pure's specialty back in college," said Sue. "He didn't care about helping animals. To him, they were research tools. He had as much empathy for them as he had for a beaker or a test tube."

"Whatever," said Pure. "You got any gauze in that bag?"

"Sure," said Cassie, fishing about.

"The real trouble began when we tried the monkeys," said Pure. "We used capuchins. We sent them through one door, but they never came out the other side. We tried attaching cameras to them, but no signal ever came out of the gates. We tried sending them through on tethered harnesses, but the tethers would pull back empty."

"That's horrible," said Cassie, producing the gauze from her bag. "How many monkeys did you kill like that?"

"None, it turns out. But I'll get to that in a moment. If you're asking how many we sent in, it was an even dozen. And you're right. It was horrible. I don't want to come across as overly soft-hearted here, but after the third or fourth failure, I kind of felt like sending the monkeys into the warp had the same scientific value as putting kittens in a microwave. The last ten exploded, but we better do another ten to be sure."

"Why, Pure," said Sue. "You do have feelings."

"Fortunately, I also had drugs. Feelings exist to be quieted."

"How did a drug addict ever wind up working in a top secret place like that?" asked Cassie as she carried the gauze over to Pure.

"Lots of practice," said Pure. "There wasn't a day in my life since college that I wasn't altering my mood with some sort of chemical. What Sue said about me being a vet in order to get the drugs is partly true. If a horse doesn't get all of its pills, it doesn't complain to anyone. Over the years I became an expert at faking drug tests."

"But still. . . , " said Cassie, unrolling the gauze and setting to work on Pure's mangled face.

"Also, I sort of had a relationship going with the head of security. Talk about messy break-ups. The last time I saw him, he tried to shoot me in the head."

"*He?*" said Sue.

"Come on, Sue," said Pure. "You're an old hippie. You can't be that shocked that I'm gay."

"But," said Sue, "You're a *Republican*."

"I just told you that to piss you off," said Pure. "I'm really apolitical, with slightly conservative bent. Except, you know, about sex. And drugs. I'd call myself a libertarian, except I've never had a job that wasn't paid for by taxpayers. I'm tough to classify."

Sue shook her head and mumbled something Pure couldn't make out.

"So what happened to the monkeys?" asked Cassie.

"I started seeing them," said Pure. "I'd be taking a shower and look out through the steamy glass and there would be a monkey sitting on the toilet, watching me. But when I opened the door it was gone. Another time I was sleeping and I felt a hand on my leg. I put my hand onto it in the darkness and was absolutely sure I was touching a monkey's paw, but when I sat up and turned on the light, nothing was there. Other times I would catch the scent of monkeys, or hear them chattering in the hallway, but any time I tried to track them down, nothing."

"Spooky," said Cassie. She turned her attention to Pure's dangling intestines. Pure did what he could to push them all back inside before Cassie started wrapping his torso.

"I couldn't tell anyone. I always knew I was playing a dangerous game, messing with my brain chemistry on a daily basis. In some ways, winding up haunted by monkeys was perfectly natural, a long delayed side effect. I tried tinkering with doses to get rid of the effect, but it wasn't working. I finally asked for some personal time and went down to Brinkley, a little civilian town about ten miles from the mountain."

"You're hardly bleeding at all," said Cassie.

"Now you've done it," said Pure, as the gauze suddenly stained red. "If I don't remember I should be bleeding, I don't."

"Sorry," said Cassie.

Pure waved his hand. "Meh. I'll be good as new soon. Anyway, I was standing in a grocery store, in kind of a half daze, high as a kite and staring at this banana. The drugs I was on are related to LSD and I was in total awe of this banana's energy fields. I'd probably been standing there five minutes when all hell broke loose.

"The air around me ripped into little rainbows. I thought I was tripping at first, but I noticed that everyone else in the store was screaming, so what was happening must have been real. Monkey paws and faces started pushing out through these little rainbow rips and grabbing at the fruit. The monkeys were screaming, half in fear, half excitement, and in my drugged out condition it was like I understood what they were saying to me. They were lost in the warp. And they needed me to get them out."

"Holy cow," said Cassie.

"So I drove back to the base, went right into the lab and went through the door. And now things get tricky to explain."

"Really," said Sue, shaking her head.

"I went into the warp and immediately saw the problem," said Pure. "There isn't one door inside, leading to Houston. There are millions of doors leading all over the world, maybe even to different times for all I know. Being inside the warp is like surfing on a wave of windows, leading to infinite possible futures. I didn't see the monkeys. The space I was in didn't look large enough to hold them, and yet, paradoxically, it seemed vast enough to hold everything, entire universes. No wonder the monkeys were lost."

"What happened then?" asked Cassie.

"I looked back at the door I'd stepped through. The room was full of security guards. Worse, Hammer was there, and he wasn't going to be happy about this. Our relationship had been kind of strained ever since I started being haunted by the monkeys. Our relationship was secret, so he had to be worried that I was getting crazy enough to spill the beans. So I decided that it wouldn't be smart to go back out the way I came in.

"I wished there was someplace safe I could go to. Instantly, the doors shuffled and whirled around me until I was looking into the backyard of the house I grew up in. I reached out and touched the window, and I was back in the real world, three thousand miles from Mount Weather. At least, part of me was back.

"Because remember how the particles are extrusions of a single particle on a higher plane? I think something like that happened to me. I think the real me, my soul or whatever you want to call it, is still inside the warp, and I'm a kind of shadow of him in the 3D world. As near as I can tell, I'm no longer alive in a biological sense. I'm a physical echo of a man who lives on a higher dimension."

"Wow," said Cassie. "My sister has definitely got to meet you."

"I can't believe you're buying his story," said Sue.

"He's awfully perky for a man with his intestines hanging out a moment ago," said Chase. "You have a better explanation?"

"He probably loaded up on rhino tranks when we weren't watching."

Pure ignored her. "Since then, I've been on the run. The scientists on the spook door project want to dissect me. I'm their new warp monkey."

"Talk about karma," said Sue.

"The one ace in the hole I have is that my relationship with Hammer, the head of security at the Mountain, was secret. Being gay is still against the rules of conduct. Unlike the public military, there's not a lot of societal pressure to update rules in a place few people know exist. With Hammer in charge of hunting me down, I think maybe, just maybe, he's not doing his best work. I think he wants me to escape."

"Is Hammer his real name?" asked Chase. "My grandfather, the one who died in the war, was nicknamed Hammer and I've never heard of anyone else with that name."

"It's a nickname for him, too," said Pure. "Hamilton Morgan is his real name."

"What a strange coincidence," said Chase. "That was my grandfather's name."

Pure puzzled over this bit of information. Certainly this was important, another clue from the higher dimension trying to tell him something. But what?

"You know," said Pure, "we might be talking about the same guy."

"Doubtful. My grandfather's ashes are on the mantel at my father's house."

"Lot's of lifers at the Mountain have their deaths faked back in the real world," said Pure. "I'm not the only walking dead man with ties to the Mountain."

Chase shook his head. "I'll buy the whole warp door thing, but I can't believe my grandfather faked his death. He had a family. Why would he do something so cruel?"

"Don't worry about it," said Pure. "I'm only speculating. Hammer never talked about his life before he came to the Mountain. It's probably a coincidence, the names. But what does it mean? What's my higher self trying to tell me?"

As if in response, a terrible wind suddenly swept through the woods, swirling the leaves around them. A pulsing, pounding rhythm swept through Pure's belly. It reminded him of the pulsing that used to sweep through him when one of the Mountain's silenced helicopters would lift off.

"I'm getting radio signals," said Cassie. "They're encrypted."

"Oh no," Pure said. "Quick we have to—"

Suddenly branches began to snap all around them. Leaves crunched beneath heavy boots. Shadows slipped and shifted among the trees. A half dozen men in black military fatigues with rifles burst into the clearing as a familiar voice shouted, "Freeze!"

"—run," finished Pure.

But there was nowhere to run. The commandos were right on top of them, guns ready, and Chase, Cassie, and Sue were all pushed down into the dirt with ruthless efficiency.

Hammer Morgan strode onto the scene, pistol drawn, aimed at Pure.

"So much for the theory that I'm secretly trying to help you escape," said Hammer.

"Maybe it's subconscious," said Pure. "That chopper must have some damn good microphones, though."

"Good enough to hear your little story," said Hammer. "You've blabbed too much. I can't let your friends go now."

The soldiers were binding the arms of the others with plastic ties similar to the ones used on the dragon. Pure noticed that the soldiers kept looking at the unconscious dragon out of the corners of their eyes.

"How about your own flesh and blood?" asked Pure. "This kid here is your grandson. You going to kill him?"

"I don't have to kill any of you if you cooperate," said Hammer.

"Generous of you," said Pure. "But, you know, even if I wanted to cooperate, I don't think it's going to happen. Earthquakes and monkey shit haven't deterred you. I wonder what he'll come up with this time?"

As he spoke, the roar of a motor tearing through the woods became ever more apparent. The soldiers melted into shadows behind the trees, turning their rifles toward a monster-wheeled van that lumbered toward them. The van shuddered to a stop. The side door slipped open and a dozen armed men in bullet proof vests leapt out.

The driver of the van stepped out, with a megaphone in hand, and said, "Throw down your weapons. You're under arrest for trespassing."

Hammer sighed.

"Told you," said Pure.

Hammer lowered his gun, but didn't drop it as he turned to the megaphone wielding man.

"I'm with the FBI," said Hammer, holding up his fake badge. "I can give you information on who to contact to confirm this. Local law enforcement should have already been notified."

"You're on private property," said the megaphone man. "Maybe you are FBI, and maybe you're not. Poachers here come up with all kinds of tall tales. I'm telling you one last time to drop your damn gun. I've got a dozen guards here with weapons ready. If you're telling the truth, we can work it out after we take you back to headquarters."

Hammer shook his head and mumbled, "Rent-a-cops."

"I'm going to count to three," said the head rent-a-cop. "If that gun is still in your hands, we will open fire."

"Screw it," said Hammer. "I'm not in the mood for this. Take 'em."

To punctuate his command he calmly raised his gun, took aim, and placed a bullet between the eyes of the megaphone guy, then leapt behind a tree before the other rent-a-cops could react. The rifles of his hidden commandoes spat out shots, dropping half the guards before the body of their leader had even hit the ground.

Pure covered his ears as the gunfire exploded around him. He flinched as a bullet knocked the bark from the tree six inches above his head. Chase, Sue, and Cassie flattened themselves into the dirt. The dragon cracked his bleary red eyes to see what all the fuss was about. As he saw the armed men among the trees, his eyes snapped open and his body tensed. As the muscles in the reptile's neck and jaw bulged, the plastic tie that bound the creature's mouth struck Pure as being woefully insufficient.

CHAPTER NINE
SPARK OF LIFE

ADAM WATCHED THE BRACELET fall through the dark water, its bright curves visible beneath the surface for a moment, growing ever dimmer as the bracelet drifted into darkness, vanishing.

Was that it? Was that all there was to do? He kept staring into the water, expecting some dramatic development. Nothing happened.

He returned once more to the corpse he'd worn only moments earlier. He moved the limbs of his former body to give it a restful repose. The absence of life mystified him. What had changed inside his former shell? He was a man of science. He understood life from the genetic level up. But the more he'd studied and understood through the years, the more he'd grown to feel that there must be something more to life than mere chemistry and genetics. He'd watched his wife fall asleep and never awaken. What had happened? Where had she gone? Her body had remained, still healthy in most aspects. Her heart beat, her lungs moved of their own power, but her eyelids never opened again. Why?

Then, there had been the dragons. If he was ever going to understand life, it should have been when the dragons actually slid from their plastic wombs. He'd felt like a god that day. Of course, the feeling had been tempered by the knowledge that of one hundred embryos, only eleven reached term. Four of the fledglings died before the day had ended. The rest had grown as expected, aggressive, strong, and smart, except for subject J-11, who'd grown too smart, and begun to speak. His superiors had dismissed it as mere mimicry, parrot-like, especially since the other dragons, even ones born in later batches with improved code, showed no evidence of speech. Sometimes, staring into the eyes of J-11, Adam had felt as if he was looking into something deeper and vaster than he'd ever understand. Could mere random variation in brain wiring explain J-11's precocious personality?

Now, here was his old body, the spark of life removed. There was no reason for it to be dead. He'd been healthy enough. If he attempted mouth-to-mouth to revive it, would there be two of him? Or could his old body be reanimated to spend countless years comatose, alive yet not alive, like Jessica?

He grew aware of a noise around him, faint at first, and distant. It reminded him of the songs of whales, which he'd listened to many nights in his bunk. The ocean grew choppy, though the wind remained still. There were lights in the deeps of the ocean, dim orbs of phosphorescence, growing ever sharper and more defined.

Suddenly, one of the orbs broke the surface of the water. It was perched atop a thin spire of silvery metal. The spire continued to rise from the water as another orb punctured the surface a hundred yards distant, then another, and another, until all around him the sea was full of these sharp silver needles, growing ever taller and thicker. The water was bubbling now, and the air grew incredibly humid. Thunder rolled from all directions. The storm wasn't in the sky.

Beneath the water, lightning arced, in long blue-white jags that raced toward the horizon before vanishing. The water groaned. The choppy waves grew more violent, and Adam clung to the mast to steady himself. With a loud crash, the boat listed violently, and water washed over the deck, threatening to tear the mast from Adam's grip. The boat continued to tilt, until at last it toppled. But the boat was no longer sinking. It was rising.

The waves rolled away as a cylindrical platform lifted the boat skyward. In every direction that Adam looked, glistening geometric shapes were rising from the retreating ocean. They reminded him of children's blocks, cubes and pyramids and cones, of enormous dimensions.

Adam let go of the mast, slipping down the wet, tilted deck, jumping onto the white platform. It had a smooth, chalky texture, warm and moist, slightly gritty. Adam lifted his fingers to his face. The tips were coated with fine white sand. And the sand was crawling. With his newly fine-tuned eyes he could see the grains of sand with astonishing clarity. Each one was a tiny crab, smaller than a flea.

Though the stars were still bright in the sky, it began to rain. Adam became acutely aware of his nudity. Even though the night was warm and the rain was soothing, he worried that he'd grow cold soon enough. He wondered if his old clothes would fit him anymore.

Suddenly, clothes weren't the focus of his attention. The crabs were starting to swarm him, washing over his toes, swirling past his ankles, stretching in long fingers toward his knees. Worried, Adam scrambled back onto the tilted deck of his boat, kicking, trying to dislodge the invaders. His efforts failed. The crabs kept swarming, engulfing his legs, his waist, his torso, and he took a deep breath, anticipating they would next move toward his face.

They didn't. The crabs swirled down his arms, stopping at his wrists, and climbed no higher than his neck. The feeling of panic left him. The crabs weren't hurting him; they didn't even tickle. They were making tiny chirping noises, like microscopic crickets, which he strained to hear amid the drum roll of the rain.

As quickly as the crabs had swarmed him, all movement suddenly ceased and they grew silent. Adam was shocked to discover that he was now fully clothed, in a clean white shirt and blue jeans, wearing a comfortable pair of gleaming white deck shoes. He examined the fabric. It resembled cotton, soft and supple. The rain beaded on its surface and ran off, leaving the cloth dry. He sat and looked closer at the shoes. They were molded perfectly to the shape of his feet, free of any snaps or clasps. He wasn't sure how he was supposed to take them off, short of cutting them off.

As he thought this, the shoe began to shimmer, breaking apart once more into the millions of tiny crabs, which fell from his feet like dust, leaving him barefoot once more.

"Hah!" he said, suddenly figuring it out. He decided he'd once again like to be wearing shoes. Once more, the crabs scuttled onto him, spinning into shoes in an instant. On a whim, he decided that the shoes would look better black. In a twinkling, with a fluid motion starting at the toes and flowing back to the heel, the shoe darkened to an obsidian hue.

"Okay," he said, wanting to test this further. "I need a new watch." Again, a swarm of crabs rushed him, passing over his shoes, vanishing beneath the cuff of his pants, emerging once more from his left sleeve. They sounded much more mechanical than before, with grinding, whirring noise as they swirled around his wrist. Slowly, a gold band resolved itself, and a smooth circle with a glass face. He watched closely as the hands formed and began to tick in a deliberate path. He recognized this watch. It was his favorite one, a gift from Jessica when he graduated college. He'd lost it years ago, when the clasp had broken while he was swimming in the ocean. He remembered details of the watch, like the diamond that marked the twelve o'clock position, and the tiny nick in the glass made from bumping it against the corner of a brick wall. The watch took on these features before his eyes.

"My God," he said, tears welling. He was happy. He couldn't remember ever feeling so happy before. It was so pure, so powerful that he trembled in gratitude to be so blessed. All from the reunion with an old watch.

Despite what Atlantis had told him, he wondered if this was supernatural. Perhaps this was heaven. He'd seen his dead body. It made sense, in a way. Except what had he ever done to deserve heaven? And why would heaven be so unpopulated? He was alone here. He wished so badly that Jessica could be with him.

By now, the cubes and cylinders were starting to grow more intricate. It was now apparent they were buildings. The windows and doors were forming as waves of crabs poured from the forms. Before him, a section of the roof fell inward with a gentle sigh, revealing stairs leading down into the interior

He followed them, leaving the relative safety of the ship. The stairs led into a lovely room with marble walls, lit by globes of phosphorescent fluid. The room was unfurnished, but as he thought this the floor began to ripple and warp, until couches were formed, and paintings hung on each wall. The room had the airy, open feeling of an art gallery.

The paintings were abstract and a bit disappointing. Adam wondered if Atlantis was somehow pulling them from his mind. He hoped not. Adam had many useful talents, but he was the first to admit he knew and cared almost nothing about art. If Atlantis was being built to please his aesthetic standards, the rest of the world might be in for a letdown.

He left the room, moving down another staircase, and exited onto a narrow, winding street. The street had an old world charm, the buildings close together, whitewashed, inviting conversation from street level windows.

There was no one to talk to.

He was still confused by what Atlantis had meant when he said he was a city. Presumably, Atlantis was the intelligence crafting everything around him, from the shoes on his feet to the towers stretching into the night sky so high he couldn't see the tops. But was Atlantis an empty city? Was all this being crafted for his pleasure alone? For the pleasure of all humanity? Or was Atlantis somehow carrying other spirits within it, alien minds that would inhabit this place? Adam wished this thing had come with an owner's manual.

"Not a manual," said a deep, hearty voice behind him. "But I hope I will be able to answer your questions."

Adam turned to find himself face to face with a marble statue of Poseidon. He was sure it hadn't been behind him when he'd stepped onto the street.

"Let's walk," said Poseidon. "The sun will rise soon and I know the best place to view it."

The statue moved, as fluid and easily as flesh, motioning for Adam to follow.

"Are you one of the Greek gods?" asked Adam. "Were the gods really aliens? Is that what all of this means?"

"No," said Poseidon. "I've lifted this image from your world's mythology. Many of those who come here will find it easier to accept if I wear this form. For others, I may choose to use a Buddha statue, or an African totem. While I'm not a supernatural creature, the human mind is hardwired to accept these archetypes. It will help ease the cultural shock of settling here."

"Who will be settling here?" Adam said, following the Greek god down the twisting alley into an open plaza. In the center of the plaza was a fountain, and beyond that was one of the enormous towers, far taller than any building he'd ever seen, massive, yet graceful, slender as a needle in proportion as it rose into the heavens.

"Anyone who wishes. All will be welcome," said Poseidon.

"That may not work out as smoothly as you imagine," said Adam. "People from different parts of this world don't always cooperate. People from the same parts of the world, even."

"I know the history of your nations. Even as humans build cultures that span the globe, you still maintain tribal identities and react to competing tribes with hostility. Natural selection has bred this into your race. It was a logical response to a world of limited resources. Here, there are no limits."

"No limits? There must be some cost to all of this. I don't mean financial, I mean in energy, in resources. How are you building these structures?"

"Far beneath this city lies a mid-Atlantic ridge. I'm drawing minerals directly from it to assemble these structures. These waters also provide raw materials for food and clothing. As you've witnessed with your shoes, when you're done with an object, I can simply recycle its components into new forms. All matter can be recycled endlessly."

"But people like to keep things," said Adam. "If you make everything people want, it won't be long before this island runs out of closet space. Trust me."

"I believe you. But again, your thoughts apply to your old world of finite resources. That watch you wear, I've crafted from your memories. If you decided not to wear it any longer, it wouldn't require storage. I would simply reclaim the minerals. Should you ever wish to see it again, it's a simple matter to recreate it. Storage no longer requires space, only information."

"All of this creation must carry a tremendous cost in energy. What is the power source? What fuels all of this?"

"Your sun, which has heated the ocean we rest upon for billions of years. The ocean is a giant solar battery, and it's a simple enough matter to draw heat from it to provide clean, nearly limitless power. There is some cost, in that the ocean will grow slowly cooler. It will take millions of years to draw off enough heat to have any environmental significance."

"This all sounds very Utopian," said Adam. "I suspect most people will have a difficult time swallowing this."

"Perhaps," said Poseidon. "But the fact that your language possesses a word such as Utopia shows that humans already have a nearly universal vision of the perfect city. Some call it heaven. Others call it Shangri-La. I'm the city your race has dreamed of since the dawn of cities."

"The thing about heaven was, there were rules to get in. How will you decide who comes here? You can't accommodate nine billion people."

"Nine billion is not an intimidating number. But, as you said, some will be skeptical. Many will not come. All who do will be welcome."

Adam couldn't quite get over the notion that Atlantis was overestimating the potential for humans to get along. There were too many questions in his mind all at once. If Atlantis could provide the world with the technology for clean, unlimited energy, was there time to reverse the environmental damage Earth had suffered? Would introducing this knowledge cause economic chaos?

But it was difficult to focus on his worries. Poseidon was leading him up broad stairs toward the tower. Adam looked in awe at the vast structure. He had no way of judging its height. He was too close. It vanished into infinity, far taller than any building he'd ever seen.

He stepped into the domed lobby. In the center of the lobby on the floor was a large black disk, so perfect in its darkness that Adam hesitated to step on it, fearing there was nothing before him but a vast pit. Poseidon walked to the center, and motioned for Adam to follow.

"This may disorient you," said Poseidon.

Adam felt his stomach turn as he stepped onto the dark circle. He was no longer standing in the lobby. Instead, he was standing on a narrow balcony, impossibly high above the city. Dizzy, he grabbed the balcony rail with a white-knuckle grip. Beneath him the city was glowing white, and he could see the plan of the city, circles within circles, punctuated by spires. He was miles in the air. His clothing instantly thickened, keeping him warm.

"What just happened?" he asked. The air here was thin. His voice fell faintly on his own ears.

"To facilitate movement through the city, all of the towers contain gateways connected through underspace. We've traveled seven miles to the top of the tower though we only took one step forward. In time, this method of travel will become second nature for you."

"Seven miles? How can we be breathing this high up?"

"There are tiny machines within you that instantly adapt your body to these conditions."

"Nanotechnology?" asked Adam.

"That is your culture's word for it, yes."

It was too much. He was standing as high as the peak of Everest, having walked here with a single step, inside a brand new body, and now he had to think about microscopic machines working inside his lungs. He realized he had gone insane after all. The talking statue before him was just a fantasy. And then the sun broke over the horizon, revealing the vast arc of the Earth, painting the city below in a palette of rose and shadows. Adam smiled in the face of such beauty.

"If only Jessica could see this," he said.

Poseidon smiled, a twinkle in his eye.

Then, on the horizon, dark specks appeared. Adam's new eyes spotted them instantly.

"What's that?" he asked.

"Fighter jets," said Poseidon. "The world has discovered us, it seems."

CHAPTER TEN
THIS IS GOING TO STING

SNARLING, THE DRAGON THRASHED against its bonds. Its mouth was sealed with a plastic muzzle that kept its jaws clamped shut, but Cassie and Chase hadn't taken its serpentine neck into account when they bound it. The beast simply snaked its jaws down toward its bound wrists and looped a single sharp claw through the cord, snapping it.

The handful of rent-a-cops who survived due to good reflexes or sheer luck had now taken positions behind trees themselves and were returning fire on the black-garbed soldiers.

The dragon used it free jaws to snap through the cords that bound its legs.

Pure calmly rose to his feet amidst the hail of gunfire. He had a good feeling about all of this. He walked over to the fallen leader of the rent-a-cops and found the knife on his belt.

"Jesus Christ," Hammer shouted as the dragon pounced toward him. From the corner of Pure's good eye, he could see the dragon crash into Hammer and knock him to the ground. Hammer's head landed on a particularly sharp looking rock and he stopped moving. The dragon didn't pause over its prey, leaping instead toward a black-garbed soldier behind a nearby tree. Pure deduced that the beast really didn't like guns or the people who carried them. A severed arm went flying overhead as the dragon made short work of his target.

Pure strode to the center of the clearing. The gunfire was definitely dying off now, as the commandos dropped one by one. The few surviving rent-a-cops were running for all they were worth. Pure heard a snap and a curse as the dragon landed on another of the black-garbed soldiers.

Using his knife, Pure quickly cut Chase and Cassie free. He was tempted to leave Sue bound, but decided not to be petty. As he cut her loose she rolled over and he saw she was smiling.

"This is better than Ontario!" Sue said, referring to a famous riot of a decade ago when the Canadians had first really gone into panic mode about their country disappearing under ice.

There was a horrible cry trailing off into a gurgle from a nearby tree and all gunfire stopped.

The dragon emerged into the clearing, covered with gore, his eyes fixed on Pure.

"That was an impressive bit of slaughter," Pure said. "They didn't mess around when they designed a predator, did they?"

"Why aren't you still injured?" asked the dragon, furrowing its brows in a confused dog kind of expression.

Pure looked down. He pushed aside the bloodied gauze to discover that his belly was intact once more.

"Huh," he said. "In all the excitement, I sort of forgot about it. He must have taken the opportunity to hit my reset button."

"What manner of beast are you?" the dragon asked.

"I'm just your average walking-dead, queer, black-ops veterinarian," said Pure, extending a hand. "The name's Alex Pure. Pleased to meet you."

"I've no patience for trickery," said the dragon. "You've shot me, fried me, drugged me and bound me. Friendship isn't easily forged in such conditions."

"Sounds like someone has a chip on their shoulder. More to the point, you've got a chip in your head," said Pure. "It causes you a lot of pain when you get near the borders of the park. Am I right?"

"What of it?"

"We can fix you," said Pure. "We can take out the chip. Get you outside of the park, away from hunters."

"And then what? I'm well aware of my status, and have long dreamed of the larger world. But I know my lot in life. I'm property, a plaything created for amusement. I can never be free, even beyond the accursed boundary."

"What kind of attitude is that?" asked Pure. "Never say never. Trust me, there are agents out there that would dream of having you as a client. We could be talking about a book deal, movie rights, the works. Once the press gets hold of you, you'll be famous, and once you're famous, you'll be the freest creature on earth. Celebrities get away with murder."

"Intriguing," said the dragon, scratching his chin with his claws.

"Make up your mind quickly," said Cassie. "One of the guards that got away has radioed this in. We'll be swarming with backup any minute."

"Very well. I shall go with you. What have I to lose?"

"Good. Get in the van," said Sue, opening the van doors. "I'll drive. Cassie, you're riding shotgun." Sue shoved the shotgun into Cassie's hands. "Get me some directions on the fastest way out of here. Chase, Pure, in the back with the dragon. Get that chip out ASAP."

"Yes, ma'am," said Chase.

"I rather like her," said the dragon, moving toward the open door.

"You got a name?" asked Pure.

"Morningstar."

They piled into the van. A John Denver song was warbling softly from the speakers, "Country Roads." Cassie switched the radio off before John could finish the last syllable of "West Virginia." A bottled water sat on one of the seats. The tiny print on the label read "Bottled in West Virginia." Bells went off in his head.

"That's two," he said. "Can anybody think of any reason we might be needed in West Virginia?"

"Not on the itinerary. We're heading straight to the Big Apple." Sue said as she stomped on the accelerator, tossing Pure, Chase, and Morningstar backwards.

"Actually," said Cassie. "I was going to suggest going through West Virginia. It's not far out of our way. We could hook up with my sister, Jazz. We're going to have every cop in America looking for us, but she's got the connections to get us safely to wherever we need to go."

"Then that's where we supposed to go," said Pure, bracing himself with one hand against the ceiling as he brandished the knife. He turned toward Morningstar and placed his fingers on the dragon's brow. Through luck or invisible guidance, he could feel the small square of the pain-chip beneath the beast's hide. "Hold tight. This is going to sting."

IN THE DISTANCE, the night sky glowed red with the fires of road crews fighting back the jungle. Pure had taken over the driving duties somewhere around the Tennessee border. Sue and Cassie and Morningstar were zonked out in the back of the van. Chase was sitting next to him, obviously annoyed as Pure kept pushing the scan button on the radio.

"Can't you just pick one?" Chase asked.

Pure said nothing. He kept his eyes on the highway, watching for the frost-backs who walked along the edges of the road. These illegal Canadian immigrants tended not to wear anything bright or reflective.

They loomed out of the darkness at the last second, casting frightened glances at the passing van. Poor bastards.

"The world's going to hell," said Chase as they passed by one of the frost-backs, his sad, hollow-eyed face ghostly in the headlights. "I wonder what it would have been like to grow up in a time when the world wasn't on the verge of total anarchy?"

"I'm sorry. Did the center not hold?" said Pure, struggling to figure out if the ghostly voice on the radio a second ago had said "Atlantis" or "Mylanta." It didn't matter, he supposed. His higher self wasn't trying to warn him against heartburn. "I bet you look around, see all of these homeless Canucks, see the jungle eating cities from the south and glaciers coming in from the north and it looks like the end of the world, huh?"

"Yeah," said Chase. "I think it might well be."

"Grow up," said Pure. "Get some perspective. The world isn't in any danger from this. Kids your age always think they're living in the end times, that things are as bad as they can possibly get. It's what people believed a century ago. Even a thousand years ago. The end of days always seems to be just around the corner."

"How can things get worse?"

"We aren't fighting any major wars at the moment; all the major powers are too broke to field armies. And how much of the world's population have we lost to plague recently? Ten percent, tops. Mostly we have some lousy weather and a tough economy. One day you'll tell your grandkids about how horrible the world was. They'll laugh and tell you how tough their world is and you'll think, 'these young whippersnappers don't know shit.'"

"You think you're funny don't you," said Chase.

"I think life's funny," said Pure. "It's just a matter of training your eyes to see the humor."

"I don't see anything funny about my life," said Chase.

"Maybe you just aren't using the right drugs yet," said Pure. "I could prescribe something that would have you giggling at funerals."

"I don't want to be giggling at funerals," said Chase. "You might not take life seriously, but I learned early on just how serious things really are. Remember sleeper flu?"

"Yeah. It took my grandmother," said Pure. "She slept for a year before it took her."

"My mom's still in a coma," said Chase.

"Really?" said Pure. "Wow. The flu was, like, twenty years ago."

"It took her just after my first birthday," said Chase. "My dad keeps her in some upscale nursing home in Pennsylvania. All the memories I have of her are of this withered skeleton lying in bed. I haven't gone to see her in years. It's too depressing."

"That's a rough break."

"But at least my Mom has a good excuse for neglecting me," said Chase. "My dad took himself out of my life with full deliberation. He only cared about his job. When I was old enough to confront him on this, he actually had the nerve to tell me the reason he worked so hard was because of Mom and me. He told me boarding schools and nursing homes aren't cheap. But he had more than enough money to get by, it turns out. He retired early and bought a boat, then set out to sail around the world alone. How's that for a remote father?"

"And that's why you're wanting to punish him by exposing him to the whole world as a monster for creating our toothsome friend back there."

"That's definitely a bonus. But really, the most important thing is that the world finds out about the potential environmental harm."

"Oh, please," said Pure. "You sound like you're reading that off a cue card. How much did you care about the environment before you met Cassie?"

"A lot. Really. I'm not faking my devotion to the cause," said Chase.

"You're so transparent I could read a book through you. I'm guessing Cassie caught your eye and you desperately wanted some excuse to talk to her. You find out she's a gung-ho enviro-freak; you just happen to know about some morally dubious genetic engineering. You aren't the first person to pretend to feel something you don't in order to get into another person's pants."

"My feelings about Cassie are none of your business."

"Oh," said Pure, nodding slightly. "*I see.*"

"You see?" said Chase. "What do you mean, you see?"

"I deduce from your tone that you haven't slept with her. She's still stringing you along," said Pure. "You never imagined you'd actually find yourself on the dragon hunt personally. You thought ratting out your dad would be enough to bed her, right?"

"I'm starting to see why Sue hates you," said Chase. "You're an asshole."

"Everyone needs an asshole to keep them from filling up with shit," said Pure. "Look, kid, I thought I was picking up some strange vibes from you two. You've got the hots for her so bad you're committing felonies to impress her. She's putting up with you while you're useful, but she doesn't have the faintest romantic glimmerings about you. I've got a feel for these things. It's a side effect of my gaydar."

"Gaydar?" said Chase, rolling his eyes. "That's real?"

"Nope," said Pure. "Not in any logical, empirical sense. But, yeah, sure. Sometimes. I get signals."

"Really?"

"Like with your granddad," said Pure. "Jesus, you think you know a guy and then you find out he has a grandkid. Sheesh."

"He's not my grandfather," said Chase.

"When he looked at you back in the forest, he had this little twitch in his cheek," said Pure. "He knows who you are."

"You're basing this on a cheek twitch?"

"I'm tuned in to Hammer on a pretty deep level," said Pure. "Really, really deep if you get my drift."

"You're disgusting," said Chase.

"You've got his eyes," said Pure.

"Are you hitting on me?" said Chase.

Pure chuckled.

They drove through Memphis in silence. Pure wondered if Chase was finally going to sleep.

About an hour before dawn, Chase asked, "So where did you meet him?"

"Hammer? As head of security, he oversees interviews of potential recruits to Mount Weather. It's not like they have an office where you go in and fill out an application. They have a secret network there to recruit people that fill their needs. They needed a vet for the lab animals and I fit the bill. I was unmarried, had no strong family ties, was something of a loner. I was apparently a pretty good candidate for vanishing from the face of the Earth and living the rest of my life in Mount Weather."

"It also makes you fit the profile of a nut who would climb a bell tower and start shooting people," said Chase.

"There's a surprising overlap. Anyway, when I was contacted by the screener, I was told that there was a research job overseas, top-secret medical work for a large pharmaceutical company. They hinted that some of the research would be illegal if done in the U.S. I told them I was the man they were looking for. I had a half dozen interviews and a battery of psychological tests."

"I can't believe that didn't weed you out," said Chase.

Pure shrugged. "Part of my medical training was on administering these tests. I know how to make myself sound good. Too good, actually. Part of the screening team was suspicious. There are six people on the screening team and I was splitting them perfectly, three to three, as to whether I was a dream candidate or nothing but trouble. So Hammer was brought in to visit me at my home and make a final judgment.

"I'll never forget opening my door to let him in. Hammer was gorgeous. He was a couple of decades older than me, but his body was chiseled. I got a nice warm shiver from the way he took over the room when he walked in, the way he stared at me, as if he was daring me to be dishonest with him. He had this take-no-prisoners gleam in his eyes and I don't mind telling you, I wanted to bite this man."

"Look," said Chase. "You can leave out the sexual commentary."

"Why? You homophobic?"

"No. But I happen to be polite enough not to talk about sex."

"Probably because you have nothing to talk about. Anyway, we're alone in my apartment and Hammer is in full-bore dominance mode and says to me, 'Mystery solved. I can smell it on you. You're a junky.'

"And I never break his gaze. I say, 'Sure. And you're queer. Is there a problem?' "

Pure felt himself drifting off into the memory. He remembered Hammer's stoic, stony face, followed by the slight wry grin.

"We clicked," said Pure. "We were two people who prided ourselves on being direct and at the same time we both had huge secrets, things that were at the core of our personalities, that we were hiding. That was what bonded us. I knew something about him no one else knew, he knew something about me no one else knew. That, and the sex was incredible. My god, Hammer has this wonderful little thing he does—"

"You're doing it again," said Chase. "I think you're trying to provoke me."

"There's something about you that makes it fun to bug you," said Pure. "I haven't put my finger on it yet."

Chase shook his head. "This is all a coincidence. My grandfather's dead. And he certainly wasn't gay. He had a wife and a son."

"Hammer grew up in the late seventies, early eighties. It was a different world then. Some gays were coming out, but lots were in denial. They got married due to societal pressures, then either lived in misery or else found outlets for their desires on the side. Hammer would always dismiss my questions about his past by telling me it wasn't important, that it was a lifetime ago. Maybe he was so unhappy with the choices he'd made that the idea of faking his death and going to live in a hidden city seemed like a better alternative."

"Whatever," said Chase, lowering his seat back another notch and turning his face toward the window.

Pure decided to let the matter drop. Maybe it was important, maybe it wasn't. He wondered if Hammer was dead now. Morningstar had done a number on him. Why hadn't he thought to check his pulse?

It bothered Pure slightly that he wasn't more worried about Hammer's fate. Had he always been this cold and self-centered, or was this only a side effect of the warp? Why didn't he know more about Hammer's past? But, it wasn't like they'd spent long endless hours on some romantic beach talking about their lives. Their relationship had been one of stolen moments, kept hidden from others. It had been exciting, romantic, but also pretty shallow. Their relationship was mostly physical. But, yowza, what a physique.

Pure turned his attention once more to the radio. This time, it was definitely a Mylanta commercial once he listened to a larger clip. But it had sounded like Atlantis at first. Something big was brewing, he could feel it. It involved Atlantis—whatever the hell that meant. Now he was heading back to West Virginia, home of Mount Weather, sitting next to his boyfriend's grandson—that meant something, didn't it? The world was like a big spider's web of connections and coincidences. Was he now so tangled in the web he was prey for something he couldn't see?

Pure shook his head. He needed to stop trying to figure everything out. Just ride the waves of weirdness that were swelling up to carry him toward an unseen shore. A week ago he would never have believed he'd be driving around the country in a van with two girls, two guys, and a big animal, trying to solve mysteries. No, wait, that was Scooby Doo. But from that moment forward, he thought of the van as the Misery Machine.

CHAPTER ELEVEN
ANGELS

CAPTAIN CHERISE WASHINGTON piloted her F-32 Navy Phantom along the coastline of the new island. The radar data from the Aegis system had been right after all. An island almost forty miles across now sat where there hadn't been one the night before. Nor was this one of the black, steaming chunks of rock that volcanic ridges would occasionally push to the surface. The beach below her was sparkling white, as if made of pearl, and to her right the gigantic towers of an undiscovered city gleamed in the sun.

The F-32 was a poor choice for a reconnaissance plane. Cherise was moving at the speed of sound, a bit fast for sightseeing. But the *USS Clinton*, the aircraft carrier Cherise was stationed on, was the closest American vessel in the vicinity of the island and the *Clinton* housed fighter jets, not spy planes. In a situation like this, any information might be useful. Already, she could tell her mission wasn't a waste. The first piece of useful information she gathered was that her radio headset spewed out only static the second she passed within a mile of the island. The island was surrounded by some kind of jamming field. She and her squadron played around for fifteen minutes, defining the static boundary. Attempting to fly over the city would leave the squadron completely cut off from radio contact.

The second important thing she learned was that the city looked empty. She had no way of telling what might be in those towers, but the beaches were devoid of any signs of life.

"Here's the plan," she said. "Skirt the radio boundary, but keep in contact. I'm going to do a flyover of the island. Maintain visual contact with me as long as possible. If I'm not out the other side of the island in five minutes, head back to the Clinton."

She banked her plane into a hard right, rocketing toward the center of the island. If the city had any sort of defense systems, she wanted to smoke it out. Passing over streets and buildings, she still saw no sign of any inhabitants.

Suddenly, her defense radar began to chime. There was something small and fast rising toward her. She banked hard left, veering close to a tower and climbing in a way that no other plane in the world could match. In seconds she'd looped around the tower completely. But the radar continued to chime. She hadn't lost whatever was tailing her. It was, in fact, gaining on her. Impact would be in ten seconds. Nine. Eight.

She twisted around, trying to see something, anything that might indicate what was on her tail. Nothing. Her helmet blocked her peripheral vision. She straightened the plane out with five seconds to go, and then punched into a dive, looking for an extra boost of speed. She pulled out a hundred feet above the ground. The thing on her tail was closer than ever. She pushed aside the guard on the ejection trigger in her joystick with three seconds to impact. She held off, waiting for the last possible second.

The last second arrived, and the radar showed the object close, but no longer on a path toward impact. Whatever it was now pulled parallel, passing to her left. She glanced over and blinked. She studied the oxygen gauge on her in-helmet display. She wasn't starved for oxygen, even with the g's she was pulling. She looked left again.

An angel flew next to her plane. Its wings were enormous, perhaps twenty feet across, three times the length of its body. It was difficult to say if it was male or female. The angel's long white hair flowed around its smooth face, and its slim, graceful body was concealed beneath white robes that also seemed sculpted from marble. The incredible wind that accompanied the speeds they were traveling barely rippled the robes. The angel smiled as it looked at her, and raised a hand in greeting.

Suddenly, the static in her headset cleared and a voice, gentle and calm, said, "I mean you no harm. In one day, we will broadcast a message of welcome to your people. If you wish to investigate closer, there's a landing strip that can accommodate your plane three miles north. Welcome to Atlantis."

The angel extended its arm toward her and gave a thumbs up gesture. Then the angel sped ahead of her, leaving behind a halo of mist as it broke another mach and darted behind one of the towers, vanishing.

"Jesus H. Christ," she whispered, then instantly cringed. In light of this development, taking the Lord's name in vain might be a bad idea.

ANTONIO LOPEZ-NELSON had been president of the United State for three years, three absolutely horrible years. In the most recent poll, his job approval numbers had been at 17%. It wasn't like the world wasn't a mess when Lopez-Nelson had taken over. But since the day of his inauguration, there had not been a single morning where he'd come into a morning briefing and been greeted with good news. This morning, he walked down the long hall toward the briefing room slowly, all alone, sipping coffee carefully. The two minutes it took him to leave the oval office and walk to the briefing room were likely to be the only quiet moments of his day. He was considering moving the briefing room even further away, to give him yet another quiet moment. Was that too much to ask?

His only consolation was that if great presidents are made during difficult times, people might one day remember him as the greatest president of all.

On the day he'd been sworn in, a magnitude 9 earthquake had struck New Madrid, Missouri, and the inauguration platform had trembled with the furthest echoes of the shock at the moment he'd been sworn in. Apparently, scientists had been warning for over a century that such a quake was possible, but no one had listened. That trembling inauguration platform had been a bad omen.

In the weeks that followed, mosquito born hemorrhagic fever struck New York City when summer-like temperatures arrived in February and stuck around. February continued to be an unlucky month. In his second February in office, war had broken out between Pakistan and India. Thanks to the nuclear arsenals of both nations, it was a very short war, but it still sent shock waves through the world's economy. The stock market had collapsed, and the dollar was so weak that the peso was now considered the world's safest currency. On top of all this, there were three separate regional rebellions going on, with Texas attempting to secede, Montana falling under control of the Freemen, and the whole Mountaineer Underground nonsense in West Virginia. Just when he thought that there was no more possible bad news, he'd woken up to find an email from David Sanchez, his largest campaign contributor, giving him the heads up that some kind of scandal might be about to break concerning genetically modified reptiles at a research facility in Arkansas. Lopez-Nelson couldn't figure out why anyone would care about such an obscure subject, and that made him worry all the more about what it was that he wasn't being told.

In front of the briefing room, he took one last sip of coffee, pulled back his shoulders, and stepped inside.

Silence greeted him. Everyone was there, his entire cabinet, but there was none of the usual chitchat. They turned in unison toward him, revealing pale, shocked faces.

Then they looked back to the head of the table. Lopez-Nelson followed their gaze, to the statue of an angel that stood across the room. Strange. No one had said anything to him about a new statue. Was this a gift from some foreign country? Didn't they know the grief the church/state separation people would kick up over an angel statue in the White House? Then the statue raised its open hand in greeting and said, "Hello."

Lopez-Nelson jumped as the statue moved and spoke. Then he slapped his thigh and started laughing. Things had been so tense lately, a practical joke starting the briefing was a welcome change. This one had really got him. He wiped his eyes.

"Hah," he said. "I really thought it was a statue. You got me. Who set this up? Ben? Was it Ben?" His vice-president was the only one not in the room. Supposedly he was visiting Houston this morning to look at damage from recent riots. But now he wouldn't be surprised if Ben leapt out from behind a curtain and yelled, "Gotcha."

All of the members of his cabinet remained silent. Lopez-Nelson studied their faces. None had even the faintest hint of a smile.

"Okay," he said. "I don't get it. What's going on?"

"I'm a representative of Atlantis," said the angel. "I've been sent to inform you that tomorrow morning the city will be broadcasting a message to all the citizens of Earth. We're paying this visit to you and to other world leaders as a courtesy. Don't be alarmed by the new land forming in the Atlantic. We mean no harm. We come to offer peace, prosperity, and security to all the people of Earth. We're aware that your nation possesses the technology to attempt an attack upon Atlantis. We wish to warn you, although we are in no way threatening you, that any attack against us will only result in the destruction of your forces."

"Ben?" said Lopez-Nelson.

MARIAH BELIEVED IN THE POWER of prayer. There was much in her life to pray for. At home, she took care of her twenty-nine-year-old daughter, Anna, who had an inoperable brain tumor. The doctors said Anna had only weeks to live. Perhaps this was so. Or, perhaps not. Mariah knew a thing or two about the pronouncements of doctors. She'd witnessed their predictions go wildly wrong many times on her job.

Mariah was a nurse's aide on the graveyard shift at Rolling Meadows, a long-term care facility just outside of Memphis, Tennessee. Each night, she took care of the men and women in the ward as they slept. They always slept, and would have slept even if she'd had one of the coveted day shifts. Caring for these sleepers gave her a perspective on the workings of God. The rooms of sleeping patients could be viewed as a message to the doctors, a message saying not to be so arrogant, not to treat people as if they were only a list of chemicals to be boiled down and studied. Twenty years of study had done nothing to wake these people. If there was another message here, it was that God treated everyone equally. Rolling Hills was an expensive facility. The patients here were from wealthy families. She could never afford to place her own daughter in such a facility. But what did wealth matter to God? The only thing that would one day wake these sleepers was the power of prayer. And so Mariah prayed, during the night, during the day, before going to sleep, upon waking, Mariah prayed. The world had become sinful and depraved, so she was in no way angry or blameful of God for the punishments he'd visited upon the world, even upon her own daughter. She could only hope that if she remained devout enough, faithful enough, that the Lord would one day bless the world and bring relief from these terrible times.

It was about an hour after dawn, nearly time for her shift to end, when she was pulled from her silent prayer by shouting from the lobby. She crossed herself and pressed up against the wall, listening. Was the facility under attack? She'd heard a woman screaming, probably Celia at the front desk, but that had stopped. Now she heard a man's voice shouting, "Who are you?" and coming closer to her. Curious, she stuck her head around the corner, into the hall leading to the main lobby.

An angel was walking toward her. Tall, magnificent, like a marble statue come to life, the angel strode down the hall, its wings moving in gentle motions that sent bright, sparkling showers of dust swirling through the air behind it. Doctor Fredrickson, the young new doctor who'd recently started on nightshift, was walking backwards before it, arms outstretched as if trying to get the angel to stop.

"You can't come in here," Dr. Fredrickson said, half shouting, half begging. "The police will be here any minute. Stop!"

The angel spoke as it continued to walk forward. "The substance I'm releasing from my wings contains microscopic machines that are analyzing the brain structures of your patients. When the police arrive, please have them wait outside if I haven't completed my work. I understand they will be armed, and I don't want them doing anything to imperil the patients."

"Is that a threat?" said Dr. Fredrickson. "You can't come in here and start making threats."

Mariah took pity on the poor young doctor. As he continued walking backward, he drew near her, and she reached out and grabbed his coat, and pulled him toward her, out of the angel's path.

"Don't try to stop it," Mariah said as the angel strode past.

"Mariah?" Dr. Fredrickson said, glancing at her nametag. "What do you know about this?"

Before she could answer, the swirling dust engulfed them. She inhaled. The air smelled of roses, and was fresh and full of wonder, the sort of air she'd breathed only in her dreams of paradise. Even Dr. Fredrickson calmed upon breathing this heavenly scent.

"My God," he whispered.

"Yes," said Mariah.

She let go of the doctor, who stood still, looking stunned, tears welling up in his eyes. Mariah had never before felt so full of purpose, so decisive. She followed the angel, who was opening the door to the private room of Jessica Morgan. Mariah slipped in through the open door, now close enough to the angel that she could touch it. She didn't dare. She didn't fear the angel, but she worried that her own, earthly touch might sully it.

The angel stood near the head of Jessica's bed. She'd not seen anything so exquisitely beautiful since she'd seen sculptures at the Vatican, forty years ago on a pilgrimage.

"You're going to wake them, aren't you?" said Mariah.

"Yes," said the angel.

"Will you also help my daughter?"

The angel studied her with stony eyes. Mariah believed the angel could see her soul.

"She has cancer," said Mariah. "She stays on a hospital bed in my living room. The doctors say she will die soon. I know you can help her."

"All who can be healed shall be healed, in time," said the angel. "For now, I've come to retrieve a specific individual."

The angel leaned over and lifted Jessica into his arms. She was little more than a skeleton, with skin pale and translucent. As he lifted her, tubes were pulled roughly from her skin, but she didn't flinch.

Then the angel tilted his face toward Jessica, brought his marble mouth to her cracked, papery lips, and kissed her.

Mariah fell to her knees, hands folded in prayer. As the angel breathed into Jessica's mouth, her body began to change. Jessica's limbs grew thicker, her skin blushed with new blood, her needle marks and bed sores closed over and vanished.

The angel drew his lips away. A halo of diamond dust illuminated their faces. Jessica's eyes fluttered, opened, then closed once more. She breathed deeply, stretching her arms, then once again opened her eyes.

"Good morning," said the angel.

"Am I dead?" asked Jessica, calmly.

"No," said the angel. "You need never again fear death."

"Mrs. Morgan, it's the rapture," said Mariah, attempting to be helpful.

The angel carried Jessica past Mariah and walked toward the lobby once more. Mariah followed, as the angel stepped outside. Behind her, people were shouting, a cacophony of voices, boiling down to one message.

All the sleepers were waking.

Outside, the angel spread its wings, and said to Jessica, "I'm taking you home."

"Heaven?" asked Jessica.

"Atlantis," said the angel.

Then, with a graceful wave of its wings, the angel lifted into the sky.

Mariah watched until she could see them no longer. She went back inside, paying no attention to the chaotic shouting from the halls. She had to get her purse. She had to go home to see her daughter. She had faith that she hadn't seen her final miracle of the day.

CHAPTER TWELVE
INTRIGUING

A S CASSIE GAVE PURE DIRECTIONS after they crossed into West Virginia, Pure experienced a sense of déjà vu.

"Are you guiding me to Billings?" he asked.

"Yeah. That's where my sister is."

"Mount Weather is near there," said Pure.

"I know. That's why she's there."

"Not exactly a friendly place for an environmentalist," said Sue. "That crazy right wing militia has taken over the place."

"The West Virginia Underground," said Pure. "Religious nuts with guns and a healthy dose of paranoia. They're nothing to worry about."

"You been following the news, lately?" asked Sue. "These zealots effectively control half the state."

"Only half now?" said Pure. "West Virginia's gotten more liberal since I left, apparently."

Almost on cue, they drove past a road sign that had been painted over. "The Underground State" had been painted in bright red letters, and a deer skull was hanging from leather cords tied through bullet holes in the sign.

"Ominous," said Chase.

"Agreed," said Morningstar, his long head snaking up over the back seat to peer out the side window. "A dear head has rather stringy meat. A horse head would be more welcoming."

Morningstar had survived Pure's pocket-knife and bumpy road surgery and had slept most of the last twelve hours, a side effect of the acyteloranethine. He now looked bright-eyed and perky in the rearview mirror.

"Morning," said Pure. "Sleep well?"

"Indeed. As well as I've slept since I was born," said the dragon.

"Look, this is driving me crazy. Why do you have a British accent?"

"My creator, Adam Morgan, told me that we weren't designed to speak," said Morningstar. "We dragons were designed to be fast, strong, and smart, with a predator's intelligence. He was surprised when some of us imitated human speech from an early age. There was some debate as to whether we were mere mimics, like parrots, or actually intelligent beings."

"You strike me as incredibly intelligent," said Pure.

"As we did to Adam Morgan. He would come to our cages and talk to us for hours, telling us that our lot in life was to hunt and be hunted. In his desire to make us intelligent, he had borrowed sections of the best mapped genetic code for intelligence, that of the human mind. He told us he wanted to stop the project once we began to speak, but that higher powers prevented this. As time went on, we saw Adam Morgan less and less, and other trainers took over. There was a woman named Cynthia who read us fairy tales and had us watch movies so that we could learn the dragon's role in human mythology. Her accent was British, as were the accents of the actors in many of the movies."

"This is sick," said Cassie. "They knew you were sentient and they still planned to hunt you?"

"It wasn't an unfair fate. We were allowed to hunt back."

"I see they bred optimism into you," said Pure.

"Nothing exists in a vacuum. As I learned from the fairy tales the roles of dragons, I also learned of chivalry, honor, and duty. And, as Cynthia was fond of saying, no matter what difficulties you may face in life, you should always face them with a stiff upper lip."

"You don't really have lips," said Pure. "Just scaly jaws."

"Which, I assure you, are stiff."

"I still think it's monstrous that they raised you just to be hunted," said Cassie. "I wouldn't blame you if you hated all mankind."

"On the contrary," said Morningstar. "You humans are born into this world unsure of your roles. When I spoke with Adam and Cynthia, it seemed as if they spent their lives in a confused quest for purpose, sometimes wondering what their creator intended. We dragons had the advantage of meeting our creators directly and receiving explicit instructions. We know what we're bred for. Our lives are to be lived on the razor's edge, to hunt and be hunted by the world's most successful predator."

"Man," said Chase.

"Indeed," said Morningstar. "It is quite elevating to know that I have emerged the victor from every encounter so far."

Pure started to point out that they had technically been the victors of his last encounter, but decided to hold his tongue.

"Despite my prowess at survival, the rewards I was promised have yet to materialize."

"Rewards? Like, a horde of gold?"

"What would I do with gold? Cynthia told me females of my species were created at the same time as the males. Only males have been released into the park; she implied that the most successful hunters would be introduced to the females for breeding. But what if these are lies? What if there are no females of the species? I sometimes feel that my struggles are meaningless as I will never have the opportunity to mate."

"Chase feels the same way," said Pure.

"Hey!" said Chase.

"Maybe once this is all over, we can get you a girlfriend," said Cassie, not clarifying if she was addressing the comment to Morningstar or Chase. "From what I know of genetic engineering, I'm certain that there would be females created. The female is the default form of any species; males are just malformed females."

"We aren't here to be a dating service for a lizard," said Sue. "Let's stay focused. Our immediate goal: Expose the men who did this and put them out of business."

"Put them out of the business of creating life?" asked Morningstar. "I'm hard pressed to imagine a more noble profession."

"There's nothing noble about this project. You're just a toy for rich hunters. If we hadn't rescued you, eventually your head would wind up as a trophy in some fat cat's den."

"This may be so, Madam, but the knowledge that I'm hunted has made me cherish every day I survive. I hold no hard feelings for those who wish to kill me."

Pure laughed. "He's got Stockholm syndrome."

"Stockholm syndrome?" asked Morningstar.

"Hostages get it. They start sympathizing with their captors. It's a coping mechanism."

"Label my opinions what you wish," said Morningstar. "I bear no ill wishes toward my creators."

"But you still chose to come with us instead of staying with them," said Pure.

"I can hardly be judged for accepting an opportunity to expand my horizons."

"Ignore him, Morningstar," said Chase. "Pure thinks he's a psychologist instead of a vet."

"I'm just clear-headed," said Pure.

And on they squabbled into Billings.

Cassie gave directions to a Piggly Wiggly that was familiar to Pure. As he pulled into the grocery store parking lot, he said, "This is it. This is where the monkeys pushed through the warp. I can't believe my higher self took such a convoluted route to get me back here."

"Maybe he wanted you to have a dragon when you came back," said Cassie.

"Yeah," said Pure. "But why?"

"Let's go inside. Jazz says she'll contact us here."

"Ah, the infamous Jazz," said Sue. "I'm eager to finally meet her."

"What's she infamous for?" asked Pure.

"She's, like, the most wanted hacker on Earth," said Cassie. "She's the one who digitally kidnapped all those telecom satellites three years ago. She also was the hacker who took down the bank of Japan. They never have tracked down all the money she's got scattered through accounts worldwide. She told me that if she were a country, she'd be the world's fifth largest economy, right behind the US."

"Sounds talented," said Pure.

"That's barely scratching the surface. She's also a whiz at robotics, bionics, all sorts of gizmos. She wrote the code for the mental joystick I use to drive my mini-choppers. I'm a pretty good hacker, but she's magic."

"Enough chitchat," said Sue, stepping from the van. "Morningstar, you wait here. Keep an eye on this for me." She lay the shotgun on the seat. Morningstar picked it up with his wing-claws, inspecting it curiously.

Pure, Chase, and Cassie followed Sue into the store. Pure noticed a lot of people staring. Did they remember him?

Pure certainly remembered the store. The supermarket looked pretty much the way it had probably looked in 1950, a squat beige cinderblock structure with posters in the window advertising the price of chicken and pot roast. Stepping through the sliding doors, he spotted the produce section, exactly as it was that fateful morning.

He wondered again if people knew he was the ghost-monkey guy. Maybe not. In the chaos of that event, perhaps he'd barely caught anyone's eye. Or, maybe he was here because someone was supposed to recognize him. He wished his higher self would be more direct in his guidance.

They paused in front of a table full of tomatoes.

"I think people are looking at us," whispered Chase.

"Not many nuns in this neck of the woods," said Pure, thinking this was the most likely explanation. "You ever think of dressing in something other than that penguin get-up, Sue?"

"This 'get-up' is a badge of my moral courage. I may be a fugitive, but I'll never be in hiding."

"So," said Pure. "What next, Cassie? Are we supposed to get a cart and start shopping while we wait for Jazz?"

"I don't know," whispered Cassie. "I expected further instructions by now."

Then there was a shout, a crash and a bang. All four of them whirled to face the front door, which was now ten feet inside the building, pushed by the grill of a battered black pick-up. The truck skidded to a halt as a half dozen men in camouflage pants and black tee shirts leapt from the back, brandishing an eclectic array of rifles, pistols, and sawed off shotguns. The door of the truck swung open and a tall man got out, easily six foot six if not bigger. He wore a floor length black overcoat and a matching cowboy hat. His long blond hair hung halfway down his back and his face sported the sort of chiseled, even features one normally found on the covers of romance novels.

"Hooyaw!" the blond man shouted. "Good morning, shoppers! We're the requisition for the West Virginia Underground. Pardon our splashy entrance, but we're on a tight schedule. If everyone stays calm, nobody will get hurt."

The blond man looked behind him, at the six men gathered in front of the truck, half of them keeping their guns pointed into the store, half staring at the cloud of steam rising from the front of the truck.

"The radiators done busted, Gabe," one of them said.

The blond guy sighed and rubbed his temples. "We don't use real names in the field, Number Three."

"Sorry," said Number Three.

"Two, Five, Six, grab a cart and round up the shopping list. I'll secure us some new wheels."

Gabe glanced over his shoulder into the parking lot as his men scrambled into the isles with carts. He looked back and shouted, "Okay, who's driving the van?"

"That would be me," said Pure, raising his hand.

Gabe walked up to him. Pure couldn't help but notice that the leader had incredible piercing blue eyes. Maybe his higher self was trying to arrange a date. *Good job, higher self.*

"Keys," said Gabe.

Pure shook his head. "You don't want the van. It's already stolen, plus it has a dragon with a shotgun in the back seat."

"I'll cross that bridge when I come to it," said Gabe, holding out his hand. "Keys."

Pure dug for the keys in his pocket, unable to think of a good reason not to.

In the distance, a faint siren slowly wailed.

The three men with shopping carts ran back to the front of the store, their buggies filled with bulk goods, bags of flour, coffee, and dried beans, and what had to be every egg in the place. They struck Pure as being rather disciplined looters, not filling up the carts with potato chips and soda.

"Shit," said Number Three as a squad car skidded into the parking lot.

Gabe shook his head sadly and said to Pure, "Looks like you and your friends have just turned into hostages."

Number Three moved behind Pure and stuck a barrel to the back of his neck as other members of the militia grabbed Sue, Cassie, and Chase. Gabe confidently strode over and grabbed the grocery carts and pushed them into the parking lot, giving them a good shove toward the van. As his men scuttled in the background with the hostages, Gabe approached the lone squad car and the two deputies, raising his arms in the classic pose of surrender.

"Stay right where you are, Gabriel," one of the deputies said as he crouched behind his car door with his pistol aimed toward Gabe's chest. Pure found it interesting that the deputies were ignoring the armed men with hostages and focusing on the big guy. Apparently, Gabe had a reputation.

"Friends, all I'm doing is walking closer to save you the trouble of coming over here to arrest me," said Gabe.

"Not another step," shouted one of the deputies.

Gabe kept walking toward the car. Pure cringed as a shot rang out. Then another. Then a whole volley, as the deputies all but vanished behind a cloud of smoke as they emptied their pistols into the approaching figure.

As the guns fell silent, Gabe stood in front of their car, none the worse for wear except for rips in his coat.

"Gentlemen, is think there's something wrong with your engine," said Gabe, as he pounded his hands onto the hood of their squad car. The hood crumpled and buckled. Gabe picked it up and tore it loose. He tossed it aside while the deputies reloaded.

"Yeah, this doesn't look right," Gabe said, grabbing handfuls of random wires, ripping them loose, and tossing them over his shoulder amidst a shower of sparks.

"Well there's your problem," he said, as the engine burst into flame.

The first deputy finished reloading and aimed his gun once more at Gabe.

Gabe grinned. "Go for it. You've heard reports that I'm bulletproof, but I understand it takes folks a little while accept this. You might not have heard that I can see the future. In about ten seconds, I'm going to feed you that gun. Nine. Eight . . ."

He didn't need to reach seven before both deputies turned and ran.

Gabe headed back toward the van, where his men and Pure and company stood watching him.

"That's showing them, Gabe," said Number Three, although there was as much fear in his voice as congratulations.

"Just get in the van," said Gabe. "More cops will come. Keep the hostages."

Number Three slid the side door of the van open and glanced inside. His grip on Pure loosened as he began to shriek like a little girl. His voice was suddenly muffled as Morningstar snaked forward and closed his mouth around Three's head.

"Don't hurt him," said Pure.

Gabe strode up beside him. He stroked his chin as he studied the dragon.

"Intriguing," he said.

"Bulletproof?" said Pure.

"We're both full of surprises," said Gabe.

"Gang," said Pure, turning toward Sue, Cassie and Chase. "This might be where we part ways. I have a strong hunch I'm here to hook up with this guy. I'm also going to take Morningstar with me, if he doesn't mind."

"Why not?" said Morningstar, his voice barely audible over the shrieking face between his teeth. Pure noticed, however, that Morningstar's voice was relatively undistorted by the immobility of his jaws. Apparently his speech organs were closer to that of a parrot, further down his throat.

Pure added, "The rest of you can hang out here and hook up with Jazz if you want."

"You're friends of Jazz?" said Gabe.

"I'm her sister," said Cassie.

"Then you're all coming with us," said Gabe.

THEY DROVE INTO PARTS unknown, up and down tiny mountain roads full of switchbacks. They were packed into the van like sardines, assuming that half the sardines had guns and another had dagger-like teeth and breath reeking of CEO and horse. Bags of groceries were stuffed into every cranny and nook not occupied by a body. Number Three, the dim-witted rebel who had accidentally said Gabe's name during the raid, stared at Pure. Pure met his stare. Number Three didn't stand a chance of winning. Being dead meant you never had to lose a staring contest.

At last Number Three averted his gaze, looking at Morningstar for about ten seconds until Morningstar started looking back. Turning pale, Number Three suddenly found the roof-liner of the van to be fascinating.

"Three's an interesting name," said Pure. "That short for something?"

Three ignored him, or pretended to, at least.

"I bet you got teased about that a lot as a kid," said Cassie.

Three shifted uncomfortably, sinking deeper into the mound of toilet paper he was leaning against.

"Don't let 'em rile you," said Gabe from the driver's seat.

The back of the van had no windows and Pure couldn't see much on the road ahead. He was lost. He suspected Cassie knew exactly where they were via GPS but he wasn't about to ask her. He didn't want to tip their captors off to Cassie's special talents.

Sue leaned toward Number Three and looked him over. "You shouldn't let yourself be dehumanized by letting people call you a number," she said. "You look like a Zeke to me. Maybe a Cletus."

"Shut up," Three said, clenching his teeth in an attempt at menace.

Morningstar snaked his head a little closer, mimicking Three's clenched teeth. Three sank back, sweat visibly beading on his forehead, and Pure figured it was a good thing the man was sitting on toilet paper.

"His name's Francis," said Cassie. "Francis Darnwell."

Three's eyes popped open. Pure knew Cassie had scored a bulls-eye. No doubt she'd been digging through databases with facial recognition software.

"As in, 'You know Darnwell?' " Chase said.

Pure grinned. The kid wasn't so bad.

Then the lights went out. Pure hadn't been paying attention to the little bit of the road ahead of them he could see, but from the sudden darkness and the loud roar he guessed they'd plunged into a tunnel. The darkness stayed solid. Pure wondered why Gabe didn't turn on the lights. They van shuddered and lurched as they took unseen potholes at breakneck speed.

Cassie leaned close to Pure and whispered, "Don't panic, but I've lost all radio signals."

"We're inside a mountain," Pure whispered back.

Morningstar's road-kill breath was suddenly next to his other cheek. The dragon whispered, "As long as we're exchanging information, you should know that Gabe shares something in common with you."

"I already know he's damn good-looking," said Pure.

"I mean, sir, that he also does not breathe."

Twin shivers ran down Pure's spine. A: It was kind of a relief to finally have someone confirm what he suspected about not breathing. B: Was Gabe like him? Had he also been through the warp?

"Ya'll stop whispering," Francis said, still attempting to sound menacing. But the squeak in his voice revealed he was scared.

Pure was scared himself. The road was bumpy as hell and pitch black. Gabe gave no hint that he understood the concept of brakes. Memories of a long-ago driving instruction video came to mind, twisted smoking wreckage where nothing was left of the vehicle occupants but a handful of blackened teeth. Just how much damage could he take before his higher self couldn't fix him? Wasn't it time for some warp monkeys to appear and take over the steering wheel?

Pitch black bothered Pure for a second reason. Sometimes, when it was really, really dark, he felt like he was somewhere else. He had the sense that he was someplace icy cold, his body stiff, heavy, and bloated, with the weight of an ocean resting on his shoulders. This was the closest he ever came to dreaming, and these dreams were always the same. He stumbled forward in the dream darkness, groping blindly, as gape-jawed monster fish with lanterns dangling from their brows swam before him.

And then, light. The ocean dream evaporated. The van slowed. Pure craned his neck, trying to make out their surroundings. The visual imagery was too chaotic to interpret, random flashes of light and shadow, devoid of context. Where were they?

At last the van stopped. The back doors were thrown open. A whole army of militiamen in black tee shirts and camouflage pants surrounded the van, guns drawn. As Francis and his cohorts pushed Pure and the others from the van, men ran up and fastened their hands behind them with plastic zip strips.

"Play along," said Pure, as Morningstar growled at the men who approached him.

The dragon stood down, and someone produced steel handcuffs, joining his wing-claws together. Pure doubted the dragon could bite through those. Still, Pure's gut told him they weren't in danger. Cassie's sister was apparently a big shot among these people judging by Gabe's earlier reaction.

"Why are you shackling us?" Cassie asked. "We're friends of Jazz. I'm her sister."

Gabe chuckled. "What makes you think we're friends with that atheist freak?"

"I told you these were a bunch of right wing zealots," growled Sue. "Jazz is a good leftie. I knew she wouldn't get wrapped up with these nuts."

"Hold your tongue, woman," Gabe said. "Or I'll cut it out and staple it to your forehead."

Pure studied their surroundings. They were in a huge cavern, with stalactites hanging high overhead. The floor of the cavern had been bulldozed flat, and now housed several military style tents. Pure searched his memory for what he could remember about the West Virginia Underground. Supposedly their leader was some kind of religious prophet. Hannibal? That didn't sound right. Hecuba? It definitely started with an "H."

"Let's take them to see Hezekiah," said Gabe, giving Pure a shove.

"That's it," said Pure. Then, in his calmest voice, "Hezekiah is a prophet, right? Legend has it his mom ran off to the mountains when she got pregnant and raised him inside a cave so he wouldn't be corrupted by the world."

"Silence," said Gabe. "The story of our beloved founder isn't for heathen infidels. He's a holy man. You aren't worthy to speak his name."

Gabe pushed Morningstar from behind so that the dragon stumbled a little.

"I'm disappointed your pet didn't put up a fight," Gabe said. "I would enjoy the challenge of ripping him limb from limb."

Morningstar's alligator-horse-face showed no reaction to Gabe's taunts. Pure remembered what had happened to the hood of the squad car and knew Gabe was actually tough enough to back up his threats.

"Leave him alone," said Pure. "Man, you seemed like a nice guy back at the Piggly Wiggly. Aside from, you know, the whole armed robbery and hostage thing."

"I am a nice guy," said Gabe. "To normal people. Not heathen swine like Jazz's friends."

Pure gritted his teeth. Gabe wasn't fitting smoothly into the fantasies Pure had entertained about him. If they ever did go on a date, Pure definitely wasn't putting out. Not all the way, at least. Well, not on the first night.

They were taken past the tents toward the far side of the cavern, where a pitch black hole in the wall awaited. It was difficult to gauge scale in the underground. His first guess was that the hole was maybe a hundred yards away, but after they had walked for ten minutes he realized the hole was huge, big enough to hide a building in, and seemed farther away than ever.

Then, at last they entered the mouth of the hole. Darkness engulfed them. Pure gritted his teeth, anticipating the return of his ocean dream. Maybe it was time to make a break for it. Just take off running and hope that his higher self would guide him toward safety. Then lights began to flicker in the gloom ahead and he decided the opportunity was lost.

Their captors halted and forced them to their knees. Sue grumbled until someone slapped her.

Then, silence. Further down the tunnel, more lights flickered. Lanterns, set in sconces on the wall, came to life. Two dark figures approached through the dim light. Pure squinted to make out details. One of the approaching men was small, dressed in shapeless, loose-fitting clothes, like a monk's robe, his face hidden under a huge hood.

The second man was anything but shapeless. Gabe was a big man, but the man who approached was a giant, seven foot tall easily, with a wide, solid build. He was dressed all in black, with a broad brimmed pilgrim's hat casting shadows over his face. His hair was long and wild, as if it had gone a lifetime without being cut, and his beard hung down to his waist. In one huge hand the monster carried a Bible, an enormous one that one might find on display on a podium. The giant held it like a paperback. In his other hand was an axe, equally oversized, its sharp edge glimmering red in the lamplight.

The giant figure strode to where Pure and the others knelt. He stared at them, then at Gabe.

With a thunderous voice that echoed through the chamber, he asked, "Gabriel, why have you brought this lot before me?"

"For judgment, Oh Great Hezekiah," said Gabriel. "They may be allies of Jazz. We would have already slain them but perhaps they have useful information. Should we torture them first?"

"Useful?" said Hezekiah. "Perhaps you're right. We can always use fresh meat to feed the hounds."

Hezekiah looked up at the small army of goons behind Pure and the others.

"Leave this place," the prophet said. "I would not have their sinful blood contaminate you as it splashes from the walls."

With silent nods of assent, the army walked away. Pure was heartened by this turn of events. The prophet looked formidable, but Morningstar could take him. Unfortunately, while the rest of the army left, Gabriel stayed behind, and he wasn't going to be a pushover. The hooded figure in the monk robes was also still present, hanging a respectful distance behind the prophet.

As the footsteps of the army faded, Hezekiah strode back and forth before the prisoners.

"This one," he said, standing before Cassie. "An abomination, as much a machine as human. A modern witch who should not be suffered to live."

"If you know who I am, you know it would be stupid to hurt me," Cassie said, sounding defiant.

"Silence," boomed Hezekiah, moving toward Chase. "A coward. A moral weakling. His lusts lead him down dark paths. Yet, salvageable, perhaps. He has committed no unpardonable sin. What say you boy? Do you renounce your wicked ways? Will you join our army as a faithful servant?"

Chase said nothing for several seconds. Pure placed bets in his head about what the answer would be.

"Screw you," said Chase, costing Pure his imaginary money.

"You've chosen damnation," the prophet said.

Then, before Sue. "A bride of the anti-Christ. Her foul faith has led uncounted souls to the pit."

"I've heard it all before," Sue grumbled. "You gonna jaw us to death or you actually planning to use that axe?"

The prophet stood before Morningstar. "It's rare to see a demon in such a naked form. Of course you will receive no mercy."

"Now, Pure?" said Morningstar. "Shall we meekly sit here and take these insults?"

"Hold on," said Pure, as the prophet moved in front of him. Pure looked up into the man's black eyes, searching for any insight into his thinking. Pure decided to chance it. He rose to his feet before Gabe could move to hold him down. He stood as tall as he could next to the prophet and said, "Sue's right. You talk a big game, but you know we're not scared of you. Let us go before you force us to do something we regret."

"Brave words," said Hezekiah. "For a soulless sodomite."

"You know what?" said Pure, looking first at Hezekiah, then turning toward Gabe. "I *am* soulless. You're facing a damn Halloween parade here. I'm a zombie. My friends are a dragon, a cyborg, the world's meanest nun, and . . . uh . . ."—Pure grasped for the first thing that came to mind—"Chase is a master of kung fu. So let us go, apologize, and we'll let you live."

He stared once more into the prophet's dark, narrow eyes. The prophet stared back. Then the prophet grinned. The monk-robed figure behind him slapped his knees and said, in a woman's voice, "Damn Cass, you got some wild-ass friends."

"Jazz?" said Cassie, rising to her feet. Gabe moved forward and silently snipped the ties binding Cassie's hands.

The robed figure pulled back her hood, revealing a woman with shocking orange hair cropped short and a tattoo of an Ouroboros in the center of her forehead. "Hey, Sis," she said, running forward and throwing her arms around Cass.

Gabe moved down the row, freeing everyone else. As Gabe unlocked Pure, Pure studied his face. He leaned in close, looking at the man's skin close enough to see the pores.

"Wait a second," Pure said, gears clicking in his head. "This is a robot?"

"Yeah," said Jazz, swaggering up to Hezekiah. She rapped him on the forehead with her knuckles. "Both of 'em. Wild, huh? Cost me damn near five billion each to get the parts. I've leapfrogged the Korean models by at least twenty years."

"But . . . but why?" asked Chase. "Why scare us like that? Why any of this?"

"The Jazz I've heard about wouldn't be associated with these wing nuts," said Sue. "She's a socialist."

"More an anarchist," Jazz chuckled. "Sue, don't you know any history? There's no army better than one fighting for the Lord. Unemployment was close to thirty percent in these mountains. There were a lot of men with time on their hands who already had high-powered rifles and camo pants. Hezekiah gives them a cause to believe in."

"What do you need an army for?" asked Pure, continuing to study Gabe.

"Wait," said Cassie. "How did Hezekiah know so much about us? I told you I was bringing friends but I never said anything about Pure. Have you been—"

"Tapping into your systems?" asked Jazz. "Duh."

"You've been in my head? How dare you?"

"Oh, come on, what sister hasn't taken a little peak into a sister's diary?"

"But my diary is *in my head!*"

"What's so special about your head? It's just another databank, and you've been eager enough to let me hack it before now."

Chase placed an arm around Cassie to comfort her.

Jazz moved to Morningstar. "Glad to meet you," she said, offering her hand.

Morningstar took her hand and shook it. "My pleasure, madam."

"Oh my God they took my suggestion," said Jazz. "You sound British."

"Took your suggestion?" asked Sue. "You've worked with Bestiary?"

"I was hacking them when Cassie was still in diapers," said Jazz. "I thought their little dragon project was the coolest thing ever. I used to spend hours digging through the progress reports and thought it was funny as hell when these things started talking. So I whipped up a fake memo from a financial backer requiring that the dragons be taught the lore of knights and dragons and that they learn it in a British accent. I had no idea they'd take it seriously."

"You've known about the dragon project?" said Sue.

"For ages," said Jazz.

"And you didn't try to stop them? You didn't put a halt to their abominations?"

"I *can* hear you," said Morningstar.

"What's so abominable about pushing the frontiers of genetics out a little further? When you were a little girl, didn't you ever dream about unicorns? Maybe with wings? Because there's a team in France getting ready to market those."

"I thought you were a defender of the earth," said Sue. "I thought you were opposed to genetic engineering."

Jazz shook her head. "In the grand scheme, it's just a higher form of evolution. Bees help design flowers and flowers help design bees. Men who never heard of DNA designed dogs, corn, and broccoli. I don't see why greater understanding of our role in species development is a bad thing. In the end, it's all just code to be hacked."

"You're as bad as Pure," said Sue.

"Ah, yes," said Jazz, turning her attention to him. "Alex Gordon Pure. Mount Weather ID# AL9874Z17. Security clearance 'Fountain.' You've been in the belly of the beast."

"I've been one damn place after another," said Pure.

"You asked why I'm building an army. Simple. I want to get inside Mount Weather."

"Really?" said Pure. "You'd be better off wanting one of those unicorns."

"Ever since I learned about Mount Weather, I've known what I really wanted for Christmas," said Jazz. "The projects they've got going on in there make my robots look like tinker toys. You were working on a warp door, right? And it *works*."

"There are some bugs," said Pure.

"You don't even know about the other projects," Jazz said. "You're clearance isn't high enough. They've got a negative gravity chamber in there. They've got stable anti-matter atoms all the way up to boron. They're even prototyping a fucking time machine."

"Yeah," said Pure. "I know about that. Don't get too excited. Everything they put in the chamber disintegrates the second they power up."

"I would think the military would be happy with a disintegration machine," said Sue. "But I'm disappointed you want such things, Jazz. You're not a fighting for a good cause. More technology isn't going to solve the harm inflicted on this planet by technology. If you're not planning to destroy the secret projects at Mount Weather, you're nothing more than a thief. I don't want any part of this."

"You just lack imagination," said Jazz. "Think of how many dolphins you could save if you had your own atom bomb. You want to take a dragon to NYC? What about a suitcase nuke? Have it handcuffed to your wrist while you stand atop the Empire State Building and tell the world what it needs to hear. I guarantee people are going to listen."

"A suitcase nuke?" Sue rubbed her chin.

"The place is packed with them," said Jazz.

"Losing control of their top secret base would be a real black eye for the government," said Cassie. "It might trigger the revolution. The good one, I mean, not what these rednecks are part of."

Sue eyes suddenly took on a far-off stare. Pure could tell Cassie had snagged her.

"This does sound . . . intriguing," said Sue. "Why don't you let us sleep on it and get back to you in the morning?"

"Morning's going to be a little busy," said Jazz.

"Why?" asked Cassie.

"Tomorrow's the day we break through," said Jazz. "West Virginia has so many mine shafts and caverns it's a wonder it hasn't collapsed. A big chunk of my army is made up of former miners. We've been tunneling through the bedrock for the last five years. Your arrival is well timed. We break through to the lowest level of Mount Weather at 10 a.m."

CHAPTER THIRTEEN
WALKING WITH WATER

CAPTAIN CHERISE WASHINGTON hadn't gotten where she was by disobeying orders. The Hollywood myth of fighter pilots as rule-breakers and daredevils in no way defined her personality. She was a careful person. She played by the rules because the rules kept people alive. But how could rules apply to a city that had sprung from nowhere overnight, to a city populated by angels? She could have flown outside the zone of static for further orders, but she doubted those orders would be to land and take a closer look. The static provided a bit of cover, but as her plane touched down she was still deeply aware that if her plane fell into enemy, perhaps alien hands, she would almost certainly be court-martialed.

After the plane came to a halt, she popped the hatch and climbed out. She took off her helmet. The city smelled of sea breezes and sunshine. It reminded her of the air on the beaches of Oregon, where she'd grown up. The city was quiet, the air still. Despite the angel she had seen, she still couldn't help but feel that this was a deserted place.

"Hello?" she called out.

No one answered. She walked to the edge of the runway, studying the city beyond for any sign of life. New young grass was sprouting on the field that separated her from the nearest tower, a bright almost neon green blanket that thickened and grew before her eyes. She knelt down and touched the grass, pressing it between her gloved fingers. The blades seemed to squirm as they continued their rapid growth, perhaps a quarter of an inch per minute.

This sort of thing didn't happen in the real world. Was she sleeping? Was this all a dream? She shook her head, certain that she was both awake and sane. Was she finally witnessing the supernatural? This place reminded her of heaven, a heaven plucked straight from her childhood dreams. Her mother had died when she was four. When she thought of her mother in heaven, she thought of a place of endless green fields. She had dreamed about that land of green fields for a long time, every time she'd thought of her mother. In her dreams, it had all gotten confused as the years passed, and she'd grown to see her mother as a creature of that field, with rose petal skin and ivy hair and clover for eyes.

The field grew more lush and green. Trees began to sprout randomly, pushing into the air steadily, several inches per minute, with branches spreading to create large patches of shade.

Cherise sat, watching this miracle field, as the sun warmed her in her flight suit until the heat became uncomfortable. She rose, removing her gloves, unzipping her flight suit to cool off a bit. Almost as if sensing her distress, a floral breeze swirled around. Then, in the corner of her eye, something moved. She turned to look. Under the shade of a distant tree, something was rising, something vaguely human in shape.

She was nervous about heading too far from her plane, but the whole point of coming here was to meet the locals. She began to walk toward the shadowy figure. She raised her hands and called out, "Hello!"

The figure stepped from the shade. It was a woman, woven from vines and flowers, with clover for eyes.

"Hello," her mother said. "Welcome to Atlantis."

PRESIDENT LOPEZ-NELSON rubbed his temples. This had turned into the longest meeting of his life. Ever since the angel had said there would be a message the following morning and had then flown back out the open window, his advisors had been peppering him with facts and speculation.

Fact: The angel had flown from Washington so fast and so low that radar couldn't track it and none of the interceptor planes sent to chase it could locate it.

Speculation: Perhaps the angel had been a hologram?

Fact: There was a city in the middle of the Atlantic Ocean. This wasn't a hologram. Radar confirmed its existence, satellite photos were pouring in. It was a city that hadn't been there yesterday.

Fact: The city hadn't descended from the sky. There were too many early warning systems for something of this size to slip through. And from the earliest satellite photos, it looked as if the city had risen up out of the ocean. There was also sonic evidence for this from submarine microphones.

Fact: The floor of the ocean where the city had ascended supported an active deep-sea-vent range and had been thoroughly photographed by research vessels only three years prior. The photos and the radar maps of the seabed showed no signs of a city.

Speculation: The city was being built somehow, at an alarming rate of speed.

Question: By whom? For what purpose? Was a human hand behind this? Or alien?

Fact: The city had already swallowed one fighter plane, now visible on a runway in the satellite photos. The fate of the pilot was unknown. The pilot was Captain Cherise Washington, a stable and levelheaded person by all reports, not someone likely to be collaborating with aliens.

Speculation: Given the level of technology on display, could the residents of this city have somehow taken over the electronics of the plane and forced it down?

"Obviously," said Lopez-Nelson, "If this thing can take over our planes, sending in more for reconnaissance is useless. Suggestions?"

"I say we do this low-tech," said General Junaluska. "Put together a landing force of marines with basic gear. Yank the computer navigation system out of personnel carriers and pilot the boats in by compass and guts."

"What about the radio silence?" said Lopez-Nelson. "What good is it going to do us to send men in if we can't communicate with them?"

"Our satellites have resolution down to six inches," said Junaluska. "We equip the men with mirrors and they can signal us in Morse code."

"You're joking," said Lopez-Nelson. Then he rubbed his eyes. This hadn't been a good day for assuming things were jokes. He trusted General Junaluska, but he also knew the old war-horse's all-purpose solution to the world's problems was to find someone to shoot.

"Okay," he said at last. "Okay, I haven't heard a better plan. How fast can we get men out there?"

"I ordered the modifications to the boats four hours ago," said Junaluska. "I already have my best men on board, and the ships under way. I can have them ashore in twelve hours."

"Do it," said Lopez-Nelson.

MARIAH ARRIVED HOME to find Anna looking sicker than ever in her bed. Mariah took her frail bony hand and said her name, but Anna didn't stir. She breathed in shallow, ragged gulps, but wouldn't open her eyes even as Mariah squeezed cold water from a wet washcloth over her brow to cool her.

On any other day, Mariah would have been frantic. She would have called the hospital, desperate to try anything to pull Anna back into the waking world. But this was the day of miracles. The angel had said Anna would be healed.

She sat by Anna's bed, her hands clasped around her daughter's hands, and prayed, and prayed, for hours, until the weariness of the night's work and the morning's excitement at last overtook her, and she fell asleep, sitting by the bed side, her head on her daughter's chest.

IN ATLANTIS, THE DOOR of the room Adam waited in swung open and Jessica entered, looking as young and healthy as she had on their wedding day.

"Adam?" she asked.

"Jessica?" he said.

They ran to each other and embraced, smothering one another with kisses. Adam felt faint with joy. His newly-minted heart skipped beats. His day-old stomach filled with butterflies. Jessica was awake. It was like he was emerging from a twenty-year nightmare. He was awake, and she was awake, and they were young and healthy once more, in this city of miracles.

Jessica pulled away, just a little, to look into his eyes. "It's okay to tell me," she said. "We're dead? This is heaven?"

"No," said Adam. "You're alive. I'm alive. This isn't heaven. It's Atlantis. It's tough to explain."

"But I was carried here by an angel," said Jessica.

"And I've spent the day conversing with a Greek god," said Adam. "But as best as I can understand it, there's nothing supernatural about any of this. Atlantis is an alien city, an artificial intelligence operating on such a high level of technology that it appears to be magic. I can grasp the basic principals underneath it all, but only barely."

"Alien?" asked Jessica. "Why is it doing this? Is it dangerous?"

"No," said Adam. "If there's one thing I'm sure of, it's not dangerous. It means us no harm. I think it was designed to serve us, to keep us safe and happy."

"Designed? By who?" asked Jessica.

"It's been a little vague on that point," said Adam. "Look, I know I'm the last person you'd ever expect to hear these words from, but who cares? We should sit back and enjoy this. Our old, sick bodies have been repaired. We're in a place designed to provide us with anything we desire. We can puzzle it out later. Right now, let's make the best use of our time together. We've a lot of lost years to make up for."

As he spoke, the room shifted and changed, and a bed grew from the wall, a huge bed with fluffy white linens. The light in the room dimmed, and candles rose from the floor, giving the room a romantic glow, and filling the room with the scent of lavender. A violin began to play, the music coming from nowhere and everywhere.

"Oh," said Jessica, a tear falling down our cheek. "It's our song."

Adam pulled her on to the bed. It occurred to him that perhaps she wasn't real. Atlantis could grow human bodies. He could read minds. Could it have made this fantasy come true? Was this merely some imitation of Jessica?

Then her lips met his, and he surrendered to faith, trusted his heart to know the difference, and once more wrapped his arms around the woman he loved.

"MOTHER? IS THIS HEAVEN?" Cherise asked as she took the outstretched hand of the woman before her.

"No," said the woman with roses for skin and ivy for hair. "You're still alive. And I did not mean to deceive you. I'm not your mother."

Cherise pulled her hand away. She was ashamed of herself for being so easily lulled into this false sense of security. Of course this thing wasn't her mother. Somehow, it was violating her mind, tapping into her deepest memories.

"I'm sorry you feel betrayed," said the woman. "I'm Atlantis. I'm a city, but have chosen this intimate form in hopes of quickly forming a bond of trust with you. Your suspicion that I'm reading your mind is correct."

"Then stop it now," said Cherise.

"I can't," said Atlantis. She motioned for Cherise to follow as she left the field and stepped upon a path of white sand that led toward the spires of the city. "You can understand from the experience of your own senses. Imagine if someone asked you to stop hearing things in the middle of a symphony? You might try to block out the sound with your hands, but you would never be fully successful. I possess over three hundred senses. I know your thoughts with the same ease that I hear your voice or feel your feet upon my sand."

Cherise looked down as she followed the woman at a safe distance. "Your sand? Possessive, aren't you?"

"I'm everywhere around you," said the plant-woman. "This body is for your convenience. But my mind is in the stones you walk upon and the air you breathe. I exist in the water flowing through the fountain in the plaza ahead."

Cherise remembered the breeze that had cooled her. The air was sentient? Was it even safe to breathe? "Okay. You said you want to form a bond. There's a few things you need to do if I'm going to trust you. First, I don't like you messing with the memory of my mother. If you have another body, I'd rather talk to that. Understood?"

"Of course," said the woman, who turned and walked away.

Cherise swallowed hard as she watched the memory of her mother walking away. But despite the pain Atlantis had caused, her gut told her that the entity had meant no harm.

She turned away from the figure of her mother and yelped to find another figure standing behind her. This was a man, formed of water, with shiny silver fish swimming in his chest. She reached out to touch him. Her fingers sank right into his arm, and pulled away wet.

"I weave these bodies together with machines too small for your eyes to see," said the water-man. "Don't be alarmed."

"I'm okay," said Cherise. "Wow. So you really are an alien."

"It may be easiest for you to understand me in these terms. But I came of age on this planet. I'm as much a child of earth as you."

"Most children of earth don't hop around from body to body."

The water-man shrugged. "I have access to technology developed over a much longer time scale than mankind has existed. I hope to share it with you openly."

"Then why the wall of static?" asked Cherise. "Why not let me call my superiors and tell them I'm okay."

"The static is intended to discourage aggressive visitors. I'm still young. Your world has mastered a primitive level of war-making that could unleash severe ecological damage to your own world. The static helps create a fog of doubt. Doubt will lead to delay and indecision among your leaders, allowing me time to neutralize their more dangerous devices."

Cherise wasn't sure she liked the sound of this.

"I know what you're thinking," said Atlantis. "You wonder what threat I pose to this world."

"Yes."

"When I'm done, human civilization as you know it will no longer exist." Atlantis said this in a matter-of-fact tone, devoid of malice. "Mankind at present is like a cancer upon this planet. Through carelessness and ignorance your race has altered this planet's ecological systems to the point of collapse. It's fortunate I arrived when I did. A century from now, it's possible your race would have ceased to exist."

"Look," said Cherise. "I know we have problems. I've been hearing about climate change and acidic oceans my whole life. But we're taking steps to get things under control. If we humans created this mess, we can fix it."

"I will fix it," said Atlantis. "I've been created to heal and nurture your race and this world."

"That's kind of presumptuous. We didn't invite you."

"This is untrue. I received permission from a representative of your species. I have technological and information resources your race has yet to develop, and may never develop on its own. Would it not be immoral of me to stand by and watch your race slowly die?"

"Unless you have some sort of technology that sees the future, you can't know what will happen to our race."

"True," said the water-man, smiling gently, like a wise teacher. "But your world contains human cultures with vastly different levels of technological access. Suppose that, deep in the Amazon, a tribe that had never before seen modern humans was discovered, and this tribe was currently caught in the midst of an epidemic that threatened to kill all its members. Would it be immoral to vaccinate the members of the tribe not yet infected?"

Cherise frowned. "It's not that simple. Yes, it would be a good thing to save the tribe with the vaccinations. But it would come with a cost. This isn't as hypothetical as you make it out. It's happened again and again that encounters with more advanced civilizations have obliterated older cultures. The tribe might survive the intervention, but their way of life would be forever destroyed."

"And so it shall be," said Atlantis. "Though destroyed is a harsh term. Transformed is less pejorative. In a few hours, I will broadcast a message to the entire human race. Soon, everyone will know of my existence. And within less than a week, human civilization as you know it will draw to an end."

CHAPTER FOURTEEN
BREAK THROUGH

IN THE PITCH BLACK BOWELS of the Earth, the massive mining machines drowned out all conversation. The heat was unbearable, every surface slick and slimy from the humidity. The rotten egg smell of coal dust was inescapable. Despite this, Pure was feeling optimistic.

They were in the fortuitously named "shaft seven," making good time. The plan was simple. Mount Weather had enormous ventilation tunnels that spread out from the central complex in all directions. Mount Weather had been designed to house a hundred thousand people, and that meant that a lot of air was required. One way of protecting the vents was to dig them deep and surface them far away from the actual site. The vent tunnel they were intercepting drew air from somewhere in Ohio. The entrances to the shafts were well hidden and heavily secured. Any attempt to invade through them would be met with locks, grates, baffles, and bombs. Random sections of the shaft were booby-trapped to collapse if invaders penetrated too far. Which was why they would be entering the shaft only a half-mile from the central complex. They would still face bars and baffles, but these wouldn't prove overly formidable. Jazz's army had plenty of former miners with experience in blowing things up.

Once they were past the gates and barriers, there would no doubt be a fierce fight against Mount Weather's security forces. Again, this didn't seem insurmountable. The men who fought for Hezekiah seemed willing to die for him, and would probably outnumber the guards three to one. Long before reinforcements could arrive, Jazz would have captured the computer core that controlled all the gates and locked down the facility. The government would find itself locked out of its own impenetrable fortress.

And then . . . then Pure would have access to the spook door again. He didn't know why this was important. He wasn't one hundred percent sure that was even what his higher self was aiming him toward. But it made sense. Physical trauma allowed Pure to briefly glimpse the warp space and his higher self, but he could never actually make contact. But what if he entered the door now? Was it possible he could reintegrate with his other half? Could he be whole and alive again? Or at least die in a respectable fashion without running around as a semi-dead adventure zombie?

Suddenly, there was a wash of cool air and swirling dust and a noticeable change in the pitch of the machinery. One by one, the grinding wheels spun down to silence.

"We've broken through," said Jazz from beneath her monk's hood. "I'm going to have Gabriel and Hezekiah lead the charge."

They were at the back of the pack of rebels. They were all dressed in the black tee shirt, camo-pants uniform of the West Virginia Underground. Hezekiah had announced that the prisoners had renounced their wicked ways and were now part of the flock, and so far none of the other members of the militia had even cast them a mean glance.

Sue looked like a natural in her militia uniform. Stripped of her nun's habit, Sue's left wing radical persona didn't bug Pure as much. Deep down, Pure had to admit a grudging admiration for the old biddy. He liked people whose convictions outstripped their common sense. It was only Sue's insistence that the Lord was on her side that bothered him. Pure had little patience for people who didn't understand their own religion.

"This is so cool," said Cassie as they followed the last of the rebels. This was the first sentence she'd spoken all day that Pure had understood. Most of the morning, Cassie and Jazz had been jabbering in lingo Pure couldn't comprehend about how Gabe and Hezekiah worked. He grasped occasional individual words, but the sum of their conversations was gibberish.

"Stacks?" asked Cassie.

"Three. Smart-jellied grope-packs."

"Ultraswank. Under that?"

"Shoe math," said Jazz, with a tone that made it clear she was saying something cool. "Veloski protocol."

"OMG," said Cassie. "Muscles?"

"All slick. Memory strings. Niners. Self-restoring; these things might still be running a hundred years from now. Hell, maybe a thousand."

"Pocalyptic," said Cassie, with a shiver of appreciation.

Chase was dead quiet and looking a little pale. Jazz had given him an AK-47, an ancient but dependable machine gun. Pure felt sympathy for

Chase. One minute you're trying to impress a girl by talking about your father's line of work, the next you're committing high treason by taking over a top-secret military base. Life had a certain momentum. Pure knew this better than anyone.

The vent tunnel was bigger than Pure had expected. It was a twenty-foot diameter tube carved straight from the surrounding bedrock and filled with about two feet of ice-cold water. The tunnel had a strong wind that whipped past the entry hole they had dug with a low, foreboding moan. Between the water and the wind, Pure could feel his temperature dropping by the second. In a way, it was a relief. The world was shifting gears for him, moving at normal speed for the first time in ages. Still, he wasn't sure what would happen if he got really cold. Hopefully they would get into Mount Weather soon.

The whine of turbines grew ever closer. Somewhere up ahead were huge fans capable of sucking air from Ohio to West Virginia. An explosion shook the walls, sending pebbles bounding off their heads, and the whine of the turbines stopped instantly.

Then, gun shots. The *pop pop pop* of machine guns as the leading edge of the militia encountered the guards. The tunnel was too cramped for Pure to see what was happening. Cassie and Jazz chattered back and forth in excitement. Pure knew they were watching the action through Gabe and Hezekiah.

The gunfire grew more intense. Cassie's expression changed from excitement to horror.

"They're being mowed down," she said, her voice choking.

"Press on," Jazz said.

"We're like fish in a barrel," Cassie said. "Hezekiah and Gabe are through but everyone else is falling the second they step out."

"Eggs for omelets," said Jazz. "We'll whittle them down."

"Send me in," said Morningstar. The dragon hadn't spoken all day, and he moved with such eerie silence that the sound of his voice right next to them caused Chase and Cassie to jump.

"Go," said Jazz.

Morningstar's long claws bit into the surface of the rock. He scampered to the ceiling and scrabbled over the heads of the combatants, disappearing into darkness.

Then, shrieking.

"Holy cow," said Cassie, looking slightly green.

"Pocolyptic," said Jazz, trailing off in a long, impressed whistle.

Then, silence.

Cassie turned and began to vomit as Chase moved to help steady her.

"Nice pet you got there," Jazz said to Pure. "He moves so fast I could barely track him. Hezekiah would look to the nearest shriek but by the time his head moved he would only see a disemboweled soldier dropping to the floor."

"Yeah," said Pure. "I've been on the receiving end."

Hezekiah's voice boomed through the tunnel. "Forward, my children. The enemy has fallen before our righteous fury. No one may oppose us."

Pure had to admit there was something breathtaking in Hezekiah's tone. It was easy to see why people obeyed him. As they climbed over the corpses of the fallen rebels at the mouth of the tunnel, Pure watched Jazz for any reaction. Cassie and Chase and even Sue were visibly shaken, and Cassie especially looked ill. Jazz stepped over the corpses without hesitation or squeamishness. Pure wasn't sure if he admired her toughness or loathed her lack of compassion.

Not that he could talk. Pure felt like he should be feeling something as he slipped and stumbled over the fallen bodies. But, deep, deep down inside him, there was nothing. Stepping over these bodies had no more emotional significance than stepping over a log. Was this a side effect of his being dead, or had he always been a psychopath? He wished he could remember. He couldn't trust his brain anymore. His memories of his own life had no more emotional weight than the memories of sitcoms he'd watched.

The room they entered was unfamiliar to Pure. He'd never gotten into the guts of Mount Weather before. The room was cramped, filled with pumps and machines that had fallen silent when the turbine blew up. Dead bodies were all over the place. Hezekiah's and Gabe's clothing was riddled with bullet holes. Morningstar sat perched atop a huge pipe, gnawing on a moist bloody hunk of meat with a shoe on the end of it.

"Yes!" said Jazz, spotting a computer terminal. She ran to it and sat down, pushing back her monk's hood in her excitement. Pure noticed that some of the militiamen were startled by her appearance.

Jazz's enthusiasm soon vanished. "Damn," she said. "This isn't connected to the larger network. It's useless. I thought this was too easy."

"Easy?" said Sue. "There's a hundred men dead to get you here and you complain that it's easy?"

Gabe walked up. "Our men understand the price they must pay for liberty."

"You," said Sue, grabbing one of the men. By chance, it was Francis from the van. "What are you fighting for?"

"The same thing you are, sister," said Francis. "The right to raise our children in the faith, uncorrupted by the forces of the Anti-Christ."

"Yeah," said Jazz, sounding deadly serious. "Anyone with half a brain can see that Lopez-Nelson is the antichrist."

"Just testing, brother," said Sue, releasing Francis and smoothing out his shirt. "Carry on."

"Time is of the essence," said Gabe. "Let's push forward."

By now, his men had cut through the heavy steel hatch with the torches. Hezekiah kicked down the door. Fortunately, no one waited on the other side. Pure guessed that the security forces would counter the attack by attempting to lock down the facility, slowing their progress until reinforcements could arrive.

They were going down a long hall, with storerooms off to each side. Pure was more than a little lost, although Jazz's army moved with a confidence and swiftness that made Pure think they were well-briefed on the layout. The demolition team had already cut through the next door by the time the rest of the army reached it.

"These guys tear down mountains for a living," Jazz said. "The doors don't stand a chance."

For the first time, they were moving into a room Pure recognized. Finally, he was able to orient himself. They were in the senate. The vast room was an almost perfect duplicate of the real senate chambers in Washington. Mount Weather had been envisioned as a functional shadow government, complete with legislative chambers, a Supreme Court, the works. At the height of the cold war, each state governor had secretly appointed two shadow senators to serve in the mountain, although that practice had been stopped decades ago. The militiamen spread through the chamber in an air of silence. The room was ornate and awe-inspiring, in contrast to the cramped, functional rooms they'd passed through to reach it.

Jazz moved to the front of the chamber, her face brightening as she spotted a computer terminal. She sat down and began tapping away. She broke into a broad grin.

"Cassie, get over here and plug in. This one's live."

"Found it," said Cassie, without moving from where she stood. "My god, this is the most primitive wireless network I've ever hacked. Cavemen had better."

"The feds are notoriously bad about keeping up to date. This stuff was state of the art thirty years ago," said Jazz. "Hee hee. There's the lock-down sequence. Poor babies."

"Got 'em," said Cassie. "Now I'm . . . uh-oh."

"Uh-oh," echoed Jazz.

"What?" asked Pure.

"Bad voodoo," said Jazz.

"Very bad," said Cassie. "Explosive."

"What?" asked Pure. "What?"

"Damn!" said Jazz. "I lost it!"

Cassie sat down in one of the padded leather chairs. According to the nameplate, she was now a senator from Idaho.

"It's been fun, guys," she said.

"They can't do this," said Jazz. "Not after five years planning. No, no, no, no, no!"

"What's going on?" Sue asked Cassie.

"We have about forty seconds to live," said Cassie. "They've sealed off this section of the mountain and are pumping in nerve gas."

"Can't you stop it?" asked Chase.

"Damn it," said Jazz. "The vent controls are on their own secured network. All hardwire, no radio. We had one of the terminals back in the turbine room and I didn't even look for something like this. We'll never make it back to the terminal in time."

"Thirty seconds," said Cassie.

"I love you," said Chase, embracing her.

"Oh, geez," said Cassie, twisting her face away from him.

High overhead, the vent doors swung open with low, ratcheting knocks.

Behind Cassie's podium, an enormous video screen flickered to life.

Then the angel appeared.

CHAPTER FIFTEEN
WE NOW INTERRUPT YOUR REGULAR PROGRAMMING

EVERYONE ON EARTH heard the message.

In cities around the world, every television, every radio, was taken over by the Atlantean broadcast.

"Greetings. I'm the city of Atlantis," the broadcast began.

IN TIBET, IN A MONASTERY where television was an unknown thing, the monks were astounded to find a giant snow leopard strolling into their courtyard. It introduced itself as Atlantis and said, "In the coming days, each of you will receive a ballot. You will have one month to make a decision."

In the far reaches of the Amazon, a woman made of water stepped onto the shore of a local village and told the villagers that she was a city, and they had a choice to make.

"The ballot will have a button," she said. "Press it, and I'll bring you to me."

In Kenya, in a camp of poachers, a gorilla with silver skin and diamond eyes surprised them by walking into their midst and beginning to speak. As the shock wore off, they tried to shoot it, but if it felt pain it didn't react. It continued speaking to them, as they fell into a hushed awe.

"In Atlantis, you will be safe from war and disease. There will be no hunger or poverty. You'll not need to toil or labor for sustenance. You may turn your energies to the pursuit of whatever you wish, be it the perfection of arts, the study of science or literature, anything you can imagine."

President Lopez-Nelson swallowed another antacid tablet as he stared at the TV screen. The message was worse than anything he'd imagined. If this thing had declared war, his country would have banded together behind him, the nations of the world would have turned to him for leadership. Instead the damn thing was offering some kind of Utopia. It had to be a trick.

"I know that some of you may be skeptical," said the broadcast. "You've thousands of years of cultural experience that leads you to believe that nothing comes without a cost. This is accurate. There are human pursuits and pastimes that will not be allowed in Atlantis. The petty tribal conflicts that rend this planet will have no place upon my shores. No citizen of Atlantis shall be allowed to use violence to achieve their goals. And there is a still greater cost."

Mariah woke when she realized the television had turned itself on. She'd fallen asleep by Anna's bed, and was still sitting upright in her chair. It took her fogged mind a second to understand what it was saying.

"Your present industrial culture is killing your world. Atlantis cannot stand idly by while this happens. In three days, the infrastructure supporting your poisonous activities will be shut down. It's the Earth's best hope for survival."

Cassie fell from her chair, convulsing.

"It's in my head!" she screamed. "It's in my head!"

"And on my monitor," mumbled Jazz. "It's everywhere. Some sort of universal carrier code. My god, it's beautiful."

On the enormous monitor, an angel was babbling about Atlantis. Pure was pretty sure this was important, but his attention was instead focused on the vents overhead, which continued to clank open. He doubted the nerve gas would hurt him, but who knew? And it would definitely kill everyone else in the room except the robots. Suddenly, he hated his higher self and whatever little game he was playing.

"Hah!" said Jazz. "I stopped the gas!"

"What?" asked Pure. "How?"

"This signal. It's perfect. It's like the ultimate machine language, and it's universal. It's a song every electronic circuit in the world is humming. It's hitting the terminals in the pump room the same way it's hitting us. Triggering the kill switch was a breeze."

Chase and Sue were struggling to hold Cassie down. She was foaming at the mouth, thrashing, screaming, "Get out! Get out!"

Jazz ran to her side and grabbed Cassie's fallen cane. She flipped open a panel on the side and whistled in awe.

"Cassie," she said. "Calm down. It won't hurt you. Stop fighting it. I'm going to use some of your cortex to record this."

"Pardon me," said Pure. "Her cortex? You're going to use her brain as a tape recorder?"

"This is an intelligent signal. I don't think mechanical media will be able to get it all. I need something organic," said Jazz, pressing buttons on the cane.

Cassie stopped screaming words and began to simply scream, the sound echoing around the chamber. A foul stench hit Pure's nostrils as she lost control of her bowels.

"She's demon-possessed," said one of the militiamen, pulling back.

Gabe and Hezekiah had grown still. Their lips moved in unison with the angel on screen though they made no sound.

"It's an angel," said another of the militiamen, watching the screen. "It's finally here. Judgment day." The man dropped his rifle, then fell to his knees. One by one, his fellow rebels joined them, and the message of the angel and Cassie's screams were almost drowned out by the prayers of two hundred men begging to be let into Heaven.

Blood was now pouring out of Cassie's nose. Pure grabbed Jazz's arm.

"This is killing her. Stop it."

"She's just going to have a headache," Jazz snarled. "Don't fuck with things you don't understand."

"Stop it now or—" Pure didn't have anything to follow the "or." What was he going to do? Punch Jazz?

Jazz looked up from the tiny monitor on the cane with a taunting grimace. "Or what?"

"Or I let Morningstar eat you," said Pure.

On hearing his name, Morningstar stuck his head over Pure's shoulder. "Madam, I don't pretend to comprehend what is happening here, but if you possess the power to stop it, now would be the time to do so."

The monitor went dark. Hezekiah and Gabe stopped lip-synching and began to stagger drunkenly in small circles. Cassie continued to thrash and scream.

"The signal cut out," said Jazz. "But the recording has set up an electrical storm in her frontal lobes. She's going to be having a seizure for another two or three minutes. All we can do is hold her down until she recovers. This isn't my fault."

Pure stared at Jazz, still holding her arm.

"She *will* recover," said Jazz.

"The second she can walk, I want her, Sue and Chase out of here," said Pure. "I should never have gotten them involved in this craziness."

"It's safer in here than anywhere," said Jazz. "Thanks to the signal, I've gotten control of all the systems in the complex. We can move about as we please. I can gas anyone who gives us trouble."

"No nerve gas," said Pure. "I'm damn serious about this. The people who work here are good people just making a living. If you're in control, let them go."

"We could use them as hostages," said Jazz.

"Do as he says," said Morningstar, drawing his head close enough to Jazz to allow his carrion breath to wash over her.

Cassie's shouts suddenly vanished. Her violent convulsions ended. She began to cry softly, her sobs the only sound in the chamber. The militiamen had stopped their prayers and were watching the bizarre gyrations of their leader and his right hand man.

"Boys," said Jazz. "Reset."

Hezekiah and Gabe stopped moving. Hezekiah straightened himself, stared into the eyes of the nearest militiaman, and said, "I am a brother to dragons, and a companion of owls."

"Yes sir," said the militiaman, quietly.

"The Lord is coming soon," said Gabe, brushing his hair back from his eyes.

"Sooner than we thought," said Cassie, sobbing. "Angel. I had an angel in my head. I can still hear him."

"Hang on, Cassie," said Chase, squeezing her hand. "It's okay. You'll be okay."

"I'm blind," she said.

"You've been blind," said Sue.

"No. Totally. I can't see the cameras. I can't see the network. What's going on?"

"Sorry," said Jazz. "I needed all the cybernetic components in your brain to capture the signal. I can't reset them until I've learned everything I need to about the code."

"Why?" Cassie sobbed. "Why did you do this to me?"

"Am I the only one who understands what we just witnessed?" Jazz asked angrily. "A goddamn intelligent alien signal just washed over this place. This is more important than *anything*."

"Nothing is more important than the holy cause," said Hezekiah.

"Of course," said Jazz, rolling her eyes.

"Listen up, brothers," said Gabe. "Show time's over. We're in the belly of the beast and we're going to be here a while. I want the C-team to get back into the tunnels and look for survivors. We'll set up an infirmary in the hall. B-team, set up a perimeter. Find all the doors and wire them. Make sure no one gets in with their hands still attached. A-team, secure the cafeteria in the chamber below. Let's eat in style tonight, boys."

A flurry of activity erupted. Sue was helping Cassie to her feet.

"Find us a room with a shower and bring us some clean clothes," Sue said.

"No problem," said Jazz, snapping her fingers. Gabe grabbed one of the militiamen and gave an order for this special mission. Jazz said, "We're in the right place for it. The senator's quarters are the most luxurious in the mountain."

"We're on the wrong side of the complex for the spook door," said Pure. "Can you lock it down from here?"

"Already done," said Jazz. "I can't wait to see it."

Pure wished he'd paid more attention to the angel. Had it really said, "I'm the city of Atlantis?"

"Atlantis rising." That was his problem. Why was it that when the small clues made the most sense the big picture always seemed fuzzier?

PRESIDENT LOPEZ-NELSON turned to General Junaluska in the wake of the broadcast.

"That was a threat, wasn't it?" he asked.

"Nuke the damn thing," said Junaluska. "I've already run simulations. Given current wind conditions, the fallout is unlikely to reach Europe."

"I should consult—"

"Mr. President," said Junaluska. "Listen to me. Every year that's gone by, I've seen this country give up more and more of its authority to the UN. If we'd acted autonomously, New Delhi might be more than a smear of black glass today. Now the world is so nuke-phobic that if you go to them seeking approval it's going to be debated for a hell of a lot longer than we have. You heard this thing threaten to destroy our infrastructure and kidnap our population. You have the authority. You don't need anyone's permission to press the damn button. Do it now, while there's still an element of surprise."

"I don't know," said Lopez-Nelson. "I should—"

"Listen to me!" said Junaluska. "You know my heritage. I'm of Cherokee blood. I'm the most American person in this room. And I'm here to tell you that even if this thing is the most benevolent being in the world, even if we storm its shores and find out it's being operated by *Santa Claus*, we must destroy it. The way of life of my people was all but obliterated by European contact. If we don't stop this thing now, there will be no true human civilization left. It will forever be corrupted by the encounter with this thing. You're the one man on the face of this Earth with the power to stop it."

"What about your landing teams? Can't we—?"

"They are still hours away. Satellites show this thing getting more developed with each moment. Stop it now."

Lopez-Nelson cradled his face in his palms. "This is madness. Earthquakes, fine. Environmental collapse, sure. A lousy economy? Just part of the job. But an invasion from heaven? There's no way to win. I'm either going to be known as the man who lost the world, or the man who nuked angels."

"History gets written by the victors," said Junaluska.

"All right," Lopez-Nelson said, with a sigh. "Bring me the football."

The football was the name given the suitcase that was never more than a dozen yards from his person. The marine sergeant who carried it unlocked the handcuff that attached it to his wrist, brought it to the President's desk, and pressed the latch. A retinal scanner rose from the suitcase's black surface like the eyepiece of a microscope. Lopez-Nelson lowered his eye to the lens.

The case clicked open.

"May God have mercy on me," he said, as he began the launch sequence.

ADAM AND JESSICA stood on the balcony in the aftermath of their lovemaking, looking out over the still forming city. Trees were growing now, and a distant tower had changed into a fountain, with a waterfall almost a mile high falling into an unseen pool. Rainbows danced within rainbows around it.

"It's so beautiful," said Jessica. "But where is everyone?"

"The city is uninhabited at the moment," said Adam. "I think we may be the only people here."

"Why?"

"Atlantis is barely a day old. I know it's difficult to understand, but the city is growing before our eyes. It's creating homes for other people who come."

"Is Chase coming?" asked Jessica. "Oh my God. Chase. I've been so overwhelmed by the angel and flying over the Atlantic and finding you that I haven't had time to think about the implications. Chase is all grown up now, isn't he? I've missed his childhood."

"He's grown," said Adam. "He's . . . a good man." He hoped it was true. He had no reason to doubt it.

"How about my parents?"

"I'm sorry," said Adam, pulling her closer.

"Then they . . . when?"

"Your father passed away about seventeen years ago. Your mother a few years after that. I think your sister's still alive. I kind of lost touch with her."

"You lost touch?"

"Honey, I'm not proud of how I've handled the last twenty years. I lost touch with a lot of people. I'm afraid Chase is one of them. I've seen him only a couple of times since he left for college."

"Why? How?"

Adam shrugged. "Things haven't worked out."

He immediately knew this was the wrong thing to say.

"Things haven't worked out?" Jessica said, her voice rising. "That is not acceptable, Adam. Chase is our son. He deserves more than a shrug and a lame excuse."

"I don't have an excuse," said Adam. "I admit this was my failing. I wasn't the best father."

"You used to always say you'd be the most devoted father on Earth," said Jessica. "You said that after you grew up without a father—"

"Stop," said Adam, holding up his hand. "You're not telling me anything I don't already know. You can't make me feel more guilty than I already do."

"I'd like to at least try," Jessica said softly, turning her back to Adam, crossing her arms.

"Don't be like this," he said.

"I want to see him," said Jessica. "That's my top priority. I want to see my son."

"I do to," Adam said. "And I think we will. This city specializes in making dreams come true."

THE WATER-MAN LED CHERISE to a small café in sight of the shore. They sat at an iron table beneath an umbrella. A robot with glass skin revealing golden clockwork within brought Cherise drinks and food. There had been no menu.

Before her sat a glass of milk and a tomato sandwich on toast. She felt a wave of sentimentality wash over her as she smelled the food, the warm bread odor, the tang of the tomatoes.

"When I was a kid this was what Granny fed us for lunch all the time in the summer," said Cherise. "But it's not real, is it?"

"Of course it's real," said Atlantis.

"It can't be. There aren't any cows here. There weren't any plants here before I landed. You can't grow a real tomato in one day."

"All matter consists of a relatively small number of elements arranged in various combinations. The milk may never have been excreted from an udder, but it's still milk by every possible test."

Cherise was hungry. They'd been walking for hours and she hadn't eaten breakfast before getting sent on the recon mission. Her stomach grumbled. Yet the tomato sandwich seemed like a dangerous thing, more menacing than a hand-grenade with a missing pin.

"Wasn't there a Greek myth? About Hades? That if you ate any of the food there, you could never come back?"

"Yes. Other cultures share similar myths. In Celtic lore, eating the food of the fairy kingdom would keep you forever a prisoner of the fairy realms. But you aren't in the fairy realms, Cherise."

The sandwich smelled heavenly. Her curiosity was also hungry. Could you make a good glass of milk without a cow?

She took a nibble of the sandwich. Its flavors exploded in her mouth, the tomato sweet yet acidic, with a hint of saltiness, the toast dry and crumbly on the surface yet sopping with juice and mayonnaise. She swallowed it down and took a sip of the milk. The milk was cold and creamy and instantly lifted away the acid of the tomato. The condensation on the glass trickled across her fingers.

"Lord," she groaned. "Nothing has a right to taste this good."

"I'm glad you enjoy it," said the water-man. Then, casually, "I hope it isn't your last meal. The United States has launched a nuclear assault on this island."

"W-what?" Cherise sputtered.

"Don't be alarmed," said the water-man. "My probability models predict a 64 percent chance that I can stop all of the missiles."

"How long before they get here?"

"Never, I hope," said the water-man.

The light grew suddenly dimmer. Cherise looked toward the sky. A flock of angels, darkening the sky with their multitudes, was rising over Atlantis.

"I gotta get back to my plane," said Cherise.

The water-man shook his head. "There's no point—"

Cherise didn't wait for him to finish his sentence. She started running. Assuming they were launching ICBMs from the mainland, she had maybe twenty minutes before they hit. That wasn't enough time to make it back to the plane and get clear. She'd walked three miles, maybe more by her estimate. Assuming she didn't get lost in a city without road signs, she would use up most of the twenty minutes getting back to her plane.

Still, there were other scenarios. Perhaps only a limited strike had been ordered. The Atlantean defense could no doubt stop the attack if it was a single missile. That would likely be followed by a no-holds-barred barrage of dozens, if not hundreds of warheads in the hope one would get through. That barrage might be forty minutes away, maybe even an hour. She could be far outside the danger zone in an hour.

Luckily, she had an excellent sense of direction. It was rare for her to become disoriented, even in a city where the buildings were still plain white shells. Only, many of the buildings weren't white shells any more. She was sure she wasn't lost, but the buildings were changing, as if phantom work crews had followed along behind them. Many of the blank white walls were now bright pastel hues. Sloped red brick roofs hung off of formerly flat-roofed cubes.

Bushes and vines were growing along walls, flowers blooming in boxes sitting in windows. The city was coming to life, only there were still no people. The streets remained as vacant as ever.

By the time she reached the fountain where the water-man had appeared, her lungs were burning and hot wires of pain lined her legs. She was almost there.

She burst into the field. Now the grass was knee-deep and her view of the plane was blocked by stands of raspberry bushes. She sprinted past around them to the runway.

"No," she said as she wiped the sweat from her eyes.

The runway was covered with ivy. Her plane was buried under the thick vegetation, like some ancient relic of a lost civilization. The light upon the dark, flat leaves shimmered.

She looked to the sky. At midday, in tropical latitudes, there was an aurora borealis. Rain began to fall around her out of a clear sky. The water pooled at her feet, then bulged, and the water-man rose before her.

"Our defenses held," said the water-man. "We've stopped the missiles before they reentered the stratosphere. We're taking defensive action against sites containing unlaunched missiles. The attack has failed. You're safe."

"I'm safe?" asked Cherise. "I think you might be confused as to whose side I'm on."

"Did you want the attack to succeed?"

"I don't know. No," said Cherise. "I believe that you don't mean any harm. But I think you're so powerful, you can do damage without even meaning to. Call off your attack on our missile sites. Put me through to my commanding officers. I may be able to talk them out of attacking again."

"I won't halt the nullification of the warheads," said the water-man. "But I will lift the radio silence. You can make your call."

CHAPTER SIXTEEN
BORN AGAIN

THE WAR ROOM WAS ABUZZ with the latest developments. An aura of despair had hung over the room after the failure of the ICBMs to reach their target. Now, the gloom of the war room had been replaced by hopeful chatter. The radio silence had been broken. Captain Cherise Washington was alive and broadcasting from Atlantis.

General Junaluska weighed the information she reported carefully. Despite Captain Washington's assertion that the city wasn't overtly hostile, the most important thing she told him was the technology levels they were dealing with. The aliens could create angels from the soil and launch them into combat against missiles. Plainly, they were dealing with a technological culture far superior to anything Earth could throw at it.

The reality of the danger was obvious. Benign or hostile, prolonged contact with such an advanced technological culture would no doubt doom humanity. Just as encounters with Europeans had all but destroyed Native American civilization, so to would the American way of life be devastated.

The path was clear. It was a slender, long shot chance. He'd held the landing boats of marines at a distance from Atlantis, keeping them out of range in case the nukes had hit their target. Now, they were the last, desperate hope. His squad had high-tech toys, but they certainly weren't dependent on them. These were the fiercest, best warriors America had to offer. Strip them naked and arm them with a knife and they could beat the best any foreign army could send against them.

Consulting the president would only waste time. It was his call to make now. The Marines were going ashore, and taking no prisoners.

"Land the boats," he commanded. "Shoot everything that moves."

ADAM AND JESSICA walked on the beach in the moonlight. They had their arms around each other, pulled tightly together as they walked along sand soft as talcum powder and white as pearls. Sea oats rustled along the dunes.

Despite the romance of the setting, Jessica had fallen silent and Adam could almost read her thoughts. They'd asked Atlantis to bring Chase to them and the city had promised that it would look for their son. This had cheered Jessica up some. Their argument on the balcony was put behind them.

Adam knew he'd never fully understand Jessica. It was a classic glass-half-full-or-half-empty way of looking at things. He was focused on the wonder of the here and now. But for Jessica, Atlantis was only a distraction from the things that truly mattered to her. No doubt her thoughts were on all those lost years. She hadn't been there for the good times or the bad. She'd missed her parent's funerals and her son's graduation. Adam knew there was nothing he could say that would ever give those back to her.

It wasn't that Adam didn't understand regret. It had been his primary emotional state for some time now. But, it's tough to feel too sorry for yourself when you have a brand-new body, when your all-but-dead wife is restored to youth and health, when you're stranded in paradise with angels and Greek gods at your beck and call.

Though it wasn't the time to say it to Jessica, he was relieved that the past was gone. His old life was dead. He'd even seen the corpse. He was born again. And this time, he knew what mistakes not to make. He intended to live this new life, to seize each day and shake out every last bit of joy it could offer him. He would never again be a stranger to his own son, never again keep secrets, or hold off on saying the important things in his heart because the right time never came up.

The irony that he was hesitant to share these thoughts with Jessica wasn't lost on him.

He was pulled from his reverie by dark shapes on the shore ahead. Large, boxy boats were smashing through the waves and sliding up onto the sand. Men were spilling out the back as a steel door opened.

"Uh-oh," said Adam. "Looks like they've sent in the marines."

Adam felt too serene to let this worry him. He was sure that the marines were no threat to Atlantis, and that Atlantis would find some way of making the marines feel welcome.

One of the marines pointed in his direction. There was a jolt and a crack, and Adam fell to his knees. He touched his chest. His hand came back wet and hot. His vision blurred as the sand rushed toward him. He never had time to say the last word in his mind: "Jessica."

Jessica screamed and fell to her knees beside her husband. Blood was everywhere. The bullet had punched straight through him. She felt faint. This was too much to take in. Her mind ground to a halt staring at the horrible scene.

A hand fell upon her shoulder. She looked up. It was the angel who'd carried her here.

"Do not be afraid," he said, as bullets ricocheted from the shield of his wings. "Come," said the angel, lifting her into his arms. "You should not see this."

"Adam," she said, staring at his body.

"He's no longer in there," said the angel.

He flapped his wings and they lifted into the air.

The men on the beach began to scream. The sound of gunfire intensified, becoming a single, thunderous drum roll. Jessica twisted to look below her and the angel moved to shield her eyes, but not quickly enough. The beach had grown teeth. Jagged, spike-toothed mouths were yawning open in the sand beneath the invader's feet. One by one, the men vanished and the teeth snapped shut.

The beach was quickly calm and quiet again.

It was the most horrible thing she'd ever seen. And it satisfied her. It satisfied her in a way that shamed her to the core. These were the men who'd snatched her husband away forever, after she'd finally been reunited. No fate could be cruel enough. And yet, no amount of cruelty toward his murderers would bring him back.

She closed her eyes as hot tears streamed down her cheeks.

"There's no reason for sorrow," said the angel.

"Adam's dead," Jessica sobbed. "Oh, God."

By now, the angel had returned her to the bedroom she'd shared with Adam only hours earlier. He placed her on the white sheets and smiled.

"Sleep," he said. "Be at peace. Tomorrow morning you'll see the futility of tears."

Jessica wanted to leap up and slap the angel. But she couldn't. Sparkling dust was falling from the angel's wings, and she could focus on nothing but the tiny particles, and the prisms they formed in the candlelight. The horrors of the previous moments slipped from her mind. She was so drowsy. She tried to fight it, tried to focus on the pain, to claw her way back to waking grief, but it was no use. She dropped away into silent darkness.

IN A WOMB DEEP beneath the surface of the city Adam Morgan awakened. He grasped his chest, as the memory of falling to the sand returned to him. He found no wound. His chest was smooth and hairless, slippery as if covered with soap. He opened his eyes to see, but there was no light. It was as dark with his eyes open as closed. Slowly he became aware that he was suspended in liquid, warm and slightly gooey, and that the fluid even filled his lungs. He tried to speak, but couldn't. He wished there was light.

And so there was light. The goop he floated in was translucent, faintly blue. His body vanished into haze as he looked down. Or was he looking up? In the weightless suspension, he couldn't be sure, but it felt like he might be floating upside down. He brought his hands to his face. They looked strange and distant, unfamiliar, completely free of wrinkles and creases, without even fingernails.

Again, he tried to speak, but the fluid flowed across his vocal cords without sufficient friction to produce noise. He wanted to ask, "What's happened?"

"Don't be alarmed," the fluid said. His ears didn't hear the voice. He wondered if he imagined it.

"You *are* imagining it, after a fashion," said the voice. "The section of your brain that allows you to remember and fantasize about sound is being stimulated. While you're suspended in the aqua vita of the womb, I can communicate with you more fully than when we're limited to sensory input."

As if in demonstration, Adam realized he knew how to play piano. It was a strange, almost exhilarating discovery. His grandmother had owned a piano and he'd taken lessons as a child, but he'd had no particular aptitude or talent for it. The parts of his head that heard the music had always been separate from the parts of his head that saw the notes on the page, and the parts of his head that told him which fingers to move. They had never flowed together as one fluid process.

Now, he was no longer floating in goop. He was sitting at his grandmother's piano in her living room. He wasn't a child. He was the man he'd always wanted to be, the man who'd traded bodies with him on the ship. And he was playing piano. Mozart's "Turkish Rondo." The music leapt from his fingers like sparks of electricity. It was a joyful, powerful experience to know that he possessed the knowledge to make such sounds.

"But I'm not really playing, am I?" he said/thought.

The living room faded. The piano dissipated into bubbles.

"No," said the fluid. "But the human brain is a wonderful thing. In my short exposure to it I've come to appreciate its possibilities. It's a marvelous tool for the creation of realities."

"I still know how to play piano," said Adam looking at his hands. "I hear music in my head and feel my fingers twitch. Why? How?"

"It's merely a demonstration," said the fluid. "I could stimulate your brain to imbue you with any knowledge you desire. You may find the aqua vita a useful medium for entertainment or communication. While sipping your planets data streams, I've discovered that your species devotes a great deal of its resource to entertainment. In the aqua vita, you could be totally immersed in the amusement of your choice. You may also communicate with other humans suspended in the aqua vita on a direct level, sharing thoughts and memories beyond the limits of language."

"I see," Adam said. "I'm not sure that's a good thing. In my experience, learning to keep things hidden from others spares them a lot of pain."

"The pain will not last. Openness of emotion and the direct sharing of experience will create joys far greater than the pains," said the fluid.

"Speaking of pain," said Adam. "Didn't those soldiers shoot me? What happened?"

"You were shot and your old body was damaged beyond convenient repair. It will be recycled. You inhabit a new body. It will be a perfect match for your old one."

"I suppose I have to believe you, since you've done it before. But how? How do you pull my mind out of my old body and put it into this one?"

"Thoughts are nothing but data. Your memories are complex interlinked chains of information stored in the physical structures of your brain. I constantly map this information. In the event of catastrophic body failure, I transfer the data to new housing."

"But then . . . wouldn't that mean—"

"You're immortal," said the fluid.

Adam felt the same detachment he felt when the doctor told him that his wife had sleeper flu and might never awaken. It was too big to deal with immediately. He would need time to think through the ramifications. With Jessica's illness, that process had dragged on for twenty years. How long would it take him to come to grips with immortality?

"Your body is finished, unless you would like to modify it."

Adam could see himself in his mind's eye better than any mirror he'd ever used.

"Modify it? Like, what, change my hair color?"

"If you wish. Change your eye color. Your height, weight, skin color. More advanced modifications are also possible, though they would require starting fresh in a new shell. You could change your gender. You could grow gills, or exchange your hair for feathers. You of all people should be comfortable with the possibilities that are open with modifications to the genetic code."

This was another item to put on the mental shelf labeled, "Deal with this later."

He looked at his hands again. They were more familiar now, the nails had returned, and the creases around the joints.

"I'll stick with this body for the time being, thanks," said Adam.

"Prepare to be released from the womb," said the fluid. "Your wife will be waking soon, and it will be a pleasant surprise for her to discover you by her side."

"Let me out," said Adam.

His feet gently came to rest on a grated surface. He'd been floating upright all along. The fluid flowed across his skin, quickly exposing his head to air. He felt sick as the fluid flowed up from his lungs, emptying through his mouth and nostrils. As the last of the fluid cleared his mouth he gasped, taking the first breath of air his body had ever experienced. By now, the goop was only waist deep. He was in a large, egg-shaped chamber. He placed his hands on one of the glassy walls to steady himself as his new legs felt the full weight of his body for the first time. His stomach felt tight and empty. Of course it was empty. His new mouth had never tasted food; his teeth and tongue were virgins. He'd never been kissed; he'd never scratched an itch or worn clothes or combed his hair. He was utterly new.

He grinned uncontrollably as hot water began to shower over him, washing away the last traces of the aqua vita.

The first word to pass from his new throat was, "Wow."

CHAPTER SEVENTEEN
DON'T HOLD BACK

PURE SAT IN THE WELL of the senate, his feet kicked up, trying to make sense of the puzzle. Why was "Atlantis rising" *his* problem? He supposed that his higher self, from his vantage point outside of reality, might have more information than everyone else. But how did that translate into a responsibility to act? What did he care if aliens and angels overran the world? If he could just get his body back to normal, he could manage all his moods with pills again and wouldn't care. Alas, shortly after Jazz had secured Mount Weather, Pure had slipped away to the pharmacy and engaged in a whole buffet of medications designed to make him forget all about the crisis at hand. They'd had no effect. He'd known this would happen; it wasn't the first time he'd gotten his hands on drugs since coming out of the warp. They were no more effective at altering his body than bullets or dragon claws. It was unfair. He'd been put on Ritalin when he was eight. Every year after that he'd added another doctor prescribed medicine to the arsenal designed to protect him from distraction, sorrow, anxiety or aggression. For twenty years, pills had provided a pleasant pillowy buffer between him and reality.

Now that this buffer was gone, he couldn't help but miss Hammer.

When they would sneak their special moments together, they weren't wasting time with chitchat about the weather or gripes about work. Mount Weather didn't have actual weather, and they both worked in top-secret jobs that they weren't supposed to talk about. Their relationship hadn't been about dealing with day-to-day drudgery, or trivia, or working out old emotional traumas. Pure had drugs for that, and Hammer had stoic repression. This meant that when they did slip away for a few stolen moments together, it was all about pleasure. Supposedly, this was the most crude and shallow form of relationship. Yet, whenever Hammer had grabbed Pure with his rough hands and pressed him up against the wall, sucking away his breath with a violent kiss, the universe hummed. The moon orbited the earth, the earth orbited the sun, all spun around the center of the universe, which turned out to be Pure. Talking would have wrecked the magic.

Pure sighed. He was supposed to be figuring out Atlantis and instead he was reminiscing about sex. That long ago diagnosis of ADD might possibly have some underlying merit.

A second distraction arose when Chase wandered into the chamber. His hands were in his pockets and his head was low.

"Howdy," said Pure.

Chase glanced at Pure but didn't say anything.

"Something bugging you?" Pure asked.

Chase shrugged his shoulders. "Cassie just told me to stay away from her. I think she's just upset. She's in a lot of pain. I just want to be there for her."

"If she wanted you to be there, she'd say so," said Pure. "You're in love and she isn't. Live and learn."

"Cassie's not thinking clearly," said Chase, walking up the stairs. "She's screaming at Jazz. She's terrified about Atlantis. She saying it's the end of the world."

"Might be," said Pure, grabbing a remote control off the seat beside him. He pressed a button and an enormous video screen lowered behind the speaker's podium and came to life. Pure began racing through the channels. "It's the end of decent television, anyway. I was flipping through earlier. Everything's all Atlantis, all the time, even though no one seems to have any actual information. At least the population is taking it fairly calmly. It looks like only half the world is rioting."

Images flashed across the screen as Pure kept clicking the clicker. The charred wreckage of an airplane. Shops with windows broken. A knife that never needed sharpening, cutting through cans. A severed arm lying in the middle of a road. Men in suits sternly addressing the camera. The Vatican, looted, smoldering. An exercise machine that would give you rock hard abs in only thirty days for a very reasonable price. The President, looking pale. Pills to enlarge your penis.

"When aliens one day intercept the last signals broadcast before the apocalypse," said Pure, "they sure are going to see a lot of infomercials."

"Do you think this is really the end?" asked Chase.

"Probably," said Pure. "I think I was supposed to stop it somehow, but I've been out of my league from the start. I wasn't cut out to be an action hero. If I'd known this was coming, maybe I would have . . . would have . . . I dunno. Actually, now that this is happening, I don't see why better choices in life would have made any difference at all. Anything you wish you'd done differently?"

"Yeah." Chase sagged into the chair next to Pure. He looked as if all life had drained out of him. "My dad. I wish . . . I wish. . . ."

"That you'd had a chance to work things out with him?" asked Pure.

"I wish I'd punched him in the nose when he told me he was leaving to sail around the world," said Chase. "That bastard. I mean, Mom's still in a damn coma, so sometimes I'm tempted to cut him some slack. I know he's had a tough life. I could always kind of see the logic in him shuffling me off to boarding schools. But now he's retired. He's filthy rich. Set off for an around the world voyage on a brand new boat. Did he invite me to come along? Make up for lost time, *blah blah blah?* Bastard. I'd like to sick Morningstar on him. Watch the big lizard eat his guts while he screams for me to help. I'd just laugh and laugh and laugh."

"Don't hold back, Chase," said Pure.

"How about you? You seriously wouldn't do anything differently?"

"Nope."

"There's not even one regret? Not one thing you'd like to change?"

Pure started to shrug off the question. He made the mistake of letting it gain the tiniest bit of traction in a distant wrinkle of his brain. Two seconds later, his shoulders sagged.

"Everything," he whispered. "I'd change every damn thing about me."

Chase looked surprised. "Not the answer I was expecting. You seem pretty comfortable in your own skin."

"I haven't really spent that much time in my own skin. I've been stoned to one degree or another since before I grew pubic hair."

"You never tried to stop?"

Pure shook his head. "Drugs gave me a structure. When I went off to college I had a whole itinerary programmed into my phone with alarms to alert me what pill I was supposed to be taking. Some people have religion to guide them through life, I had pharmaceuticals. I don't want to pretend that it didn't have some benefits. I was always a straight A student, very focused and studious. Most of the meds worked as advertised. And, some of the side effects were pretty helpful. Lower libido, for instance; I didn't spend all my teen years thinking about sex."

"I gotta get me some of them pills," said Chase. "I've spent pretty much every hour thinking about it."

"You a virgin?"

"That's kind of a personal question."

"You've confessed a desire to watch your father die violently. I'm confessing that I regret being an addict. I think we're pretty deep in the territory of personal questions."

Chase nodded. "Yeah. I mean, I went to a male-only high school so I didn't have a lot of opportunity to meet girls until college."

"I really don't see a male-only school as an obstacle to losing one's virginity," said Pure.

"Don't go there."

"I mean, when I was your age, I'd been hooking up with other guys on the internet since I was fourteen."

"I thought you said the pills kept you from thinking about sex."

"I said I didn't think about sex all the time. But the few hours each week I did think about it, I was usually just a few text messages away from a hook-up. I'd had at least fifty partners before I went off to college."

"That sounds pretty dumb. You're lucky you didn't get AIDS."

"You know there have been precautions against that for decades, right? Having anonymous sex doesn't have to be dangerous. I've never caught so much as a cold."

"That's nothing to brag about," said Chase. "You obviously didn't fall in love if it was all anonymous."

"True. At least until Hammer. I think I loved him. A little. Sort of. But maybe love is overrated, if a few pills can take its place." Pure tilted his head back and scratched his neck. "Screw it. The more I think about it, the more I'm sure I wouldn't want to change a thing. My life has been warped from the start, but what the hell. I'd rather face the apocalypse as a perverted warp monkey than as a love-sick virgin."

"There's no need to be insulting," said Chase. "I thought we were bonding."

"So did I. It scared me. I don't want you begging me to make a man of you when the angels come back."

"Dream on," said Chase.

The door to the chamber opened with a loud clank. They looked up to the top tier and saw Jazz coming toward them.

"Great timing," said Pure.

"Am I interrupting something?" Jazz asked.

"No, I meant 'great timing' on your takeover of Mount Weather. If the angel's to be taken seriously, you've got about two and a half days left to enjoy your conquest."

Jazz came down the stairs. "I'm taking the angel very seriously."

As she spoke, she wriggled free of the backpack she was wearing. She tossed the backpack onto the desk in front of Pure. It landed with a solid thump.

"This, gentlemen, is a nuke," said Jazz.

Chase jumped up. "Holy shit! Is it radioactive?"

"Calm down, kid," said Pure. "It wouldn't be hot. And you can't detonate one by dropping it."

"I can't detonate it, period," said Jazz. "You have to input a code on the keypad. Without the code, it's only dangerous if I use it to bludgeon someone to death."

"I thought code-breaking was your specialty," said Pure.

"Ninety percent of hacking involves attacking the weakest link in the system, the idiots using the computers. I got plenty of the passwords I used to attack the banking system simply by calling up people and asking nicely pretending to be with their IT departments. Guessing a string of random numbers is a little time consuming. Since you worked here, I was hoping you might tell me who would know the codes."

"Christ, how would I know? I didn't even know we still had nukes. I thought we'd disarmed twenty years ago."

"Why do you need a nuke?" asked Chase.

"We need nukes and worse if we're going to stop Atlantis. This thing is the product of an alien civilization far more advanced than our own. It will destroy us if we don't stop it."

"What if it really is here to help?" said Chase.

"Even if it has the most altruistic of motivations, it can still destroy us," said Jazz. "Guns and smallpox dealt Native Americans a severe blow, but it was the missionaries who came in to feed them, clothe them, and save their souls who obliterated all but the barest traces of their culture. We've got about forty-eight hours to figure out how to stop this thing."

"Stop it?" The shout came from behind them, a shrill, piercing voice that made them all cringe. It was Sister Sue, who'd been coming down the steps so slowly and quietly none of them had noticed. "This isn't something to be stopped. This is something to be embraced! Didn't you hear this thing? It's the vindication of what I've fought for my whole life. We've screwed up the planet so badly that we require outside intervention. I can't see a single downside."

Pure's mouth slowly dropped open. He tried to think of something mean to say, but couldn't. It wasn't worth the effort. Sue simply lived in a different world than he did.

"Sue," said Jazz. "Did you know you were one of my personal heroes?"

"Heard it before," said Sue.

"That song Bob Dylan wrote about you," Jazz said. "Man, I listened to it a million times growing up. You're a legend. You fight for what you believe in, you speak truth to power, you answer to no earthly authority as you battle for what is right."

"I did what I had to," said Sue. "Anyone can see the world is going to hell. I've felt like Don Quixote tilting at windmills for the last eighty years. I can't tell you how good it's going to be to finally see those windmills fall."

"I can respect that," said Jazz. "But I can't let it happen."

"If we're picking sides," said Pure, "I vote for the course of action that most pisses off Sue."

"To hell with both of you," said Sue. "Even if you wanted to stop it, you couldn't."

"We've got a suitcase nuke and a spook door that says differently," said Pure. "Jazz, you're right, we have to find a way to arm this bomb. I suddenly know what it is I'm doing here."

CHAPTER EIGHTEEN
SWIRL

JESSICA AWOKE TO FIND Adam sitting by her bed.

"Good morning," he said.

She sat up. "You're . . . was I having a nightmare? It seemed so real."

"It was real," said Adam. "I was shot. Atlantis fixed me."

"Fixed you? How could it fix you? You were . . . you should still be in a hospital."

"I *should* be in a morgue," said Adam. "But the rules are different here. What would you say if I told you we were immortal?"

"I've always assumed I was," said Jessica. "I've never believed death was the end. I think there's a world after this one."

"You'll never have to find out," said Adam. "You know, back in grad school I used to hang out with people who believed immortality was possible. The cellular causes of aging are pretty well understood. It's a matter of ever-shortening telomeres."

"Telomeres?"

"They're segments on the ends of our genes that serve the same purpose as the little plastic bands on the end of shoe strings. As cells divide, the telomeres grow progressively shorter, and eventually they're gone, and the gene sort of unravels. This is a simplistic description, of course, but it helps visualize what happens to our genes as we age."

"I'm following you," said Jessica.

"So the guys I hung out with were working on therapies to stop the telomeres from unraveling. If the breakdown on a cellular level could be controlled, life could be prolonged indefinitely. Combine this with our ability to clone new organs from stem cells for transplants, and they believed that our generation might see the first immortal humans. It turns out they were right. It's just that Atlantis has beat them to the punch."

"We can't die?"

"The body you saw shot on the beach died," said Adam. "But Atlantis grew me a new one. The city possesses the technology to record all of our thoughts and move them to new bodies."

"How awful," said Jessica.

This wasn't the reaction Adam had expected.

"Awful? I'm telling you we can't die! How is that awful?"

"It's recording out thoughts? What about our privacy?"

Adam raised his eyebrows. "Privacy is more important than eternal life?"

"After you were shot, the angel told me to sleep, and I did, even though I was upset. I think it was controlling my mind. How can we trust this thing if we can't even trust our own thoughts?"

"I'm surprised this is a problem for you, given your upbringing."

"What?"

"Being raised a Christian. Didn't you learn as a child that you always had God watching your actions and reading your mind? Were you concerned about your privacy then?"

"I can't believe you're saying this," she said.

"What?"

"Having God know what I'm thinking is one thing," said Jessica. "But this thing isn't God. It's some kind of alien. It makes my skin crawl."

Adam stood, throwing up his hands as he turned away.

"I don't believe this," he said. "Atlantis has awakened you from a twenty-year coma. *It brought me back from the dead.* How on Earth can you not trust it?"

"What if it's controlling your mind?" said Jessica.

"If it's controlling my mind, why isn't it controlling yours? If it's as sinister as you think it is, it could rewire your brain to make you love it."

"I didn't say it was controlling my mind now. I said it did last night."

"And I didn't say you're mind was being controlled, I said it wasn't."

Simultaneously, they each said, "You never listen to me."

Adam scratched the back of his neck.

"Look, I'm not sure you're going to be open-minded about this, but what if there were a way for me to listen to you more fully than has ever been possible before?"

"What's so tough about listening?" said Jessica. "Other people do it, but you make it seem like some impossible feat."

"You're right," said Adam. "I'm a terrible listener. But when I was being, uh, regrown, I was in a . . . a machine, I guess, that can let people directly share their thoughts and emotions."

Jessica crossed her arms. "It's so typical of you to think that we need a machine to talk to one another."

"Forget I mentioned it. I knew it was a mistake the second I said it."

Jessica sighed. "I'd forgotten this," she said. "How much we used to fight."

"I hadn't," said Adam. "Every time I would go to see you at Rolling Meadow I would sit by your bed and replay every argument we ever had in my head. I'm not just a terrible listener. I'm terrible at talking. I'm terrible at keeping quiet. All our fights were because I'm just so bad at making a connection. I'm sorry. I wish I could have said it then, so I'm saying it now. I'm sorry."

"The arguments weren't all your fault," said Jessica, shaking her head. "Don't be such a martyr. Yeah, you're screwed up. I think growing up without a father messed you up. But, everyone's messed up. I wasn't always an angel. You don't have a monopoly on sorry. I'm sorry too."

"Huh," said Adam. "Are we really going to argue about who's most sorry?"

"Let's not," said Jessica.

"Okay," said Adam.

"In fact, let's try out this machine you're talking about."

"Really?" said Adam.

"I've twenty years to catch up on," Jessica said. "Maybe sharing your memories will help."

"Come on then," said Adam. "Let's return to the womb."

THE ANGELS STARTED QUIETLY, delivering ballots to those most in need of deliverance. They rose from the stone floors of third world torture chambers, they walked the halls of asylums, they appeared on death rows in the dark of night.

Victor Wayne Johnson was condemned to die. He'd been on death row in Texas for seven years. His death was scheduled only a month away. He wasn't sleeping well anymore.

He woke from a feverish dream to find an angel above him. The angel looked down at him and said, "Your mind is an awful place."

"Jesus Christ," said Victor, halfway swallowing his tongue as he sat up and scrambled backwards, pressing his back against the concrete wall.

"Look at it," said the angel. "Its neural pathways are completely snarled. Your life experiences and brain chemistry allow you to delight in the suffering and pain of others. Almost require it, in fact. You've raped and murdered seventeen children. And I can see how much this delights you. Despite any protestations of remorse or shame, in your heart you believe your actions were justified, even heroic. You would kill again if given the chance."

"Don't send me to hell," Victor blubbered. He lost all control of his bladder. He'd expected this moment all his life, lived in white-hot fear of it. Death had never held any terror, but what waited beyond strangled his heart like ice-cold, bony hands.

"I'm not here to bring you to hell," said the angel. "I'm from Atlantis. I'm here to offer you the choice of coming with me. This is your ballot."

Victor saw the ballot as a golden key. He took it with trembling hands.

"Y-you're saying you're gonna get me out of here?" Victor said, wiping his tears. "Why? How?"

"Everyone will be offered the opportunity to embrace Atlantis."

"Ain't that the place under the sea? Where Aquaman lives?"

The angel smiled.

"What the hell—oh excuse me—what the heck am I asking questions for? Of course I want to go. I'd go to the dam—I mean darn moon to get out of here."

"Very well." The angel nodded. "But not in this body. Not with that poorly wired brain. You must be remade."

The angel placed his hands upon Victor's head. With a sharp twist, it ended Victor's old life.

In Atlantis, Victor opened his eyes, crying. He tried to move his arms, but couldn't control them. He tried to speak, but his lungs would do nothing but force loud bawls from his mouth. An angel moved into his field of vision and lifted him.

"Welcome to Atlantis," said the angel. "You were once a murderer named Victor. Now you're an infant once again. You'll be raised under careful supervision. Families are coming who will be glad to adopt you. Memories of your previous life will fade as you focus your attention on learning to master your new form. We hope that this life will be more felicitous than your last one."

Victor kept crying. But he had an increasingly difficult time trying to recall what he was crying for.

THE FLUID SWIRLED into Jessica's lungs but the sensation wasn't one of panic. She felt embraced by the fluid, hugged gently. She grew weightless. Her eyes strained to make out the dreamy, gauzy lines of her body. Even if she was young and healthy again, she still didn't quite trust her physical form. It had failed her, allowed her to sleep for twenty years. For the first time, she realized how much she hated it.

No, hate wasn't the right word. But her body had provided certain limits on her life. Floating in the blue fluid, she discovered that her body no longer had any hold on her. She was free. She slipped from her body with the ease of unzipping a pair of pants and letting them fall to the floor.

She was now outside of her body, outside of time itself. Her whole past life stretched out behind her, the hundreds of people she had known passed in a steady parade, and she was startled to find out how small this gathering truly was. She'd spent over half of her life asleep.

Slowly she grew aware that she wasn't alone in the fluid. Adam was here, beside her, invisible, present only as a warmth. He was outside his body just as she was. With her own invisible, intangible hands, she reached toward him.

And then she was him. She raised her hands. They were large and masculine. She was somehow inside his body. The memories in the brain she occupied were completely new. They were his memories.

She looked around, weightless in the goop, and saw a woman floating beside her. It was her body. It's eyes were closed as it hung, sleeping, almost lifeless. Then, the fingers twitched.

Her old eyes opened.

Both bodies smiled.

INVADING MOUNT WEATHER at the same time Atlantis had arrived had one upside. The government hadn't been able to devote the time and resources to a counterattack. Jazz reported that all the entrances to the mountain were under heavy guard from the outside. The missile launching tubes had been welded shut. The government had taken steps to insure that nothing was getting out of the mountain, but had made no moves to get back inside.

Pure went to the infirmary to check up on Cassie.

"How's she doing?" Pure asked.

Chase shook his head. He was sitting next to Cassie, who lay on a hospital bed under a clean white sheet. Cassie was pale, sweating profusely, her eyes half open, darting back and forth rapidly. Chase held her hand.

"She's getting worse. She keeps drifting in and out of sleep," Chase said. "I don't want to leave her side. I feel so guilty about this."

"You? Jazz is a lot more to blame than you."

"I'm the person who told her about the dragons. I'm the person who got her all worked up about the idea of exposing my father."

"Oh right. I guess this *is* your fault."

Chase grimaced. Before the kid could say anything else, Pure asked, "Have you seen Morningstar?"

"Not for a while. Why?"

"It's time for me to open negotiations with Jazz. If she gets to have two android supermen at the table, I should at least have a dragon."

"I'll come with you," said Chase.

Pure laughed, a quick, sharp bark of surprise. "That will really tip the balance of power."

"Don't be such an asshole," Chase said. "I only want to help."

Cassie stirred, reacting to their conversation.

"Chase," she whispered, her voice raspy.

"Yes," he said, leaning close, tightening his grasp on her hands.

"You're such a whiner," she said. "I've never liked you."

Taking advantage of the awkward moment, Pure left the room.

HE FOUND JAZZ before he found Morningstar. Her robotic henchmen were nowhere to be seen. Her trail had been easy enough to follow. Open door after open door led through parts of Mount Weather he'd never had clearance to visit. All the halls and rooms had the same white, sterile monotony.

He finally found her in an empty chamber large enough to serve as a hanger for a fighter jet. The ceiling, walls, and floor were studded with metal disks, sensors of some sort. Jazz stood at the bottom of a perfect hemisphere about 15 feet in diameter. The floor of the sphere was carved directly out of bedrock. Floating in the dead center of the hemisphere was a platinum donut. Jazz was underneath the donut, studying it. She held a broomstick in one hand as she reached up to tap the object. The end of the broomstick sizzled away as it made contact.

"What's that?" Pure asked. "Some kind of anti-gravity device?"

"Nope," said Jazz. "Gravity has nothing to do with it. The disk is being held off the ground by tachyon pressure. This is the time machine."

"Holy cow," said Pure. "Are you certain?"

"Duh," said Jazz. "Walk around the perimeter. Tell me if you spot anything strange."

Pure walked, keeping his eye on the donut. Only, as he walked, it no longer looked like a donut. Ninety degrees around the circle, the donut morphed into a cylinder. At one hundred eighty degrees, the cylinder changed into a pretzel. And at two hundred seventy degrees, it changed shape into a perfect sphere the size of a tennis ball.

"Weird," said Pure. "Why's it changing shape?"

"It isn't," said Jazz. "You're looking at a four-dimensional object. Your three-dimensional eyes can't make sense of it."

And yet, he almost could make sense of it. He had a déjà vu sensation of looking down on the object from a higher place and seeing it all at once, the sphere, the pretzel, the donut, the cylinder, all merged into a single object like a twisted egg.

"Do you know what a Bose-Einstein condensate is?" Jazz asked.

"I know who Einstein was," said Pure. "And is Bose the speaker guy?"

Jazz rolled her eyes. "I don't waste my breath explaining this stuff to people who are never going to get it."

"I feel that way about my entire life."

"For what it's worth, I doubt I'd be able to converse about this with

Einstein himself. We're way beyond spooky action at a distance at this point and well into the realm of spooky action here and now."

"Explain it to me anyway," he said. "I promise to ask a lot of dumb questions and you can come away from the conversation feeling all superior. It's all upside for you."

Jazz nodded. "The Bose-Einstein condensate is a type of matter that exists only the barest fraction of a degree above absolute zero. People have been making these things for close to half a century, but they're pretty esoteric. They don't have much use in the day-to-day world, but one nifty thing you can do with the condensate is stop light."

"I can stop light with a window shade."

"A window shade absorbs or reflects light. But the condensate actually freezes a photon dead in its tracks, until the condensate goes out of phase and lets the light move on, as if it had never been stopped."

"Okay," said Pure.

"The time-geeks here at the mountain have gone a trick better. They've created the condensate in an extra-dimensional jar and instead of stopping photons, they catch and hold tachyons."

"I know about tachyons, in a Star Trek kind of way," said Pure. "They move faster than light."

"Correct," said Jazz. "And they move backwards in time. Except for this jar, tachyons never interact with the real world." She made little quote marks with her fingers as she said the word "real."

"So the tachyons get caught in the jar and power the time machine," said Pure.

"That's somewhat simplified, but yes. You put a little energy into the time jar, the condensate goes out of phase, and the tachyons spill out. For a brief second, there's a chain reaction. The delayed tachyons can interact with surrounding matter for a negative fraction of a second. Any atoms the tachyons hit as they come out of the jar get pushed back in time."

"I'm either smarter than I thought or you're good at explaining stuff. What you're saying almost makes sense. So why did I hear so many rumors that the time machine didn't work? And if it does work, why can't we use it to go back and undo what you did to Cassie? That's what I came here to talk to you about. I think I've kept quiet too long. I acknowledge up front that you're presently my strongest ally if I want to stop Atlantis. But I want you to fix Cassie. You had no right to do what you did to her brain."

"I've no right to do anything I ever do," said Jazz. "I find the whole concept of rights to be a crutch. There's no creator granting us rights to life, liberty, and the pursuit of happiness. The one so-called right that is universal is that we may do whatever we wish to do as long as we're stronger than anyone who would try to stop us."

"Are you saying might makes right?"

"That's a bit simplified, but, yes."

"I'm confused," said Pure. "Are you a left wing nut or a right wing nut?"

"I'm the only sane person on the planet," Jazz said, with a wink. "This is why I plan to rule the world. The rest of you need me to save you from yourselves. As for Cassie, I'll help when the time is right. Believe it or not, I care for my sister. Unfortunately, Atlantis is a more urgent problem."

"Understood," said Pure. "And now we have a time machine. How do we use it to go back and stop all this from happening?"

"Ah, there's the rub," said Jazz. She ran up the side of the hemisphere and grabbed the rim, dragging herself back to the man floor. "Come to the control booth."

Jazz led Pure into a small room filled with video screens. She tapped something out on a keyboard and pointed to one of the monitors. The room they had just been in was on screen, looking whole and unspoiled. The time jar sat on a platform, surrounded by a bird's nest of wires and sensors. There was no hemispherical hole in the floor. Then, a flash of white. Suddenly, the platform, the wires, and a big chunk of floor were gone.

"Ah," said Pure. "The machine disintegrates stuff."

"Nope," said Jazz. "It's all intact. I've run the calculations, read the notes. Pump energy into the time jar and you send matter back in time. Unfortunately, due to tachyon wavelength, it turns out you don't go back very far. Five minutes, tops. If you pump more energy in to knock loose more tachyons, you just get a bigger physical area of time displacement, not a bigger time jump. You'll notice this first hole in the floor is only about five feet across. Luckily, they were testing with about one watt of power. If they'd pumped in enough energy to light a sixty watt bulb, they would have taken out this control booth."

"So . . . I don't get it. If things are going back five minutes, then what? Why don't they appear?"

"Here's where the Mount Weather scientists overlooked the obvious," said Jazz. "You should see some of the math they were doing to explain their results. It's pretty funny. They thought that, with matter moving backwards only five minutes, it was colliding with itself. Obviously, if the atoms of the floor go back in time five minutes, they must be running into the floor atoms that were already there, right?"

"Makes sense."

"And maybe the collision of the present matter with past matter releases energy that destroys the present matter?"

"Good theory," said Pure. "I guess that does explain why things disintegrate."

"Nope," said Jazz. She had a smug, satisfied look on her face. "Things are moving back in time five minutes and surviving the trip. But the tachyons move objects through time, not space. Since Earth is moving around the sun at about 18.5 miles a second, it's traveled over 5500 miles in those five minutes. Add this to the Sun moving around the galactic center at 150 miles per second, and you get another 45,000 miles on top of that. These are just off the top of my head of course. But I'm 99.9% sure the time machine works flawlessly. It may even have some practical uses. Launching things 50,000 miles into orbit at the flip of a switch could be very useful."

Pure frowned. The time machine was a dead end. He considered arguing with Jazz more about Cassie, but didn't see the point. Sadly, she was right. Atlantis was the most urgent problem.

"We'd best get back to work on finding the code to that bomb, then," Pure said. "Then I can use the warp door to deliver it to Atlantis."

"I like that plan," said Jazz.

IT WAS THE SEVENTY-FIRST HOUR. Pure wasn't precisely certain what was going to happen in the seventy second hour, but it was looking more and more like he was going to find out. Ever since he'd figured out his attack plan on Atlantis, he'd been tearing up the security offices in the mountain, looking for any clue to the code to unlock the nuke. So far, he'd had one major success. He'd located a tiny electronic key that synched with the warheads. The key constantly generated random numbers, but if the right security code was put into it, it would generate a successful access code for the warheads. Jazz was attempting to hack the key, but since it was the only one they had found she didn't want to do the sort of destructive testing that would produce guaranteed results but also destroy the hardware.

Pure felt certain that he'd find the password. In addition to housing top-secret black ops projects and a shadow government, Mount Weather also warehoused an astonishing collection of paper. Imagine duplicating every form ever collected by the government. Double that number, then triple that. Mount Weather had so many stuffed filing cabinets it was difficult to believe there was a tree left standing on the planet. In one of these filing cabinets, Pure hoped he'd find the answer he needed. The population of the mountain had a fair share of compulsive note keepers. Somewhere there was a yellow sticky note on the inside of a folder with a string of numbers that would solve all their problems. Why else would his higher self have led him here?

As Pure dug through the folders, he heard a slight scuff of a shoe against a floor. He turned around. He had an excellent view of the barrel of a pistol, held by a familiar hand, and beyond this a familiar face.

"I would have not a single regret if I killed you," said Hammer Morgan.

"I'm glad to see you too," said Pure. "I thought Morningstar had finished you."

Hammer looked half-dead, about as dead as Pure felt. He was pale, haggard, and covered with bandages. He wore a greenish hospital gown with a large brown stain plastered to his stomach. He was shivering, although years of practice kept his gun hand rock steady.

"They med-evaced me back to the mountain. I'd come out of surgery when Jazz told everyone to evacuate or get gassed. I've been holed up since, crawling through vents, looking for a clear shot at Jazz. Then I saw you. You're going to take me to her, or I'll kill you."

"Don't be like that," said Pure. "Look, if you were going to kill me, you wouldn't have made the speech. Put that silly thing down and let's make up."

"After all the damage you've caused?" asked Hammer. "Why have you done all this? Why have you betrayed your country? Why did you betray me? How did you get involved with a terrorist like Jasmine Robertson without me knowing about it?"

"Your arm's going to be tired by the time I explain everything," said Pure.

"Make it fast."

"I know this is a leap of faith, but I think my soul is trapped in a higher dimension and has been guiding me toward something important. A series of weird clues led me around the country until I met Jazz. I think all along I was being guided here to help her stop Atlantis. Wanna help?"

Hammer lowered his gun.

"I can't do it," he said.

"Can't help?"

"Can't kill you, damn it. Your crazy weirdness was always the aspect that charmed me."

Pure held open his arms, inviting a hug. Hammer didn't move toward him. Hammer no longer even looked at him. Pure stepped forward and embraced him. For a few seconds, Hammer was stiff and unresponsive, like hugging a telephone pole. Then Hammer softened and sagged into the hug, wrapping his arms around Pure. Pure felt the weight of the gun against the small of his back.

"I never meant for you to get hurt," Pure whispered.

"I really thought I could shoot you," Hammer whispered back.

Hammer broke the embrace. "Look, I'm dead serious. You know I have to stop you, right? You and your friends have had a good run, but you can't honestly hope to get away with this in the long term."

Pure glanced at his watch. "Long term is about ten minutes. Then Atlantis delivers the ballots. Whatever that means."

"I caught some of this Atlantis nonsense on the TV in the infirmary. I assume it's some kind of media hoax?"

"That would certainly be convenient, but, no." Pure filled Hammer in as best he could. He was frustrated by how few actual facts he had, how much was mere speculation. He concluded with his plan for taking a nuke through the warp door to kill Atlantis before it could destroy human civilization.

"That's not a bad plan," said Hammer. "Did it ever occur to you that maybe you should have turned Mount Weather over to the rightful authorities so that they could implement it?"

"Huh," said Pure. "What a strangely obvious idea. Somehow, I don't think Jazz will play along. But I wonder if—"

An announcement over the loudspeaker interrupted him.

"Everybody get to the senate chamber," said Jazz. "We're under attack by a damn angel."

Later, Pure would learn that the electronically sealed doors had simply swung open as the angel approached. The angel had first visited all the soldiers guarding the outer doors and given them their ballots. Some of the men had fired on the angel. It had no effect.

The angel had then moved into the mountain. The members of the West Virginia Underground had provided no resistance. They'd simply bowed before the angel, accepted their ballots, and let the angel pass.

In the senate, Jazz was waiting with Cassie. Cassie was in a wheel chair, her arms strapped down to the chair arms, her legs also bound. Her scalp had been shaved and wires ran into ugly blue bruises. She gurgled inarticulately as Jazz sat behind her, tapping furiously on a keyboard. Stacked all around them were dozens of computers and monitors, displaying streams of numbers.

"About time you got here," Jazz said without looking up as Pure helped Hammer into the senate chamber. "Things are about to get exciting."

"This is inhumane," snarled Sue from where she sat. She and Chase were sitting in seats reserved for the senators from New York. They were being guarded by Gabe and Hezekiah. "How can you do this to your own sister?"

"You're killing her," said Chase, choking up. He attempted to rise but Gabe pushed him back into his chair.

"Let's hope not," said Jazz. "If she dies, we're screwed. Who's your friend, Pure?"

Pure helped Hammer into a seat.

"I'm Hammer Morgan." With an effort that showed on his face, Hammer lifted his gun and sat it on the table in front of him. "You're all under arrest."

Jazz laughed. "You must be the patient that went missing from the infirmary. Evacuation records showed the head count was off by one. You're pretty good at hiding, though. I couldn't find you in any of my scans."

"I'm head of security," said Hammer. "I know this place better than anyone."

"What are you doing to her?" Pure asked, approaching Jazz.

"I've almost got that signal decoded. I think I can dupe it now. And, as much as I hate to do this to Cass, her brain is the only computer I have access to that has a hope of handling this. I hope you're not as squeamish as those two, Pure."

"Where's Morningstar?" asked Pure.

"I was going to ask you the same . . ."

Her voice trailed off as she looked up the stairs.

Pure followed her gaze.

There was an angel in the room.

In utter silence, the angel approached Pure and handed him a ballot. The ballot looked like it had been carved from a seashell. One side had a button that said "yes" and the other had a button that said "no." The angel moved on, handing a ballot to Hammer, who accepted it without saying a word.

The angel then moved toward Sister Sue.

Jazz yelled, "Gotcha!"

The angel paused. "Curious," he said. "I can no longer hear Atlantis."

"I've jammed the signal!" said Jazz. "Take him, boys."

Gabe and Hezekiah attacked. Hezekiah was the fastest, swinging the enormous axe over his head, producing a loud *crack* as the metal bit into the angel's stony face. As the angel staggered backwards, Gabe followed up with a kick to its chest. Before Gabe's leg could move away from the chest, the angel grabbed it with both hands. The angel steadied itself with spread wings, then gave the leg a fierce yank. The leg came free of Gabe's body in a shower of sparks and a gush of fluids.

"Shit," said Jazz, as Gabe tumbled to the floor.

Hezekiah struck again, and again the axe found purchase in the angel's head. The angel countered by punching out, placing his fist into Hezekiah's huge torso. When the angel drew out its hand, it held a mass of wires and tubes that burst and sparked as the angel squeezed. The mighty prophet Hezekiah went weak in the knees, then fell.

The angel looked a little unsteady itself. It placed its hands on the huge gash in its forehead and said, "Local damage severe. Request repairs."

"They aren't coming," said Jazz. "I've cut you off from your alien masters. Now I'm hitting you with signals that disrupt those tiny machines you are made of. You're dead."

The angel shook its head. "I'm designed to serve and protect humanity, but your assault on me cannot be tolerated."

The angel flapped its wings and flew across the room in a single bound, landing in front of Jazz and Cassie. The angel's skin was beginning to crack and flake, but it showed no sign of pain. The angel took Cassie's head into his stony fingers and said, "She's the source of the signal. I apologize for what I must do."

Then a snarl, and a flash of feathers, and the angel was no longer standing in front of Cassie. Instead, the angel was on the floor underneath a large, angry dragon. Morningstar raked furiously at the angel's guts with his hindclaws as he gnawed the angel's skull between his saw-tooth jaws. With a snap, the angel's head burst, shattering to gravel. This made the angel mad. Its vocal qualities unimpeded by its missing mouth, the angel growled, "Graaaaaagh!" as it grabbed Morningstar by the throat and tossed him roughly across the chamber.

Morningstar spread his wings in the middle of the arc of his involuntary flight, whirling up and around, flapping to gain altitude. Then it dived as the angel struggled to its feet. With a sound like a tree trunk snapping, Morningstar collided with the angel's left wing, tearing it off. Morningstar whirled again, raking his hind claws across the angel's damaged back. Large seams were spreading across the angel's torso. The damaged angel swung out at the dragon, but his left arm fell off just below the shoulder. Morningstar struck again and the angel shattered, falling to the floor as a mound of gravel.

Everyone stared silently as the dragon stood in the midst of the settling dust, its eyes fiery with reflected light.

"Now that I'm not on the receiving end," said Hammer, "that's one impressive lizard."

"I like him," Pure said. "Good job, Morningstar."

"I don't want your praise, Pure," said Morningstar. "I sought you out because I grow impatient. When will you keep the promise you made to me in the forest? When will I see my attorney and my agent?"

"Agent?" asked Hammer.

"Don't ask," said Pure.

ON THE DAWN of the third day, the world was pulled apart, as Atlantis had promised. The angels rose from the island's still changing sky line and moved ever higher, above the levels where they'd destroyed the missiles, high into the vacuum of space. They sought out the satellites that allowed the inhabitants of the blue world beneath them to communicate with one another. One by one, they shoved them from orbit, to burn in the atmosphere below.

Around the world, phones went dead, radios fell silent, and televisions broadcast only static.

When the last of the satellites fell, the angels moved to carefully calculated positions around the globe. They unfurled their wings. Then they exploded, in fantastic bursts of electromagnetic radiation.

Around the world, lights went out. The static-tuned televisions went black. Cars ground to a halt and the thick air that hung over the roads stank with the odor of burnt wire.

Boats chugging across the ocean had their propellers fall lifeless. Inspections of fuel tanks found all the fuel gone, replaced with pale blue dust.

Planes lost all response from their engines and began to fall. Angels appeared and positioned themselves beneath the wings of the crippled aircraft and guided them to the ground.

In the powerless hospitals, where even the backup generators had failed, nurses rushed into rooms to check on their most seriously ill patients to find them sitting upright in bed, healthy and whole, with angel feathers still drifting from the open windows.

It was around then that people began to discover their ballots.

Mariah experienced a typical discovery. She'd finally left the bedside of her daughter and had been fixing coffee when the lights went out. She'd looked out the window, noticing that the whole neighborhood appeared to be without power. This wasn't ground for panic. There'd been rolling blackouts all summer long.

She had gone in to check on Anna.

Anna was no longer in her bed.

"Anna?" Mariah had cried out.

"Mother?" Anna had said from the bathroom.

Mariah went in. Anna stood before the mirror, staring at her face. Her skin was flush, her eyes wide open and clear. Anna's legs were sturdy and supported her without a trace of weakness. Only moments before she'd been a pale, blind, skeletal thing.

"It's happened!" Mariah shouted.

"I'm better," said Anna. "I thought I was going to die and then I dreamed there was an angel telling me I would be well and then I woke up. I-I don't think I'm sick any more."

"It's a miracle," said Mariah.

Anna looked at her, her face a mixture of fear and joy. "And there's something else strange," said Anna. "When I woke up, I had this in my hand."

Anna held out her palm. In it lay a pale pinkish spiral disk, like a snail's shell, only much thinner. It was about the size and thickness of a half dollar. There was writing on the surface and in the center of the disk there was a button.

Mariah recognized it instantly. Though she had never seen it before, she knew there was one in the pocket of her apron. She took it out. On one side it read "yes" and on the other it read "no."

And, never having seen it before, she understood fully what it was and how it worked. If you pressed the button on the yes side, you would be taken away to Paradise. If she pressed the side that said no, she would remain here, in the world she knew, only it would no longer be the world she knew. There would no longer be cars or busses or trains, no longer be supermarkets or television, no phones or fire trucks or credit cards.

What shocked Mariah the most was discovering what a difficult choice that was.

PRESIDENT LOPEZ-NELSON looked at the ballot he held with the same expression he might have possessed if he'd found a scorpion in his hand. Atlantis was taking away all of the foundations of human civilization, like electricity and communications. He would never again address the American people via television. All the things that made America great, the armies, the banks, the teaming cities, were crippled or gone, flicked off like a light switch.

In the silent White House, Lopez-Nelson leaned back in his chair and sat the ballot on his desk. He knew he would press "no," if he bothered to press the thing at all. America was more than its tanks and fighter jets, more than balance sheets and budgets with nearly endless strings of zeroes. He wouldn't abandon the country he loved in the time of its greatest need.

If Atlantis thought that by crippling the nation's technological infrastructure it would draw citizens to it, it had greatly miscalculated. People would fight this. He was sure of it. He was ready to lead that fight.

CHAPTER TWENTY
ONE SMALL HITCH

"SO I GUESS YOU AND I should talk," said Hammer.

Hammer was in the large kitchen off from the research quarters. The room was dim, the lights half out. He'd been restless, in too much pain to sleep, yet feeling good about the pain. His body was knitting itself back together. That always hurt, but pain and progress were intertwined in matters of healing. He'd come to the kitchen to get some water and found Chase there, standing in front of the open refrigerator.

Chase looked back at him. "So it's true," he said. "You're my grandfather."

"Yeah."

"Does Dad know the truth?" asked Chase. "Was I the only one kept in the dark?"

"No one knows," said Hammer. "When I was approached to work in the security force here, I was offered a variety of cover stories. Nobody is allowed to put Mount Weather on their resume. So the residents here have cover stories that allow for a certain remoteness. For the short timers, some claim to be stationed in Antarctica, others claim to be part of submarine crews, and, of course, for lifers, there's the option I took. Once you've been declared dead, there's no going back. You're part of the mountain forever."

"Why did you do it?"

Hammer leaned against one of the stainless steel tables. He looked down at the floor and took a deep breath. He focused momentarily on the ripping sensations within him, as if his insides had been fastened together with fishing hooks that dug deeper with each breath.

He sighed. . "You've heard by now that I'm ... I have ... a preference. For men."

"Yeah," said Chase. "That doesn't matter to me. Does it matter to anyone anymore?"

"I grew up in a different time," said Hammer. "Things weren't as clear cut. From an early age, I wanted to be a soldier, but back then, homosexuals weren't allowed in the military, not openly. And, at the time I wasn't one hundred percent sure of my orientation. A lot of decisions I made in my life were decisions of convenience. It was more convenient to be heterosexual. My parents thought I was straight, and I did what I could not to disappoint them. Your grandmother was a girl I'd known since grade school. I even took her to the prom. She was the first person I kissed. It wasn't a tough decision to marry her. Our sex life was kind of pathetic, but I didn't have anything to compare it too. It wasn't until I hooked up with a guy overseas that I discovered what satisfying sex was supposed to feel like."

"Lately, everyone is being far more blunt with me than they need to be," said Chase.

"Sorry. Suffice it to say my home life was a mess as I began to explore my … um, interests. The fact that your grandmother had gotten pregnant only dug the hole I was in even deeper. I devoted my energies to my career to avoid being home as much as possible, since I had this terror that one day in a moment of weakness I would tell her the truth. My dedication to my career caught the attention of covert services. When I was offered the chance to shed my old life … I took it. I don't know of any more concise way to say it."

"You abandoned your son," said Chase.

"Yes," said Hammer. "It was the best decision possible. I would have been a lousy father if I'd kept living a lie. But when Mount Weather faked my death, my family received a very generous insurance settlement. I was a better provider dead than alive. I've followed Adam's career. It looks like he made good use of the education the money bought him."

"That sounds like something my Dad would say to me," Chase said. "That his selfishness and distance is all for my benefit. Meeting you explains a lot."

"Sorry," said Hammer. "I wasn't a good role model."

"It's too late for sorry," Chase said. As he uttered the words, his voice broke, as if on the verge of crying. Setting his jaw, Chase closed the refrigerator and walked out of the room.

Hammer took another deep breath, just to feel the fishhooks.

MORNINGSTAR MOVED through the mountain with the grace and silence of a cat. His serpentine body was perfect for slithering through ventilation shafts. No part of the mountain was closed to him.

He remembered the fairy tales of his youth. Dragons made their homes in caves. Morningstar could see the appeal.

It had been a few days since he'd last eaten. Earlier he'd talked with Pure in the kitchen, where Pure was making something he called a "burger." Pure had tried to explain the advantages of cooking meat, something about microbes, but Morningstar hadn't paid close attention. Fresh killed meat was his menu of choice. Since there were no horses in the mountain, he found himself idly wondering which of the humans he would devour. Probably Sue. Morningstar had never eaten a woman, but most of the horses he'd eaten had been female, and he wondered if female humans tasted better than the males. Plus, Morningstar liked Pure and Pure hated Sue. No doubt Pure would be grateful. Perhaps he'd even like to share the liver or some other choice morsel.

As he contemplated his future meal, Morningstar caught Sue's scent. Curious, he crept through the vents until he found the room her smell was coming from. Even without looking inside, he could tell she wasn't alone. The girl was with her, Cassie.

He peeked through the vent.

Cassie was stretched out in on a hospital bed with tubes in her arm. Cassie was paler than when Morningstar had last seen her. Morningstar instinctively recognized that her condition was worsening. She would be dead soon without intervention.

Sue stood beside Cassie, holding something in her hand. Morningstar looked closer. It was one of the small disks the angel had dropped. A ballot.

Sue placed the ballot into Cassie's hand.

"I don't know if you can hear me," said Sue. "But I want you to use this. I want you to go to Atlantis. I think they can help you there. They can fix what your sister has done to you."

Cassie said nothing. The ballot lay in her limp fingers.

"I can't go with you," said Sue. "Atlantis sounds wonderful, but the promise of what will happen to the rest of the world . . . that truly sounds like Heaven. Think of it. A world without automobiles or phones or skyscrapers, a world without highways or television or plastic. A paradise as fresh and pure as the one the Lord created. It's a dream I've had all my life, but never believed I would see."

Morningstar's nostril's twitched. Someone else was approaching, the boy. Chase was low on his list of people to eat. He struck Morningstar as bland and unappetizing.

Chase entered the room and asked, "How's she doing?"

"I don't know," said Sue. "I don't even know if she can hear me."

"I can't believe Jazz did this. You know, all the months I've known Cassie, it's always been Jazz this and Jazz that. Her sister was her hero. But this is the most awful thing I've ever seen one person do to another. Given my own family history, that's saying a lot."

"We have to get her out," said Sue. "I'm a little unclear on the specifics, but Jazz is hiding us from Atlantis. We need to get her outside the mountain, so that Cassie can use the ballot and get to Atlantis."

"I'll help if you have a plan," said Chase. "But I don't have a clue how to get out of here. This place is like a maze. Plus there's all of those militia guys to get past. But I'll do whatever it takes."

Morningstar thought the matter through. He'd studied the vents and passageways sufficiently to know that leaving the compound was simple. You could follow the vents to one of the missile silos and leave without ever encountering one of the militiamen. He could see that the silos had been welded shut, but this didn't strike him as an insurmountable obstacle. Assisting a damsel in distress was the purest form of chivalry.

He pushed aside the vent cover and lowered his head into the room. Chase jumped backwards as Morningstar hissed, "Might I be of assistance?"

EVENTS WERE NOW MOVING at a rapid clip. The world finally made perfect sense to Alex Pure. All the random pinball careening around the country finally stood revealed as part of an important and urgent mission. Obviously, his higher self in the warp had some ability to see the future. It knew Atlantis was coming, and had put together all of these elements to stop it. He'd collected the dragon to stop the angel. He'd hooked up with Chase to get to the dragon, which hooked him up with Cassie, which hooked him up with Jazz to get him into Mount Weather, which happened to have the best weaponry to stop Atlantis in its tracks. As near as Jazz could determine, Mount Weather was the only place left on Earth with electric lights. She'd refined the signal jamming, so now Mount Weather was invisible to Atlantis. The EMP's that had wiped out power above ground were harmless against Mount Weather's shielding. They were Earth's last, best hope. There was, sadly, one small hitch.

"I don't have the codes," said Hammer, toying with the nuke key in his hand. "I'm chief of security, not the president. I can't unlock this."

Pure couldn't believe his higher self was playing with him like this.

He turned to Jazz. "You say if you attempt to hack the code, the bomb will detonate?"

"Yes. This isn't like the movies. This isn't a 'should I snip the blue wire or the green wire' situation. You touch any wire on this thing without inputting the right code and it will go off. The government was worried about terrorists getting their hands on these and back-engineering them."

"Then triggering it really isn't a problem," said Pure. "It must be what I'm here for. I go to Atlantis, yank wires, and boom. Pretty obvious."

"I see where you're making your mistake," said Jazz. "When I say it will explode, I mean the detonation charge, not the nuclear material. It will blow up everything within fifty feet and spray plutonium everywhere, but we aren't talking doomsday device."

"Yeah," said Hammer. "It's not like they let someone trigger a nuclear warhead simply by yanking on a long string."

"Then we're screwed," said Pure. "What a colossal waste of time."

Jazz snapped fingers. "Time!"

"What?" said Pure.

"We don't need an atom bomb," Jazz said. "We need a time-bomb."

Hammer asked, "This helps us how?"

"The time field back in the chrono-lab. It spreads out from the actuator in a distance proportional to the energy that's put into it. We can hook the actuator to the bomb. The detonation charge will spread the field for miles. I need to do the math, but I think we can shove the whole damn island into space."

"What if Atlantis came from space?" asked Hammer. "Will that kill it?"

"You got a better idea?" Jazz asked.

"It will work," Pure said. "I feel it. It's like the last piece of the puzzle. I'm here to carry the time-bomb through the warp."

"That is an option," said Jazz. "But a better option is to have one of my robots do it. I've got Hezekiah and Gabriel in the repair tanks right now. Hez should be operational a few hours. He can take the time-bomb through."

"Won't work," Pure said. "The higher dimension responds to consciousness. Your robots will probably work the same way that tossing in a baseball does. They'll just come out in Texas."

"I've been to Texas," Jazz said. "I wouldn't mind throwing it into outer space."

"Stay focused," said Pure.

"You're right," said Jazz. "This is the best plan I got. If you're willing to die to make this happen, I'm not going to stop you."

"Your plan sucks," said Hammer.

"Why?" asked Pure. "What won't work?"

"I didn't say it wouldn't work."

PURE LIFTED THE BACKPACK. It was heavy as hell, easily a hundred pounds, but not all that big, really. Strip away the Kevlar covering and it was a metal sphere about a foot around. The actuator for the time-bomb was barely the size of a donut, wired into the metal sphere in what looked like the Gordian knot's uglier older sister. Pure was glad that Jazz understood how this crap worked. He sure didn't.

"I've rechecked the figures," she said. "This thing is going to create a field a dozen miles in radius. It's going to shove Atlantis, plus a hefty chunk of ocean out into space. Anything left of the island will be destroyed in the resulting tidal wave."

"Let's do this," said Pure, slinging the pack over one arm.

It was a long, quiet walk to the spook lab. The codes had been changed since Pure had worked there, but Jazz made short work of all the pass codes and security locks. Ten minutes later, they were back in the control room. Jazz took her seat behind the main controls.

"Everything is fired up," she said. "I'm going to try tracking you from here. The Houston end of the connection is off line, obviously, but if what you're saying is right that shouldn't matter. If we power up the door here, the duplicate door also powers up, right?"

"That's how I understand it. It's not a duplicate door. It's another aspect of the same door."

"Alex," said Hammer, placing a hand on his shoulder. "This is a brave thing you're doing. I'm proud of you."

Pure took Hammer's hand and held it against his cheek. It was rough and warm. It reminded him of earthly pleasures almost forgotten. Was he really going to be dead in five minutes? Not zombie-dead but actual dead-dead? Or could he survive even this, and wind up drifting among frozen ruins in orbit? Would he ever have another moment of tenderness with another human?

"Let's make this one count," Pure said, kissing Hammer.

Hammer resisted at first. Hammer wasn't the sort of person who engaged in public displays of affection. But then, just as Hammer had surrendered to the hug in the filing room, he surrendered to the kiss. It wasn't long. No tongues were pushed around, no lips nibbled. This wasn't a kiss to arouse passion. This was a kiss to say something that had never been said between them. A kiss to say something neither of them would ever be able to say.

Pure pulled away. Without a word, he turned, as Hammer turned away as well.

Through the open door, there was a shadow. Sister Sue stepped into the doorway, her hands behind her back.

"Off to bomb Atlantis, eh?" said Sue.

"Yeah," said Pure. "Here to wish me good luck?"

"I thought you knew me better than that," said Sue.

She moved her arms in front of her, revealing her shotgun.

She placed the double barrel under Pure's chin.

Pure felt the cold, hard metal circles against his throat. "Is there something you're trying to tell me?" he asked.

Sue fired both barrels and Pure's head became a gleaming pink mural against the ceiling.

HAMMER TACKLED SUE, who went down hard. Hammer felt the stitches in his gut tear loose, but he couldn't stop. With a grunt, he pried the shotgun from her hands and flung it across the room.

"Are you crazy?" he shouted. "Do you know what you've done?"

"I saved the damn world," Sue said, before biting Hammer on his wrist.

"Ow," Hammer said. The old woman had sharp teeth. Hammer used his free fist to clock her in the side of the head. He didn't knock her out, but the blow did shake her free.

"Saved the damn world," she muttered.

An alarm went off on the phone Jazz had holstered on her hip. "What the hell?" she asked, looking at the screen.

"What is it?" asked Hammer.

"An Atlantean signal," said Jazz. "Coming from just outside one of the silos."

"It's the ballot," said Sue. "The angel dropped one when your robots attacked. I gave it to Cassie once you left her alone. Chase and Morningstar are helping her reach Atlantis. They'll save her there, undo the harm you've done."

"Damn it," said Jazz, slamming her fist down on the console in front of her. "I need to stop her."

Jazz got up and stalked toward the door as Hammer ripped away bits of Sue's habit and used them to tie the old woman's hands.

"There's no time to deal with that now," said Hammer. "Let Cassie go. Atlantis will be a gone in another two minutes. I'm taking the time-bomb there. I'll finish Alex's mission."

"Let's hope you can navigate the higher space," said Jazz. "No offense to your boyfriend, but Pure was a little insane from the experience."

"He wasn't a poster boy for sanity before," said Hammer. "The only thing that kept his thoughts organized were the pills. But, if he could navigate the warp, I'm sure I can."

"What do we have to lose?" asked Jazz.

"My life. The world," Hammer said. "But we're out of options."

Jazz pulled a small plastic capsule from behind her left ear.

"This is a long shot," she said. "But take this. I've been using it to listen to the Atlantis signal. Normal Earth signaling technology couldn't penetrate the warp, but maybe this will. With luck it can serve as a homing beacon."

"Luck? I haven't heard you leave anything to chance yet."

"There's a first for everything."

Hammer rose, leaving Sue struggling and cursing against her bonds. He went to Pure's body. Only the hands were recognizable as the man he once knew. There was nothing left above the neck but a few stringy remnants of flesh and hair. Hammer rolled the corpse over and worked the backpack loose. He struggled to lift it. With all the blood he'd lost, he felt dizzy, about to topple. He was shaking hard, dead on his feet. Only sheer will allowed him to pull the straps over his shoulder. Spots danced before his eyes. His legs turned to rubber. He fell, but strong hands caught him and lowered him gently to the floor.

"Sir," said Morningstar, as Hammer's vision cleared to find the big lizard's face right before his. "What's happened to my friend Pure?"

"This bitch blew his head off," Jazz said, pointing at Sue.

"That settles the matter. I'd debated eating her prior to this. Now I shall do so to avenge the death of my friend."

"Later," Hammer said. "There's no time now. You need to help me. Pure would want you to help me."

"He's right," said Jazz. "You must help Hammer get to Atlantis."

"Very well," Morningstar said, lifting the pack from Hammer's shoulder. "I saw that Pure had a great deal of affection for you. I shall assist you."

Morningstar held the hundred pound pack like it was weightless. Hammer rose, steadying himself. Then he willed one foot in front of the other as he leaned toward the pitch-black spook door.

PURE FELL. THAT IN ITSELF was a novel experience. His previous excursions into the warp had felt like rising. But this time, as his headless body hit the floor, his consciousness had kept falling, passing through the ceiling of the room below, into the test animal enclosure, through the empty monkey cages, through the floor, and into the bedrock. He was falling through darkness and heat, through brimstone and silence, and for the first time in a long time he was genuinely afraid. He'd failed. He hadn't stopped Atlantis, hadn't saved the world, hadn't accomplished one damn thing that his higher self had spent so long orchestrating. He'd earned this fall into hell.

"Oh, don't be so melodramatic," said a voice he recognized.

Pure emerged from the darkness into a womb of light. He blinked (a curious act, given that he had no eyelids, or eyes) and struggled to see anything amid the glare.

"I should have figured you'd fuck this up," said the voice again.

Now Pure could see the source, a vaguely human outline, glowing brightly, but not as bright as his background. It was the higher Pure, glorified and naked, sitting on a throne made of subservient monkeys.

"I'm having a hard time seeing you," Pure said, raising his non-existent arm to shield his non-existent face.

"That's because you're still conceptualizing sight in terms of organs. You're thinking of the kind of sight that uses corneas and retinas and brain activity. Too bad you don't have those things any more."

"I remember . . . I remember Sue and her shotgun," Pure said. "The cold metal under my chin, a loud noise. I think . . ."

"You think she blew your brains out," said the purified Pure. "Your memories are dripping from the ceiling even now."

"Can you fix me?" said Pure. "You fixed my other injuries."

"No. A physical brain isn't all that important here in the warp. But back in the physical world, it's a necessary vessel of consciousness. It housed the memory your body used to repair itself. You won't be going back to that body now."

"Oh," said Pure.

"Bummer, huh?"

"I was prepared to die," Pure said. "I figured the bomb would kill me. But I hate that I didn't stop Atlantis."

"You idiot," said purified Pure. "I'm so ashamed of you I could spit. I worked so hard putting all this together and you blew it."

"I tried to get the bomb through the warp," said Pure.

"Yeah. Good thing Sue stopped you."

"Good thing? But I thought . . ."

"What? You thought what? That I was trying to guide you toward stopping the salvation of Earth? Idiot. You weren't there to stop Atlantis. You were there to stop Jazz! You picked the wrong damn side!"

"Huh?"

"Good thing I have a backup plan," said purified Pure. "Here, let me help you out with that brain thing."

Suddenly the world around Pure snapped into focus. Only it was two worlds. One world was dark and cold and heavy, the ocean-floor world he would sometimes dream of, while the other world was the here and now of light and rainbows where he was weightless and alive. The purified Pure held out his arms, beckoning him closer.

Pure moved toward his higher self. He felt like he had a body again, although that body was cold and stiff and damp. But his higher self still glowed with radiance, his higher self was still angelic and beautiful.

Pure reached him, on the monkey throne, and held out his stiff, cold fingers to stroke the glorious, beatified face. The mask of illusion fell away, revealing his higher self as something far from Pure.

The man sitting on the throne was little more than a bloated cadaver. His skin was splotchy with bruises and boils, his red eyes sagged in their dark orbs, his lips were swollen and cracked, revealing a mouth full of rotten, snaggled teeth. Long needle tracks scabbed both arms.

"Lovely, yes?" the Pure on the throne said.

"My god," said Pure. "What happened?"

"You happened, idiot. I happened. This is what we've done to ourselves."

"I don't understand . . ."

"What? You thought years of swallowing horse pills were good for you? You hid it well. You knew how to balance, how to maintain. But the damage was always there, underneath the surface. When you stepped into that warp, you were a year away from dying and didn't even know it. You had tumors in your liver. If you'd gone sober for even one day you might have noticed how damn rotten you felt. For the record, *this* is how damn rotten you felt." The diseased Pure waved his bony hands over his awful body.

"My God," said Pure.

"Don't talk about God," said diseased Pure. "You don't believe in him. You don't believe in anything. You're selfish, shallow, weak-willed, and dumb. No wonder you couldn't figure out the clues."

"Hey," said Pure. "In my defense you're a damn lousy clue maker. Why the fortune cookies and crossword puzzles? Couldn't you just send me a damn e-mail?"

"You see a computer in here? I can't affect anything in the real world, other than occasionally putting ideas in your head."

"What about the earthquake in Charleston?" asked Pure. "Didn't you cause that?"

"No. But I did know it was going to happen. And I knew you'd survive it. I steered you there in hopes of getting Hammer off your trail. In one version of events, he assumed you were dead after the quake. Alas, the events collapsed differently."

"Events collapsed differently?" asked Pure. "What do you mean?"

"Look around you," said the Pure on the throne.

Pure looked at all of the rainbows that swirled around him. He looked down at his feet and felt suddenly like he was surfing on the swirling light, riding a wave of windows each opening into tiny glimpses of the real world.

"What am I looking at?" Pure asked.

"Everything," said the other Pure. "Literally everything. Through these windows you can see every point on Earth. Even more intriguingly, you can see every point in the present, and the futures."

"Futures?"

"It's difficult to comprehend. But from inside the warp, reality looks like a funnel. There's a vast ocean of possibilities lying ahead of us. The present plows into this ocean, tossing most of it aside, forcing some of it into the narrow stream that turns into the past. I'm still learning to look at the future. It's not easy. It's like, I don't know, trying to look at every last bit of information on the internet in one glance. You can track down one bit of information, but that information is tied into other bits, which are tied to other bits, and before you know it there is too much information to ever follow or comprehend. But, intriguingly, the future also has a funnel. All these possible futures start to hit a wall about fifteen minutes from now. Take a look."

Pure tried. He couldn't make sense of what he was seeing. Fields of lava, forest on fire, clouds of ash. Then ice. Ice everywhere.

"You are looking at the mass extinction of life on Earth," said other Pure.

"Why?"

"Jazz's time bomb works. But she hasn't thought through the implications. She's about to carve a giant chunk out of the planet. She's taking not just Atlantis and a bunch of water and atmosphere, but miles of ocean floor and bedrock. The world will experience tidal waves like it's never seen."

"Actually, she mentioned tidal waves."

"Did she mention what happens when the Atlantis chunk smashes back into the planet?"

"I don't think she mentioned that."

"This huge block of rock and ice is going to be spinning wildly in a shadow path of Earth's orbit. Eventually, gravity is going to pull it back.

In seventy-five days, it lands smack in the middle of Colorado. A global wildfire is triggered by the impact. The dust from the collision plus the smoke from the fires plunge earth into endless winter. Not even the cockroaches survive."

"Wow," said Pure. "When I screw up, I do it in style."

"I hate that about you," said other Pure. "This flip attitude. I show you the doom of mankind and all you can offer is a glib remark?"

"You hate that about me? I am you! And you got something better to offer than my attempt at levity? 'Cause I don't have a lot of ideas."

"Of course I have something better to offer. Watch the windows. In one future, you've stopped Jazz. Human civilization thrives on the city of Atlantis. It's humanity's golden age. Soon, people leave Atlantis to terraform and colonize other planets. Thanks to the city, mankind doesn't merely survive, it flourishes. And you were going to put a bomb in the middle of it? Unbelievable."

Pure tried to make sense of the chaotic images swirling before him. He was seeing dragons sitting on gilded thrones, and medieval castles rising high over a rocky river. In another window he saw himself, sitting by a campfire, sharing a cup of coffee with Sister Sue, who was wearing buckskin pants. Not exactly heaven on earth. Still, it beat mass extinction.

"I guess Sue comes out of this looking pretty good," said Pure. "She stopped me from taking the bomb through, and by extension she's stopped Jazz. Atlantis wins, right?"

"Wrong," said other Pure. "Take a look."

Through one of the rainbow windows, Hammer Morgan was staggering toward the warp door. Morningstar was by his side, steadying him, and carrying the time bomb.

"I should have known," said Pure. "So, stop him. Sick the warp monkeys on him."

"The warp monkeys helped you out because they like you. They act on their own urges. They don't have any clue of the larger stakes here. If I'd been watching the right window to the future, maybe they would have stopped Sue. I didn't anticipate her getting back from helping Cassie so quickly."

"Then let's talk to Hammer when he comes into the warp. We can convince him to stop."

"Wrong again. Atlantis has introduced a new factor into the warp equation. It uses tesseract-like higher dimensions to facilitate travel through this underspace we dwell in. It has warp doors that actually work, unlike the crude toy we were playing with. Jazz is sending the Atlantis carrier signal into the warp. Hammer will be guided by this signal to the tesseract gates. His warp experience will be nothing like ours."

Hammer hit the door and vanished.

"We're screwed," said Pure.

"Not completely," said other Pure. "Remember the thing that makes spooky action at a distance so intriguing is that a single particle on a higher realm has two reflections in the material world."

"Yeah? So?"

"So there's another one of you. I've had your second body walking along the ocean floor to reach Atlantis for months now. You're floating to the surface even as we speak."

CHAPTER TWENTY-TWO
TELL ME ABOUT IT

HAMMER CLOSED HIS EYES but it didn't help. Warp space was a maddening kaleidoscope of color and fractured images. The waves of possible destinations whipped past at cyclone speed. The signal from the radio receiver in his ear could be seen pulsing before him like a serpent, moving too fast for him to reach out and catch it.

Then Morningstar caught his right arm in the iron grip of his hindclaws. The dragon's magnificent wings were spread, slowing their headlong plummet through the shattered dimensions.

"This is most unpleasant," Morningstar shouted.

"Do you see the signal?" Hammer asked, pointing to the writhing rope that lay beyond his grasp.

"Yes. And I can see in the distance, it exits through a window, and beyond that window is a city."

"Follow it," said Hammer.

Then, before he felt any sense of motion, they were rudely dumped back into the real world, landing in the middle of a marble floor with a rib-cracking smack.

Hammer rolled to his back, looking up into blue sky. He was in what looked to be a Greek temple, with marble pillars framing the view. Everything was still, save for the gentle noise of distant surf.

Morningstar rose from his rough landing with a series of grunts. He untangled the backpack that held the bomb. Looming over Hammer, he said, "Let us make haste. The stone beneath us is murmuring. The city knows we're here."

PURE FELT AS IF his chest would burst.

He'd been pushed from the warp, back into the physical world. He was underwater, his lungs full of fluid, his eyes straining against the darkness. His guts felt distorted, full of sharp knives; his limbs were leaden. He kicked and waved as best he could, though he moved with turtle slowness. Above him, the faintest lessening of darkness could be seen. He rose, lifted by gasses in his swollen belly. He floated up to the light.

Pure calmed. The ocean was beautiful, the light filtering down to reach him like a gossamer curtain. He brought his hands toward his face. His fingers were swollen and wrinkled, as if he'd been in a tub for the last year. Algae darkened his nails. He brushed his tangled hair, pulling away chunks of seaweed.

Then, air. He tried to gasp, but couldn't. His lungs were still full of water. He bobbed on the surface, disoriented and dizzy, as the waves carried him toward shore. In the corner of his vision, he saw a city of tall crystal spires beneath a cerulean sky.

Slowly, he remembered why he was here. Hammer was coming, was possibly here already. He had a bomb. Pure needed to act, but he felt so cold, so slow, so lost.

His back bumped against sand. He flailed about, feeling ground beneath him, and soon was on his feet, knee deep in surf, stumbling toward a shore white as sugar.

On dry ground at last, he fell to his knees and coughed up gallons of dark, salty water. Tiny shrimp writhed in the run-off. He kept belching between coughs, as the gas in his belly fought to free itself. The sun was hot on his back. He felt like a bloated corpse, but, thanks to the sun, a warming, bloated corpse. The extra heat gave him strength. Pure pulled himself up and began to walk. He didn't know his destination. He had no idea how to find Hammer. He could only wander and trust that the part of him still in the warp would guide him.

He staggered onto streets paved with pearl. All around him were throngs of people, laughing, singing, weeping with joy. It looked as if all the people of the world had pressed yes on the ballot. There were men and women of all races and nationalities. Pure blinked, wondering if he was dreaming. The scene was chaotic and beautiful. Women in snazzy business suits stood next to pygmies in loincloths. An Inuit man peeled off his seal parka in the shade of an orange tree. A group of Japanese schoolgirls in tidy uniforms ran around giggling. Any second now, every one of these people would be dead, freezing in the vacuum of space.

Pure moved on, gaining speed with each moment spent beneath the hot sun. He wandered through streets filled with music and light, past tables heaped high with delicacies, past pools in which children splashed. He wandered near a garden of sculptures that sang his favorite songs as he passed. He crossed through an orchard, filled with lemons and apples and kiwis and pears, grapefruit and cherries and plums and bananas, and countless other fruit he couldn't recognize. The air around him fractured into little rainbows. Bony monkey hands snatched greedily at the bananas. Pure kept moving. Ahead of him was something like a Greek temple, a square rimmed with marble columns.

And in the square, a man hunched over a shiny bomb, as a dragon spread his wings to shelter the man from the sun.

Pure tried to shout, but his voice didn't find any traction. Slime clogged his vocal cords. He coughed and spat, darkening the marble squares with gobs of green spittle. At last he managed the barest squeak as he tried to shout, "Hammer!"

It was enough. Hammer looked up, then recoiled at the sight of Pure approaching, seaweed draped, barnacle encrusted, corpse-pale. Hammer drew his gun as Pure attempted to run toward him. Pure's legs couldn't quite master the task, and he only staggered a bit faster.

Hammer lowered the gun.

"Alex?"

Pure was only a few yards away now.

"It's me," Pure said, with his broken voice. "Don't use the bomb."

Hammer shook his head. He knelt back over the bomb and said, "I don't care what kind of trick this is."

"It's not a trick," Pure said. "I've seen the future. Use the bomb and the whole world dies."

"The real Pure is dead." Hammer removed the cover plate of the bomb to reveal its tangled internal wiring. Hammer dug his fingers into the wire.

Pure lunged forward, falling, his hand reaching out to grab Hammer's wrist. His momentum pushed Hammer's hand away, luckily without damaging any wires.

"Please," Pure said, dragging himself over the exposed wiring. "Give me five minutes to explain."

"Get off," Hammer said, tugging at Pure's shoulders.

"Angel," said Morningstar.

A shadow fell over them as a lone angel descended from the sky. The angel was frowning.

Hammer raised his gun and shot the angel in the face.

The angel didn't flinch.

Morningstar leapt up to meet the angel, grappling with it, worrying the angel's head within his toothy jaws.

"Morningstar," Pure croaked. "Don't fight him. Listen to me."

But events, and bodies, had their own momentum. Morningstar and the angel smashed against a marble pillar, toppling it. Morningstar tried to leap free as the bulk of the pillar tumbled onto the angel, hiding it in a cloud of dust. A chunk of marble the size of a basketball caught Morningstar in the back of the neck. He crashed to the courtyard and lay still.

Hammer grabbed Pure by the hair and began to pull. He grunted and grumbled as he tugged Pure off the bomb.

"Another thing you got wrong," he said, panting. "Pure wasn't this heavy."

"That's sweet, but I'm not letting you trigger the explosion," Pure said, rising to his feet, placing himself between Hammer and the bomb.

Hammer calmly aimed his gun and put a bullet into Pure's left kneecap.

Pure toppled, cursing. He struggled to rise to a sitting position.

"This place is going to be swarming with angels any second," said Hammer, kneeling before the bomb. "Maybe you are the real Alex. I don't know. But there's no time left for debate. At least we'll die together. That has a certain romance, doesn't it?"

With a grunt, Hammer tugged away a fistful of wire.

Nothing happened.

As the dust of the collapsed pillar settled, the angel was revealed to be unharmed.

"That's a dangerous toy," said the angel, as he strode toward Morgan. "Primitive, easily aborted, but still dangerous."

Hammer snarled and punched the angel hard in the stomach. Pure winced as he heard bones crack all the way up to Hammer's shoulder. Hammer fell backward on the white stone of the square, sucking in his breath.

"We can fix you," said the angel, smiling at Hammer. The angel lifted the bomb. The outline of the metal began to shimmer. It turned into pink blossoms and blew away on the breeze.

Hammer fired three bullets into the angel's torso.

The angel shook his head sadly. "There's no need to struggle any more. Sleep."

Hammer closed his eyes and went limp.

"Don't hurt him," Pure said. "He's a good man."

The angel looked at Pure. A quizzical expression crossed his face.

"You aren't completely here," said the angel.

"Tell me about it," said Pure.

The angel's stony eyes cut angles and arcs as it studied the air around Pure. "Your math is broken. You're trapped outside conventional dimensionality."

"That's one impressive diagnosis," Pure said.

"Here," said the angel, reaching into the air near Pure. "Take my hand."

Pure didn't move. The world twisted and shattered around him as if he were standing in a kaleidoscope. He realized his hand was now in the angel's hand. He was standing up, his body no longer waterlogged, his knee whole again. The shards of the world slipped and clicked together like a puzzle. His vision cleared. A dozen monkeys fell from the air around him, yelping and chattering as they scampered away.

Pure felt dizzy. Spots danced in front of his eyes.

"Now that you're no longer in the warp," the angel said, "you'll need to breathe again."

Pure gasped, tasting the sea breeze, feeling the blood in his veins. He felt strange. But it was a familiar strangeness.

"I'm alive!" he said.

"I've removed the dimensional paradox that kept you divided," said the angel. "Welcome to Atlantis."

Pure looked up into the bright sky, lifted his strong, healthy, unblemished arms and shouted, "I'm alive!"

"Alive, and with a choice to make," said the angel. "Do you accept the promise of Atlantis? Do you wish to dwell here forever?"

"Gee," said Pure. "This is a no brainer."

CHAPTER TWENTY-THREE
ONE MONTH LATER

I-77 THROUGH WEST VIRGINIA was a good road for biking now that the traffic was gone. Chase had been riding 70 to 80 miles a day for the last three weeks and his body was starting to show it. His legs were thicker and there wasn't a hint of fat anywhere on his torso. All in all, Chase felt better physically than he ever had before.

Chase was part of the communications system for the town of Billings. His job was to travel the highways in search of people who'd chosen to stay behind. In the aftermath of the Atlantis ballots, three quarters of the population of the town had simply vanished. Those who stayed behind had enlisted able-bodied men like Chase to help contact scattered relatives they suspected might also have refused the offer of Atlantis. The people who remained behind were an odd bunch, mostly from groups who had existed on the fringes of the community. There were a surprising number of Wiccans coming out of the woodwork, and he would never have guessed West Virginia had such a large population of Buddhists. In any case, the remaining townspeople had pulled together to deal with the day-to-day problems of survival.

Problem one: No electricity. Atlantis had unleashed electromagnetic pulses that had crippled the entire North American grid. No one knew if it would ever be up and running, or if power did return, what would keep Atlantis from shutting it down again.

Problem two: No gasoline. Some sort of chemical agent unleashed by Atlantis had turned all gasoline into powder. The electromagnetic pulse had fried the motors of electric cars, save for a few sheltered in underground garages, but these had no convenient way of being recharged. People were once again traveling by horseback, or bicycle, or on foot.

Problem three: No phones, or radio, or television. No one was sure what was happening in the broader world. This was the strangest thing to get used to. His whole life, Chase lived in a culture that took instantaneous dissemination of information for granted. There was something exciting about living in a world where you didn't have twenty different ways of finding out tomorrow's weather.

Chase coasted down an exit ramp. There was a gas station at the bottom of the ramp, abandoned and looted. The windows were smashed in, glass and trash littered the pavement. Chase pulled to a stop near the open door, and called out, "Hello?"

The rustle of wind was the only answer.

The place looked pretty well smashed up but Chase thought it might be worth looking around. He unstrapped the pistol from under the seat of the bike. He stepped cautiously into the gloomy interior, his eyes adjusting to the shadows. The interior was gutted. The drywall had been pulled loose, wires and light fixtures had been stolen, for who knows what purpose. The shelves were completely empty save for some empty cardboard boxes and tons of candy wrappers. Chase quickly came to the conclusion he was wasting his time. He went back into the light.

An angel and two strangers were waiting by his bike. Chase kept his pistol held low, careful not to make any aggressive moves. He knew the weapon would be useless against the angel, and he didn't want to give this creature any excuse to take the weapon away. The two humans with him, a man and a woman, were smiling, yet also looked slightly scared. There was something familiar about them, especially about the man. Chase realized with a start that the reason the man looked familiar was that he'd seen the face in the mirror. The guy looked a lot like him. And the woman . . . actually, she kind of looked the way his mother had looked in old pictures, back before she fell into a coma.

"Son," said the man.

"Oh, Chase," said the woman, rushing forward suddenly and wrapping her arms around him.

"Do I know you?" he asked.

"Yes," the man said, moving closer. "I'm your father, Chase. And this is your mother. The angels have healed us."

"Mom?" Chase said, pushing her away and holding her arms. He studied her face. Her eyes were wet with tear of joy. "Oh my God, Mom! You're awake!"

"I'm all better," said Jessica. "The angel fixed me. But, oh, Chase, I'm so sorry. I'm so sorry I wasn't there all those years. It had to be so hard on you."

Chase let go of the woman who claimed to be his mother and turned away, gritting his teeth. "No," he said. "I don't believe this. This isn't happening."

"It's true, Chase," said Adam. "Atlantis can cure any wound. Your mother and I are fresh and new, healthier even than the day we were married."

"Atlantis told us you didn't choose to come," said Jessica. "Why?"

"I know you couldn't know that we were there," said Adam. "And I know that I hadn't given you a lot of reasons to come visit me. I wasn't the best father. That can change now. We have all of eternity to be a family."

Chase swallowed hard. He scrunched his eyes closed, not daring to look back.

"You're not them," he said, his voice trembling.

"Chase, please listen," said Adam. "This is a second chance. Atlantis doesn't give second chances. The ballots were a one-time process only. The city used them to select people who would be open to a new life, and to eliminate people who might not adapt well. Millions of people have begged for a second chance to contact loved ones and relatives who didn't come to Atlantis. We were only given this chance because Atlantis feels a special connection to me. Come back with us."

"No," said Chase. "I knew what I was doing when I decided to stay behind. Whoever you are, I ask you to respect that."

"But why?" asked Jessica.

"Not so long ago I thought I was in love with this girl," Chase said. "I wasn't. She didn't love me. But because of what I thought I felt, I did some pretty stupid things. Now that I've had time to think about it, I can see how I fooled myself so badly. I wanted to love and be loved. So pardon me if I'm a little skeptical of an alien city coming to Earth and promising love, love, love. I'm not falling for it."

"Son," said Adam. "Don't be so bitter. I truly did love you."

"I love you too," said Jessica. "I know I haven't been there for you, but you're my son. Please come back to Atlantis with us. Atlantis is giving us forever. We can make up for lost time."

"It's perfect there," said Adam. "Like Heaven. There's no hate or want, there's no need the city doesn't provide. Whatever pain or emotional scars I've inflicted on you over the years . . . Atlantis can help. It can help us understand each other in ways I can't even describe. We can be a family there, Chase. We can be whole."

Chase chuckled, and turned back to the people claiming to be his parents. Looking at their faces, their hopeful eyes, he knew it was all true.

"I believe you," said Chase. "I believe you're my mother and father. And I believe in that Atlantis is like Heaven. Maybe it is Heaven, and everyone there can love because no one's hungry, or hurting, or sad."

"So you'll come back with us," said Jessica, her voice bright and happy as if he'd already said yes.

"No," said Chase. "It's seductive, it's tempting, but it's wrong. So people love each other in paradise. So people love each other when all their physical and emotional needs are met, when they've got nothing to worry about. Big fucking deal. It's learning to love here in the real world that's the challenge. It's learning to love when you're sick, or traumatized, or just too damn busy. Because if you don't have to work at love, then what's it worth?"

"You don't understand," said Adam.

"I think I do. And . . . I want it. I want us to be a family. So; let's do it," said Chase. "Let's be the family we should have been, living together, sharing everything, getting to really know each other. But let's do it here. Forget Atlantis. Love me in my world."

"If that's what it takes," said Jessica, opening her arms once more to hug her son. "I'll stay. There's no promise of eternity that can keep me from you after this second chance."

Chase wrapped his arms around her and started to sob. Something in his chest had snapped, a floodgate opened as he thought of what she was sacrificing. Was he being selfish? Selfish or not, this was more than he'd ever dreamed of. His mother was alive, and she loved him, and nothing could ever go wrong in the world.

Chase kept expecting his father to join in the hug.

He opened his eyes.

Through a blur of tears, he could see that his father and the angel were gone.

CASSIE SAT ON THE BEACH, watching the waves. The sensation of vision was still a miracle to her. The city offered countless seductions and distractions, riots of colors among flower gardens, sleek and graceful lines in the architecture, and sometimes it was just too much to take in, and Cassie would come down to the beach to reduce the world to a blue-gray plane of water fading to a blue-white plane of sky, with a handful of sails dotting the horizon.

It hadn't only been her sight that Atlantis had fixed. She'd always considered herself healthy, but Atlantis had fine tuned her body, correcting a minor curvature of her spine that had sometimes given her back aches, restoring upper ranges of hearing she didn't know she'd damaged with her tastes in loud music.

The only thing Atlantis couldn't fix was her sister's betrayal. All the physical evidence was gone now, but Cassie still couldn't believe her sister had treated her so callously, like another one of her toy robots. Jazz hadn't come to Atlantis as near as she could tell. It was strange. Other people could instantly find out which of their friends and relatives had come to Atlantis and which had not. But the statues she'd talked with acted like they didn't even understand her question when she inquired about Jazz. Jazz seemed to be the one person on the planet they'd lost track of.

A crab was scuttling over the sand toward her. Cassie took a closer look. The crab was strangely shiny, like it was made of metal. She looked again. It *was* made of metal. It was a little robotic crab.

The crab stopped on the sand before her and said, "Hi."

It was her sister's voice.

"Jazz?" Cassie asked.

"You busy?" the Jazz/crab asked. "I was hoping we could get together."

"Get together? Where are you?"

"I'm here. On Atlantis. It was a bitch to track you down. So, how about it? You busy?"

"Not particularly," said Cassie. "But I don't know if I want to see you."

"Yeah," said Jazz. "I thought that might be the case. Look, I know there's no excuse for what I did. I'd like to talk about it with you."

"Fine," said Cassie. "Where?"

"There's a marina on the east side of the island. All kinds of sailboats. I'm on a Chinese junk with a green sail. The crab can lead you."

Cassie followed the crab for miles. As she wandered the pristine beaches, she was again struck by the emptiness. In a city of billions, she'd expected people to be jammed in elbow to elbow, for space to be at a premium. She'd anticipated crowd scenes like Hindus packed up against the Ganges.

"The city won't let you crowd," said the crab.

"What?" asked Cassie.

"You were noticing how open the city was. There's a sinister reason for this. The city monitors and shapes thoughts. It prevents a billion people from simultaneously having the urge to hit the beaches."

"It's reading my mind? You're reading my mind?"

"Yeah," said the crab. "I have to in order to feed the city false data from your senses. I don't want it to hear us talking, do I?"

"Get out of my head," said Cassie. "Get out or I turn around right now."

"Okay. Jeez. Don't be so shy. You have nice thoughts. Nothing to be ashamed of. There. I'm not watching them any more."

Cassie wondered if she should believe this. At the same time, there was no way she was turning back. Jazz had revealed an underlying mystery of the city, something that had bothered Cassie ever since she'd arrived. She'd never stood in line at a restaurant here, never been to a concert so crowded and noisy you couldn't hear the band. Could the city really be controlling everyone?

The green sail of the Chinese junk was now visible. There were a thousand sailboats here, of all sizes and styles, from single sail catamarans to six-masted windjammers. As she walked down the dock she spotted Jazz on the deck of the ship, in a hammock strung between the mast and the cabin. She was sunbathing in a green bathing suit that matched the sails. She also wore a jade bead necklace, with a long slender black pendant. She took a sip from a tall glass of iced tea as Cassie approached. Gabe, still dressed in the same long black trench coat he'd worn when he robbed the Piggly Wiggly, stood next to Jazz and waved as he spotted Cassie.

Cassie stepped aboard the gently rocking boat, accepting Gabe's hand for balance. The crab nimbly leapt between the dock and the deck, then disappeared into the cabin.

"Weird," said Cassie, looking at Jazz. "I've never, ever seen you in a bathing suit. Is it my imagination, or are you getting a tan?"

Jazz shrugged. "I've gone native."

"I'm really surprised you pressed 'yes' on the ballot."

"I didn't," said Jazz. "I sailed here on my own. Well, not entirely on my own. Gabe did most of the work. Whipping up a little sailing code wasn't too tough."

"Where's Hezekiah?" asked Cassie.

"I had to leave him behind," said Jazz. "Sadly, he'd developed a weird system glitch and I didn't have time to debug him. He was stuck in his fire-and-brimstone prophet mode after his self-repairing circuit brought him back on-line. I could have wiped his drives and reprogrammed, but I was kind of pressed for time. Since Hammer and Morningstar obviously blew the mission, I'm the last, best hope of stopping this thing."

"You've come here to destroy Atlantis," Cassie said.

"Maybe," said Jazz. "First I plan on stealing everything I can. There's an astonishing machine intelligence behind all this. It's going to take years to figure everything out."

"I thought you needed my brain to understand Atlantis. Well, tough luck. You can't use it. Atlantis has taken out the circuitry anyway."

"I'm using my own brain. Now that I've had time to study the signal it's no longer destructive."

Cassie wanted to scream. What her sister had done to her was unimaginably cruel and arrogant. But something else was bothering her.

"It's really controlling our minds?" asked Cassie.

"Control might be a little strong," said Jazz. "Let's just say it coordinates the scheduling of your urges. For instance, you won't get hungry until around 8:17 tonight. You'll walk into the café just as the person who was hungry at 7:17 has left."

"If it reads my thoughts, why are you telling me this? Even if it can't hear us now, won't it find this conversation in my memories later?"

"Nah," said Jazz. "I'm invisible to the city. I've hacked a dead zone into its perceptions. Since I'm using the city's own codes to hide myself, I'm like a cancer in a body that can hide from the immune system because it's part of the body."

"The one thing I don't understand about the city is why?" Cassie said. "It's confused me ever since I got here. It's done so much for me, and so far has asked nothing in return. But it must want *something*."

As she spoke, Gabe vanished into the cabin.

"You're the city's pet," said Jazz. "It keeps you happy for the same reason some people have a dozen cats. I don't know why it's been designed this way, but the city feels pleasure when it's helping others. It's happy making you happy."

"I guess," said Cassie. She sat against the ship's rail. "But . . . I don't know. I don't know if I'm happy."

"I doubt it," said Jazz. "Living in this city is like a permanent vacation. But vacations are meant to refresh you, to revive you so you can get back to more challenging things in life. The city has erased challenges. I mean, there are still things that look like challenges. Right now, there are people climbing those huge spires from the outside. There are people who've gotten gills from the city and are now swimming alongside sharks. There are people mastering musical instruments, writing novels, painting pictures. But life's big struggles, to find food, shelter, safety . . . these are gone forever. And I don't know that most people can be satisfied with that. There's a difference between challenge and entertainment."

"Maybe we can learn to be satisfied," said Cassie. "Maybe even you can learn. You look pretty relaxed."

"I am relaxed," said Jazz. "And I'm not a hundred percent certain that I'm going to destroy Atlantis. Eighty percent, maybe. But maybe a city where the biggest challenge is boredom is the fate most of mankind deserves. I'm open-minded. I'm thinking it through."

"You haven't changed," said Cassie. Gabe had returned from the cabin now, and handed Cassie a glass of iced-tea. "What makes you think you could destroy Atlantis if you wanted to?"

"Electronically, I think I can hit its systems pretty hard. And physically . . . it's pretty humid here," said Jazz, picking up the ebony pendant that lay between her breasts. She lifted it, so that Cassie could see that it was actually a tiny vial, packed with black powder. "Mega-mold spores. This place would be one big puff ball inside a week."

THE WEST VIRGINIA MOUNTAINTOP was the picture of serenity. No one who ever walked among the forest could ever guess that beneath a thin layer of soil a heavy steel gate covered a missile silo. No one was there to witness it when the soil began to shake, flying wildly in response to a powerful knocking from beneath the earth. As the soil danced away, the steel plate was exposed, denting outward with each blow, the bulge rising, rising, until it burst, and the head of an axe poked through. The chopping continued, widening the rift. At last the noise stopped, and two sets of thick fingers grabbed the rent edges of the metal, tearing the hole wider. The metal groaned, then snapped, leaving a jagged hole as wide as a manhole cover. A thick, heavy Bible was lifted from the hole and laid upon the ground. An axe was tossed through. Then Hezekiah, the prophet, crawled from his tomb. He stood, gathered up his book and axe, wiped the dust from his black robes, and wandered into the night to find his flock.

THE INSIDE OF THE TANK smelled worse than a locker room by the time General Junaluska and his men reached the Smoky Mountains. Atlantis had somehow wiped out petroleum products, but Junaluska's handpicked team had scavenged enough vegetable oil from abandoned restaurants along the way to keep the diesel engine chugging along for the long trip back to his home.

The other thing they'd scavenged had been books. Bookstores had all but disappeared years ago, but there were still public libraries filled with these paper relics. Of course, now they weren't relics; for the time being, they were the most advanced means of storing and transmitting data left to mankind.

Atlantis may have thought it had dealt a deathblow to mankind by destroying modern infrastructure, but it was mistaken. Sometimes, ancient infrastructure was more resilient. Everything mankind knew had been written down. The books of the world contained all the knowledge they would need to rebuild. His mission would be to protect those books, and that knowledge, so that mankind would one day return to glory. It might take ten years, or fifty, or five hundred. But Junaluska was prepared to play the long game. He might not live to see Atlantis fall, but perhaps his grandchildren would, or their grandchildren. When the time came for men to once again take their rightful place in the world, he would make certain that his descendents were ready.

MORNINGSTAR WEDGED the deer carcass into the fork of the tree. He slipped among the branches, all but invisible against the setting sun. He watched the two riders in the distance growing closer. He could smell their horses on the wind. He glanced back at the deer above him, its glassy eyes staring at him. He loved deer, especially their livers, and a fine meal awaited him this night. Still, every time he caught the scent of horse, his mouth watered.

The riders drew nearer. Morningstar sprang, stretching his wings, catching the wind in his feather-scales. The wind was warm, tempting him to rise higher, ever higher, but dinner awaited.

Morningstar dropped to the ground before the two humans. The horses stayed calm. By now they were used to him. It hurt him a little. He missed the fear-scent he'd engendered in the old days. Of course, Pure and Sue would be upset with him if he ever actually ate the horses. Sue, especially, would give him an earful.

"So," said Pure. "How was hunting?"

"Magnificent. A fine buck is lodged in the oak up ahead."

"Sounds good," said Sue. "I'm starved. I'll start the fire."

Pure admired the deftness with which Sue's aged hands could coax fire out of a piece of flint and a pocket-knife. Pure hadn't mastered the skill, and probably never would. Fortunately, he had about fifty boxes of matches stashed in his saddlebag. He'd never mentioned them to Sue. He didn't want to spoil her fun.

It had taken the end of the world to reveal Sue's better qualities to Pure. She could start fires, tan leather, tell time by the sun, and navigate by stars. She was a 107-year old girl scout.

Since the collapse of civilization, Sue had gotten over her vegetarianism. Hunting deer and catching fish for sustenance apparently was morally acceptable in a way that raising cows and chickens hadn't been. Sue had discarded her habit and robes for buckskins and moccasins, her white hair tied into long braids.

When the angels had first taken Pure and Morningstar back to Mount Weather, there had been some hard feelings between Pure and Sue. The whole business about shooting his brains out had made their conversations awkward at first. But Pure had wanted to go out and explore the new world and Sue had a destination in mind. Since Hammer had decided to stay in Atlantis, Sue had proven to be a sympathetic ear during those long nights of Pure griping about how he could have been so wrong about a person. He'd never pegged Hammer as the sort who would choose to be coddled and comforted, to turn into a docile pet for the big bad city from outer space.

Sue didn't grate on him now that she wasn't calling for the overthrow of western civilization. And he had to admit, he'd changed as well, becoming less abrasive with her, less of a smart-Alex. He'd been given a second shot at life. When the angels had put him back together, he felt better than he could remember, better than the best high he'd ever gotten on any drug he'd tinkered with. His newly repaired body was uncontaminated by pharmaceuticals and he planned to keep it that way.

That night, they were looking up at the stars, and Sue said, "We're close. A day or two more, at most."

Morningstar paused from gnawing on the deer's skull and said, "I concur. I smell it on the wind."

"The Ozarks do have a certain aroma," said Pure.

The following noon, they found a knight's rusted armor in the bend of a stream, and Morningstar let out a yelp of joy. Pure scanned the horizon, at last spotting the castle.

They were back in the park where they'd found Morningstar. Pure and Sue pushed the horses to full gallop, trying to keep up with Morningstar as he flew toward the castle. The huge stone mansion was abandoned now, with weeds and vines already intruding upon what must have once been carefully landscaped grounds.

Inside, the castle looked more like a movie set than the real thing. When Pure tapped the stone walls, they gave a thud that indicated they were thin concrete over a hollow form. But the upper levels of the castle were only for show, a little flair for the super-rich hunters who'd flocked to the place. Like Disney World, the real heart of the operation lay below, in the depths of the earth.

Within the basements were labs, and within these labs were dragons. Pure didn't know if they would still be alive after so long without power or lights. Then again, Morningstar was so resourceful and clever that if the dragons below had a fraction of his intelligence, some of them would have found some way to survive.

They descended the emergency stairs near the elevators, until they arrived at the hospital-clean corridors below. Pure carried a lantern to help guide them through the darkness. Morningstar scurried ahead, his eyes suited to seeing in the gloom.

"I smell them," said Morningstar, stopping before a metal door. "I hear them."

Pure studied the door. It looked like something you might find on a submarine, riveted together with thick steel plates, with a wheel for a handle. Pressing his ear against the door, Pure could hear distant voices, faint murmurs, though he couldn't make out the words.

Pure handed the lantern to Sue and grabbed the wheel.

"You're sure about this?" she asked.

"Me?" said Pure. "I thought coming here to free any surviving dragons was your idea."

"Open it," said Morningstar, impatiently.

"It was," said Sue. "You're right. Do it."

Pure hesitated. Who knew what would happen when he turned the wheel? It could be that a flood of hungry dragons would pour forth, and his brief, wonderful life would come to a rapid and messy end.

But Pure liked living in a world where getting up in the morning was a gamble. The safe, rounded corners of Atlantis could never provide him the rushes of adrenaline that were his one remaining high. Grinning broadly, Pure spun the wheel.

ABOUT THE AUTHOR

James Maxey's mother warned him that reading all those comic books would warp his mind. She was right. Now an adult who can't stop daydreaming, James is unsuited for decent work and ekes out a pittance writing down demented fantasies about masked women, fiery dragons, and monkeys. Oh god, so many monkeys.

In an effort to figure out how Superman could fly, James read books by Carl Sagan and Stephen Jay Gould and Stephen Hawking. Turns out, Superman probably wasn't based on any factual information. Who would have guessed? Realizing it was possible to write science fiction without being constrained by the actual rules of science proved liberating for James, and led to the psuedo-science fiction of the *Bitterwood* series, superhero novels like *Nobody Gets the Girl*, the secondary world fantasy of the *Dragon Apocalypse* series, and the steampunk visions of *Bad Wizard*.

James lives in Hillsborough, North Carolina with his lovely and patient wife Cheryl and too many cats. For more information about James and his writing, visit jamesmaxey.net.

Made in the USA
Middletown, DE
07 October 2017